deep UNDER

A
WALKER SECURITY
NOVEL

NEW YORK TIMES BESTSELLING AUTHOR
LISA RENEE JONES

*everafter*ROMANCE

Book 1 of the WALKER SECURITY series
A spinoff of the Tall, Dark, and Deadly series which includes:
Hot Secrets
Dangerous Secrets
Beneath the Secrets
Full length, loosely connected prelude: *Secrets Exposed*

Disclaimer: This is a work of fiction, and while the state of New York does not allow the Death Penalty now, it did when this story was originally written.

First edition April 2016.
Print ISBN: 9781682302262
eBook ISBN: 9781682303955

The Walker Brothers...

Tall, dark, and deadly, these three brothers run Walker security. Each brother is unique in his methods and skills, but all share key similarities. They are passionate about those they love, relentless when fighting for a cause they believe in, and believe that no case is too hard, no danger too dark. Dedication is what they deliver, and results are their reward.

Prologue

MYLA

FOURTEEN MONTHS AGO...

Entering through the employee door at the back of one of the three San Francisco located Shivers, a "something for everyone" kind of restaurant, I still can't believe the "something" for me is a job. At twenty-five years old, I'm supposed to be progressing in my career, not taking food orders. But then, waiting tables wasn't exactly what I had in mind when I'd packed up my car in Texas and used my savings to get here for a job that fell apart before I even arrived. I knew being a fashion designer was still a long reach for me, but a move from merchandiser for a smaller retailer to one of the largest on the planet would have been a step in the right direction.

Shutting the door behind me, I cut left into a small locker room, stopping at the first of twelve metal doors. Grabbing the lock, I turn the combination, and open the door, quickly sticking my purse inside before grabbing the pink apron on the hook. Fitting it over my jean-clad hips, I wish like heck it covered the low V of my hot pink "Shivers" t-shirt. But then, unlike some of the girls here, I prefer using my brain as an asset to get ahead in the world over the DD's. Though I guess I should thank the girls, since I'm fairly certain they are why I was hired, considering my boss, Eduardo, spends way too much time looking at them for my comfort. I might not like that reasoning, but I need to pay my bills.

I shove the locker shut and set my lock in place before turning and all but running into a big, broad body. "Eduardo," I gasp. "I didn't hear you come in."

He gives me one of his heavy-lidded stares, his thick arms crossed in front of a broad chest some might think is rather stellar. I, on the other hand, think it's as creepy as the way he looks at me. "The CEO of the chain is in the house tonight, in the private, lower-level dining room. You'll be attending his needs."

"Me? I'm still learning."

"He'll like you. That's all that matters." He settles his hands on his hips. "There's a two-thousand dollar bottle of tequila with Joe at the bar waiting on your service. And make it fast. He's thirsty." He turns and leaves and I stand there for several beats before I shake myself and start moving, following in his footsteps, down a long hallway past several offices.

Exiting into the main restaurant, the clusters of wooden tables and bar booths are half-filled, but considering it's Friday night, I am certain they will soon be at capacity. That means big tips I pray I don't miss out on for an owner not likely to tip at all. Turning right, I head to the end of the horseshoe-shaped bar and Joe meets me at the counter, setting two glasses down in front of me. "Don't spill this. It's liquid gold."

"I don't even know where the downstairs is."

He motions behind me and I glance over my shoulder to an archway and then back at him to discover he's already walking away. Inhaling, I pick up the two glasses and head in that direction. Right now I really wish I was back in Texas, where at least I had a job in my field, and I'd still have Sally, my best friend, who was recently married and now pregnant. Exhaling, I head down about a dozen stairs and reach a landing to cross to a large archway. Entering, I find a cave-like room with a long rectangular booth horizontal to me that could easily seat a dozen, but leaves no walking room in the small space. There are only two men present. My boss, who has his back to me, and a Hispanic man in an expensive looking suit, who is facing me.

"You must be Myla," the man says, an arrogant, worldly air to him, the slight graying at his temples aging him to what must be his forties. "Come," he adds, lifting a hand. "Bring me my drink." There is something about this man's command that is powerful, almost sexy, and yet...he is sinister. Scary even. I walk toward the table and set both men's drinks in front of them. "Thank you," he says, and surprisingly, he does not look at my cleavage. He just looks at me, and does so with uncomfortable intensity.

I force my hands to my hips, when I really want to hug myself. "Can I get you a menu?"

"How old are you?" he asks, as if I haven't spoken.

"Twenty-five."

"Why are you waiting tables?"

"I moved here to start a new job that fell through during my relocation, but I assure you I need the work, and I'll work hard."

"I am quite certain you will. Leave us to talk, but when my business is done here you'll join me for dinner. In other words, you are to remain free of other obligations."

"What? No I—" He arches a brow and I quickly amend. "I'm sorry. I just…I need the tips tonight. I do appreciate the offer though."

"I'll be leaving a five-hundred dollar tip. So you'll have dinner with me. Now, leave us."

I jolt with the command, my heart thundering in my chest, while my feet move of their own accord, leading me up the stairs. Once I'm there, I'm not sure what to do with myself. I'm more than a little uncomfortable with being ordered to dinner, but considering the cost of living in this city, I need that five hundred dollars. Not sure what to think of any of this, my gaze scans the restaurant and catches on Heather, a waitress who befriended me my first day, heading in my direction. I dart forward and intercept her before she reaches the bar.

"Why do you look panicked?" she asks, blowing a lock of blonde hair from her eyes.

"The owner of the restaurant is here and—"

"Michael Alvarez is here?"

"Yes and—"

"Do you know who he is?"

My brow dips. "What do you mean?"

"The leader of one of the biggest cartels in the country."

"What? He's the leader of a cartel?"

"Oh yes," she says. "He has money and he's kind of sexy, or so I hear. He never comes in, but I Googled him, and he's scary. So very scary." She touches my elbow. "I have a cranky customer. I'll be back in a minute. I need to get him his drink." She darts around me and I stand there, shell-shocked, and well...shell-shocked. It takes me almost twenty seconds to realize that I should be calling my sister who's an FBI agent.

I rush toward the hallway and the offices, cutting down the hallway, and instead of going to the employee locker room, I enter the bathroom to my right. Walking to the last stall, I enter and shut the door, locking up before leaning on the solid surface, already removing my phone from my pocket to punch in my sister's number. It starts ringing and dang it, it goes to voicemail, the way it often does for months on end when she's undercover. I don't even know if she will get my message but the beep sounds and I say, "Kara. It's Myla." The bathroom door opens and I silently curse being forced to leave a generic message. "Call me. Please."

Leaning my head on the hard surface, I wonder what it is about this family that sends us into a collision course with really bad people, which has me considering my options. Alvarez is the kind of man that my father and sister have devoted their lives to shutting down. The kind of man who killed my parents. So I should get the hell out of here, leave and go to a temp service tomorrow, and for those very reasons, and more, I'm justified and smart for doing so. No one knows how dangerous Alvarez is, simply because of *what* he is, more than me. Decision made, I decide to call anyone I can in the FBI to reach her, the instant I'm out of here. Pushing off the door, I open it and gasp to find a man with a long scar down his cheek standing in front of me.

"What are you doing in here?"

"Mr. Alvarez requests your company, which means I'll need your phone, and I'll need to search you."

"What? No. No. I don't agree."

His lips twist in an evil grin. "I don't remember asking."

Chapter One

KYLE

PRESENT DAY – DALLAS, TX

"Holy hell," I murmur, glancing in the rearview mirror of the black classic Mustang I'm driving, my gaze catching on the white pick-up two vehicles back, and the outline of two familiar people inside it. Scowling, I grab my cellphone from the drink holder to hit the call button. "Siri," I command. "Dial Whataburger," I say, my favorite burger joint, code for the number connecting my temporary phone to Royce Walker's.

"Dialing Whataburger," Siri replies, and I decide right then that she's the only woman in the Walker Security regime that actually follows orders. The ex-FBI agent in that damn truck behind me sure doesn't, but then neither does the ex-ATF agent sitting next to her that I usually call my friend and boss. Royce ordered him to hold down the fort for Walker

Security in New York.

"Yeah?" Royce answers gruffly.

"Blake and Kara are here, tailing me, and if they don't know I'm about to meet with a bigwig inside the Alvarez cartel, they will if you don't get them off my ass."

"He was just at a wedding in Sonoma. How the hell would they know we're in Dallas?" I can almost hear him scowl at the question before he says, "Don't answer. He's my fucking pain in the ass younger brother, which means he figured out the case I pulled you in for is really about Alvarez, and hacked every electronic device we own."

"Like I hacked my way into finding out that Alvarez is alive," I say, a skill I share with him, as surely as I do a bloody history. "They can't know Alvarez is alive. If they find out, that gives them hope that Kara's sister is as well, and we have no idea if that's true."

"She's alive," he says. "She might not be the flavor of the month at his side, but he wouldn't kill her. Not when he could push her into the sex trafficking operation."

"You don't know that, Royce, and I was there the night Alvarez blew up a helicopter and made us all think he and she were dead. It was hell for Kara and I saw how Blake responded. He has a lot of pent up hate for Alvarez. Give him a reason and he will kill him before we save the rest of the women."

"It's been almost three years since Whitney died, Kyle. He has Kara now."

"Three years, since his then-fiancée was slaughtered by Alvarez feels like yesterday, if you open the wound. Believe me, I was there when that happened, too. You don't want that Blake to return."

He is silent for several beats in which I turn a corner, and so does that damn white pick-up. "I'll contain them," he finally says.

"*Contain* them?" I demand, scrubbing my newly shaved face, having given up my beard for this assignment. "Tell me that means you're getting them the fuck out of here."

"I'll evaluate when you let me off the damn phone."

"I need to cancel the meeting," I say, certain this is going to get us all killed. "I'm pulling over."

"You will not pull over," he orders, pulling the hard-ass boss routine. "You know damn well that if you do, Blake will follow, and you risk your cover being blown. We both know you aren't going to do that. And you say you know Blake, so you know that means he's not following you on a hunch. He *knows*. I'm not going to trick him into thinking this isn't about Alvarez."

He's right. "Fuck," I growl.

"Yeah," he concurs. "Fuck. And for the record, you and I might share an FBI background, but you don't understand the *fuck* about me if you think I can't handle my brother. Get to that meeting and get inside Alvarez's operation. Be the guy they hire to be the notorious bodyguard those with big secrets hire when they need protection. Then be his worst nightmare."

"I'm already sold as that guy." I shift back to what's important right now, in this moment. "You're close to this too, Royce. This isn't a job we took for Walker Security. It's family."

"You're right. It is. And you're our family now, so focus on your damn job or you'll end up dead, in which case I'll drag you out of your grave to kick your ass." And in typical

Royce fashion, he assumes my compliance, as he does everyone's, and hangs up, giving me no time to question if I should back the hell out of this meeting tonight.

But I'm not backing out. I'm going to get this done and over with, for all of us, once and for all. Bodyguard isn't exactly the kind of infiltration Blake once had as a security expert that could shield Alvarez's entire operation, but it's an in. I'll make half a million dollars for eight weeks of work, which says I'm reaching fairly high up the chain. The hotel is now in my line of sight, and it's time to pray Royce has this handled.

"Siri," I say, pulling into the driveway of the Ritz.

"Yes, Kyle," Siri says. "What can I help you with?"

"Clear all phone and text logs," I say, eyeing my rear mirror with no white pick-up in sight.

"Clearing all phone and text logs," Siri confirms, and I stop at the door, grabbing my phone and confirming her work.

"At least you're reliably compliant, Siri."

"I'm afraid I can't do that, Kyle," Siri says.

"Of course you can't," I grumble, scrubbing a hand through my blond hair that screams outsider to a Mexican cartel, or so my contact Juan told me at our first meeting. But then that was the point of shaving my beard, too. I'm supposed to be the outsider they need on the inside, and it's worked or I'd never have made it to meeting number two and now three.

The doorman opens my door and despite it being February, I step outside into the year round Texas humidity of my childhood, my roots here helping establish my cover story. "Hello sir," the fifty-something, rather stately, man greets me. "Will you be staying with us tonight?"

"Just a few hours," I say, offering him my keys before I smooth down the navy jacket of one of my "go to" suits from my days in the FBI. "Keep her safe."

"Always, sir," he assures me, offering me a ticket, his face completely straight as he adds, "But I shall fantasize about driving her on the highway at a hundred and forty miles an hour."

"I've had that same fantasy," I assure him, and considering I used this job as an excuse to buy the gorgeous beast, I revel a bit in the idea that I can actually do it. "I need to get on that."

"You do indeed, sir."

"Kyle," I say, palming him a large bill. "Sir makes me feel like my father."

"Kyle," he repeats, "and I'm Les Gordan, should you need anything."

"Thanks, Les," I say, heading toward the double doors, and entering to find shiny tile beneath my feet, a centerpiece table filled with a couple dozen vases of flowers and a glass chandelier above my head. It's dripping money, and for some that would make them regret what they don't have, but not me. I have money, beyond the income I make at Walker Security, which I don't touch for one reason and one reason only. It's blood money.

Cutting left into a bar area, where a thick, blue and gray swirled rug sits beneath clusters of tables with high back chairs, my contact is nowhere in sight. As I'm about to turn back and call him, he slides out of a booth and waves me forward, his suit 70's pale blue, but expensive. At the same moment, a woman wearing a slim-fitted white dress, with long, dark hair, slides out of the seat across from him and walks toward the bathroom. I discreetly suck in air, the idea of this being Myla, impossible to ignore, but that's ridiculous. It can't be her. Could it be her? Could it be this easy to have her land in my lap?

I step forward, closing the space between myself and Juan, who is thirty-nine, five years my senior, and my research tells me that all those years were spent doing very bad things, with zero remorse. "Glad you made it," he says, as I reach him, eyeing his watch. "You're five minutes late."

"You told me about the meeting thirty minutes ago. I'm fifteen minutes earlier than I should have been, considering I had a woman in my bed at the time."

"At least you came up with a good excuse," he snaps, the lights in here doing his sun baked skin no favors, giving it a kind of raisin-like quality.

"I don't do excuses," I say, about to sit down when another brunette, dressed in jeans and boots, walks by...and holy shit. It's Kara, and she's headed straight for the archway the other woman disappeared around. "And actually," I add, "I need to make a quick phone call to a paying client."

"We're going to be paying clients."

"I'll put off the ones that already are when I have the cash." I don't give him time to argue, making fast tracks in pursuit of Kara, rounding the corner and finding an alcove with two doors, one marked Men, while Kara exits the second one marked Women, her hand pressed to her face.

"What the hell are you doing?" I demand, stepping toe-to-toe with her.

She jolts and looks up at me, having been unaware I'm even present until now, and considering what a badass investigator she is, that's saying a lot about where her head is. "Kyle," she gasps, hugging herself, defeat in her face. "I'm sorry. I just thought…I thought it was her, but it wasn't."

Not only do her words confirm she and Blake know about our hunt for Alvarez, but their revelation punches me in the gut. I wanted that woman to be Myla, too, for Kara and for all of us. "Even if it had been her—" I begin.

"I know," she says quickly, holding up a hand. "I know. I was stupid to rush in here. Blake's furious with me and I need to go before that woman, whoever she is, comes out of the bathroom."

"Yes. Go. Now."

"Thank you for trying to find Myla," she whispers, but she doesn't step away. "But first a warning. The woman I followed has deep cleavage, and I know that doesn't mean much, but my gut, which is good, says that she's either meant to test you or reward you." She doesn't wait for a reply, darting around me and disappearing, after delivering what I am certain is a spot-on assessment of the setup in the works.

Nevertheless, I'm pissed as hell that she was here, and I snag my phone from my pocket, and dial Royce. "Kara was just here. What the fuck happened to *contained*?" I've barely issued the question when the woman Kara had followed exits the bathroom, her cleavage indeed deep, her features harder and darker than Myla's, but none of these things matter. What matters is the way she pauses, looking at me like she expects me to walk her back in the bathroom and fuck her here and now.

She points and says, "I…I'll see you back at the table." She rushes past me, but not before I spy a certain familiar mix of fear and desperation in her eyes that has me flashing back to the past. To the moment when a helicopter that was supposed to have Myla inside exploded, and Kara had let out a blood-curdling scream at the loss of her sister. Then to a moment later that night when I'd watched the security footage of Myla just before she walked to the rooftop where the incident had taken place. She'd passed a camera and looked right into the lens, and there was no mistaking the fear and desperation in her eyes that spoke to me. I wanted to save her. I *needed* to save her, and then the damn helicopter had blown up, leaving her dead in everyone's mind but mine for some reason.

"Kyle," Royce snaps. "Are you there? Is your cover blown? Are you in danger?"

Shaking off the memory, I return to the present. "No and no," I reply. "I have to get back to my meeting. I'll call you when I can and no sooner, but no more fucking surprises." I end the connection and clear the record of the communication, already walking as I do.

Slipping my phone back into my pocket, I re-enter the bar, and make my way to Juan and the woman who now sits across from him, in the spot that would be mine, obviously meant to force me to choose to sit by one of the two of them. Not about to be forced into anything, I grab a chair from a nearby table and place it at the end of the booth, effectively putting me between them both.

Juan arches a brow. "You have a problem sitting with us?"

"I prefer a workable distance." I eye the woman and then him. "Is she my new assignment?"

"She's my sister," he says, the announcement shifting my gaze back to him.

A sister who hates her life and wants to be saved. He's a bigger bastard than I imagined. "You want me to protect your sister?"

"I protect my sister," he corrects.

"Then why's she here?"

"To see how easily you're distracted," he says, confirming she was a test.

"I'm not. Now what?"

"You're very white in the midst of a Mexican operation," he comments, the change of topic obviously meant to rattle me. It doesn't work.

"For an extra million I'll get a tan," I promise dryly.

"You stand out," he says, as if I haven't spoken. "You draw attention to us we don't need and I don't like that you're ex-FBI."

"And here I thought you enjoyed turning law enforcement against its own. If I make you nervous—"

"Not nervous," he snaps. "Suspicious and yes. We like corrupting the supposedly incorruptible, but this is too close to comfort for me."

"And yet we're on meeting number three."

"The closer you are, the easier to put a bullet in your head," he counters.

My lips quirk. "Had I known we were going to talk dirty tonight, I'd have had a drink first." I don't give him time to reply. "Why am I here?"

"Because the powers that be think this is a good idea," he says, no doubt referencing Alvarez.

"Does he win this conflict, or do you?"

"He always wins, but I influence him." He pauses. "Strongly."

My eyes narrow, finding a bluff in his call. "Time is money. Two free meetings is all you get, and this is number three." I repeat and I start to stand.

"Wait," he says, stopping me midway to my feet. "You're hired."

I hesitate several beats for effect, then slowly ease back into my chair. "I thought I was a sore thumb FBI agent?"

He ignores the remark. "A million dollars for eight weeks of work."

It's double the named price, which tells me the person I'm mean to protect is closer to Alvarez than I'd thought. "Who am I guarding?"

"Does it matter? You're making a million fucking dollars."

"Do you want the person protected or not?"

His eyes glint hard and he reaches into his pocket, handing me an envelope. I accept it and open it, finding a contract for the money discussed with the terms for which I will perform my duties. The jest. No one gets killed, captured, or wounded, or I pay the money back times two, while further consequences will be considered.

"I need to meet the person in question before I sign this."

"We'll be in touch." He stands and so does the woman, whose name I don't even know at this point, and they leave.

Standing, I follow in their footsteps, dialing Royce as I do, and stating, "Where do you want to meet?"

"Your buddy's bar," he says, naming a spot downtown, which one of my ex-FBI pals now runs. It's also a place I know I've been followed to many times, making a trip there expected rather than suspicious. A perfect place to have a one-on-one with the ever hard-headed men of Walker Security.

• • •

Twenty minutes later, I pull into the parking lot of "Dan's" and while I don't find any familiar cars, I'm confident Royce and Blake are present. Reaching across the vehicle, I grab my Walker Security phone from the glove box, and stick it in my pocket, before exiting, and crossing the parking lot. Entering the bar through the back door, I've made it all of two steps when Dan, as bulked up and Hulkish as ever, greets me.

"Downstairs," he says, motioning toward a stairwell between us, his graying dark hair aging him to forty when he's actually in his thirties like me. "I'll lock the back and watch the front."

"Thanks man," I say, stopping toe-to-toe with him, shaking his hand, our grips strong, as was our bond for five years in the same Texas field office. "Come to work for Walker Security and you'll get paid for shit like this."

"You've been home a month, and said that at least six times. You know my answer. I'm retired."

I press my hands to my hips. "Thirty-four is too damn young to retire."

"It's also too damn young for a lot of things," he says softly, referencing the cascade of blood that's been his life, far more than it has mine.

"That's why we stick together."

"That's why I'm getting the damn door and you're going downstairs."

I rub my jaw, a light stubble forming, and he steps around me, successfully shutting me down once again. "I'll keep asking," I say, heading down the steps and entering the concrete cellar that is wrapped in wine-filled wooden shelves.

In the center is a long wooden table, with Royce on one end and Blake on the other, with Kara by his side.

"Anything on Myla?" Kara asks, shooting to her feet the moment she sees me.

"Nothing," I say, stopping at the side of the table, hands on the back of a brown leather chair, "and that's exactly why I didn't want you involved. There may never be anything, Kara."

"She knows," Blake snaps, standing, while Royce does the same, both brothers big and broad, their long hair tied at the nape, but Royce is bigger, his features harder, his attitude all about control while Blake's is all about daring.

"I do know," Kara adds, hugging herself as she had back at the bathroom. "I know, but I have to try to find her."

"What do you think Royce and I are trying to do?" I look at Blake. "No one knows more than you how dangerous being too close to something can be. How can you want her here?"

"I don't fucking want her to be here," he snaps. "She came on her own. We were in Sonoma for the Chris Merit wedding, and she disappeared. I chartered a plane and got here just in time to catch her as she was following you to the meeting."

"And yet you didn't fucking stop her."

"Stop saying FUCK!" Kara shouts. "Stop. I hate the way you always say fuck, Blake. And fuck you! This is my sister. You knew they were doing this and you didn't tell me. I found your notes. You kept this a secret from me."

"I was waiting to see what they found out before I got your hopes up," Blake states. "I didn't want you to feel everything you're feeling right now."

"You don't get to decide what I feel or don't feel. You just get to be there to help me deal with it. Do you understand?"

Blake turns her to face him, his hands on her hips. "We've talked about this. We're both too close to this case to be objective. We're both known by the Alvarez inner circle. I trust my brother and I trust Kyle. Let's let them handle this."

"I don't want to let them handle this," she hisses.

"If Myla is alive," he says, "one wrong move and she could be dead. Think about it, Kara."

They exchange some sort of silent communication, the air crackling around them, before she says, "I need to control this."

"I know," Blake says softly, "but you can't. I have a lead on the Ella Ferguson case. Let's get on a plane and go to Italy where I think she may be. We'll find her while they find your sister. Distance will help you in ways you can't understand now."

"You have a lead on Ella?"

"I do and it's solid. Let's go be the ones who find her, while Kyle and Royce try to find Myla."

He cups the back of her head, their foreheads coming together, while Royce motions me toward the stairs, and we quickly leave them alone. I've only just made it to the top of the landing when my phone rings, and I glance down, then up at Royce. "Juan. I told him I wanted to meet the person I'm guarding before I take the job."

"A call this soon has to be a good sign."

"Kyle," is how I answer.

"That meeting you wanted is on. Back at the Ritz. Come prepared to take over tonight."

"I haven't agreed to take the job."

"Be that as it may," he says. "That decision happens tonight, and you need to be ready to stay the night."

"That gives me no time to prepare."

"Go by your apartment. Get your things. That's all the preparation you need. I'll meet you at the hotel elevator in an hour. Don't be late this time."

"An hour and a half."

"An hour," he repeats, and hangs up.

I shove my phone in my pocket. "Whoever I'm guarding is at the Ritz waiting on me. I told them I want to meet the person first. They've agreed, but expect me to come prepared to stay the night."

Footsteps sound and Blake joins us, stepping between myself and Royce. "We're going to Italy, but fuck you both for not telling me you'd found Alvarez."

"Blake, man—" I begin.

"Fuck you, Kyle," he says. "We're brothers. All of us. You don't fucking keep secrets like this." He looks at Royce. "And you, brother. You have a wife. You know Kara changed everything for me. I put Kara before revenge."

"I also know from having a wife," Royce says, "that secrets are poison. I didn't want you to have to choose to keep one from Kara. I wanted to know if this was real before we told you."

"I have to go," I interject, and knowing that if Blake hacked our records he knows everything. "I'm meeting the person they're paying me to guard."

"So you're in," he says, his tone flat.

"I'm in," I confirm. "I'll make this count, Blake. If I can find her—"

"I get Alvarez," he says. "I get to be the one who

kills him."

"Blake, damn it—" Royce begins, and before he finishes Blake is flattening him with a stare.

"Don't tell me how killing him will blacken my soul or some fucking bullshit like that, big brother. I'm killing him. And right now, I'm leaving the country with Kara on this job, which will be long enough to save everyone you can before I do it." He turns around and walks down the stairs.

Royce and I look at each other and I sigh. "I guess that's as contained as he gets."

"No," Royce assures me. "It isn't. And as I said, I'll contain him. You just go do your job."

"Right. I'm leaving, but from this point forward, I'm keeping only the phone line I purchased for this job on me." And because undercover is what I do well, I reach into my pocket and hand him my company phone I use for about everything, but undercover work. "I don't want it on me." He nods, accepting it and I add, "Tell Blake how to reach me and I'm sure I don't have to say this, but I have to say it. Make sure he knows we're using only non-traceable lines, from this point forward."

"Copy that," he says. "Just for confirmation. All calls will come from a line that be routed to a disconnected message if called by an unknown number. And all calls made from the line will be automatically purged by our team."

"Excellent," I say, turning and heading for the back door, and doing so, with the world on my shoulders. Blake's world. Kara's world. And maybe, just maybe, Myla's life, but that would be a good thing. It would mean she's not dead and I have the chance to save her. Exiting the bar, the hot air suffocates me, but my adrenaline is pumping, my desire to know where this is headed, high. Clicking my locks open, I have the tingling sensation of being watched.

My lips quirk. Like I don't know Alvarez's people have been following me everywhere I fucking go. I climb into the Mustang and settle my phone into the holder connected to my dash. "Siri, text Whataburger."

"Yes Kyle. What would you like to say?"

"Eyes on the bar," I say, starting the engine.

"Texting: Eyes on the bar. Text sent."

"Clear text, Siri," I say, putting the car into drive.

"Text cleared, Kyle."

And now I'm ready to find out who is worth a million dollars in eight weeks to Alvarez, and why.

• • •

An hour later, I've picked up a week's worth of clothes, and handed my keys off to Les again. I also palm him a hundred dollar bill. "My bags are in the trunk. Make sure you're the only one who touches them and bring them to me when I'm ready."

He glances down at the bill, and gives me a short nod. "With pleasure, sir."

I leave him and make my way inside, then to the elevator, where Juan waits on me, sans his sister. "You didn't need your chick bait this time?" I ask.

He punches the elevator button and arches a brow. "Chick bait? I'm sure I don't know what you mean."

"You wanted to know if I could be bought or bribed with pussy, which I assume is because of certain aspects of your business." In other words, their sex trafficking operation.

"Among other things," he concurs, and when the doors open we both step inside the car, where he sticks his key in the slot and punches in a floor. "You are here for business. You get your pleasure elsewhere unless you're offered compensation outside of cash."

"By the powers that be."

"Yes."

"Which would be who?" I ask, since he's yet to tell me Alvarez is alive.

"To you, that's me. You get all your instruction from me and through me."

"And this person I'm protecting is important to you or your boss?"

"Whatever, and whoever, is important to my boss, is important to me. Enough for me to bleed."

"No one bleeds when I'm around, unless I want them to," I assure him, but of course, I want him to, and a perk of no longer being with the FBI is that there's no longer any paperwork and reviews to follow when he does bleed.

His eyes narrow on me, as if he's reading my mind, the intelligence in his stare declaring him a dangerous and worthy adversary, poorly placed between me and the powers that be. The elevator stops moving and he steps forward, expecting that I'll follow, and it's then I decide he's not all that smart after all. You don't put a man you've indicated you don't trust at your back. I damn sure wouldn't.

But he has, and I follow, falling into pace with him as we find our way to a double-door entrance into a suite. "You have fifteen minutes to decide if you want the job." He slides his card and opens the door, making it clear that I'm to enter alone.

"That should be plenty of time," I say, stepping into a long hallway that seems to walk a path through a massive suite, which must be bigger than many houses. The kind I've stayed in as a protective guard for a few elected officials and a movie star, compliments of Walker Security.

I shut the door behind me and flip the bolt shut, ensuring my fifteen minutes is alone, and extended, should I wish to stay longer. Instinct has me sliding a hand under my jacket, just below my gun, and the one at my ankle is more cool comfort. I start down the hallway, cautiously inspecting an empty office, several bedrooms and bathrooms, before finally reaching the end of the path, opening to a living room wrapped in windows. It's there in the archway that I pause, sucking in air, at the sight of a woman with her back to me, staring out of the window, her petite body silhouetted in a fitted black pant suit. Adrenaline surges through me at the realization that, even without her ever turning, I know her identity. A year of searching and I've found Myla, but I don't shout for joy, nor will I grab her and just get her out of here, because nothing too good to be true, is ever true. For all I know, she's one of the Alvarez clan now and that could make her lethal to everyone in the Walker family circle, including me.

Chapter Two

KYLE

I step behind a lounge-style chair that frames the living area while Myla seems to sense me, or hear me, turning to face my direction. Her eyes, that I know to be a pale green, land on me, and the realization that this really is Myla, who had become real to me in ways I can't begin to understand or explain, downright punches me in the chest. She's in the room with me, alive, rather than the one place I couldn't have saved her from, which was death. And beautiful. So fucking beautiful, and while I knew this, she is far more striking in person than in her photos, or even on the security feeds I've replayed of her, over and over again. But she is thinner than she was, her cheekbones more defined, and oddly, somehow softer and yet stronger than I expect in the same moment. It's a contradiction I do not completely understand, nor do I try. Not yet, but I will, when I have time and space to process this moment and this event.

She grabs the back of one the sofas, and the entire living room of furniture divides us. A square table. Another couch to the left. Two chairs to the right. She is uneasy, seeming to welcome the separation while I do not.

"I guess you're my new bodyguard," she says, as if this isn't her first rodeo.

"If I decide to take the job."

"Why wouldn't you take the job?"

"Surely you know protecting you and failing is equivalent to a death wish?"

"Why would you fail?"

"Why would I fail?" I ask. "Not why is this job a death wish?"

"Isn't that obvious?" she asks, laughing, the sound a nervous but somehow musical note. "If you die, I died first."

My lips quirk. "That is a good point."

"I'd prefer neither of us die at this moment in time," she says, "but of course, I don't know you and you don't know me."

"In other words, you might prefer me dead tomorrow?"

"Or you me."

There is a rebellious lift to her chin with those words, the action not quite echoing the far more uncertain look in her eyes. "I won't want you dead, unless of course you're actually trying to kill me."

"Fair enough," she says, though she makes no promise not to try to kill me, which I assume is because she believes I work for her captor. "You wanted to interview me," she adds. "I assume you have questions?"

I do, but I don't immediately reply, my mind still on her

motives, on her living in luxury. Perhaps she's been swayed by the money and power to embrace the dark side. It's not an idea I relish, and I shove it aside. "Let's sit," I say.

"That's a yes to questions," she concludes, rounding the couch to claim a seat on the chair.

I join her, but choose to sit on the table, directly in front of her, our knees a few inches from touching, her perfume teasing my nostrils with some tantalizingly floral scent, while her eyes go wide. "You're sitting very close to me," she says, sounding confused, and a bit breathless, a detail I'm man enough to admit, I fucking love.

"I want to look into your eyes," I declare.

She purses her lips and when I expect her to scoot away or cower, she surprises me and leans forward, her elbows on her knees. "What do you want to know?"

I mimic her position, leaning in as she has, the space between us narrowed to a margin that without question, sizzles between us. "Why am I protecting you?"

"Because someone hired you to do so."

"What's your story? What's your name?"

"I know they told you my name."

"They didn't," I assure her.

Surprise flickers in her eyes, several beats passing before she finally says, "My name is Myla," and we linger there, our bodies a reach or a sway from touching, while questions sway and swerve in the air, and they are not just mine. She is sizing me up, looking for something indefinable in me that I try to understand and never get the chance.

She leans back abruptly, while I stay where I'm at, offering her no further distance and reprieve. "What else do you want to know?"

"Your story," I say. "Who you are. What you are. Why you're important enough to pay me the insane amount of money I'm being paid."

"Who am I? What am I? Those are questions people ask about themselves all their lives, and often can't answer. Why is that important?"

"That death wish connects us. I need to know you aren't a loose cannon about to explode in my face."

"I'm not."

"Prove it," I challenge. "How did you come to be where you are at this moment in time?"

"I was down on my luck and this rich, handsome, older man stepped into my life, and everything changed."

"That man is who?" I ask, looking to confirm the identity of the powers that be.

"Alvarez, of course," she says quickly.

"Of course," I say, though it's not quite the absolute confirmation that he's alive that I'm looking for. "Am I protecting him as well?"

"He has his personal guards," she says, giving me my confirmation, and telling me he travels with more than one security person.

"Why aren't they guarding you?"

Her eyes become wise. "Did they really tell you absolutely nothing or are you testing me?"

"They really told me absolutely nothing."

"Then maybe Juan is testing me."

"Why would he test you?"

She cuts her gaze and then looks at me, her stare and voice steadier. "I'm here for my own personal business, while Michael is tied up with his."

It's not an answer, but the use of Alvarez's first name in an intimate, familiar way, is another punch in the chest, and now I sit back. Her eyes flicker a moment, telling me she's noticed and questions why, but I give her nothing, while I work to extract what I need. Proof she isn't a willing part of this world. "What business?" I ask.

"I'm starting a clothing line. I'm hiring models for a show and setting up my first store here. It's all very exciting."

Only her voice doesn't say it's exciting, when it should be. "Why in Dallas, Texas, rather than New York?"

"Texas is economically strong." Her answer is quick and practiced. "And it's becoming quite the fashion expo here," she adds.

"And this is your dream?"

"Yes," she says softly. "And if you're guarding me you'll get to have models and share the excitement with me."

"I don't care about models or excitement. If I'm guarding you, it's you I care about."

"I guess Michael can make that worth your while."

"Once I take a job, it's no longer about the money. It's about the person."

"Until you're told otherwise."

"That's not how this works."

"Yes it is, but luckily Michael wants me protected."

"Others want you dead?"

"Everyone is always after Michael and looking for any weakness."

"Like getting to his woman," I say, looking for her to declare herself no such thing, but that isn't the answer I get.

"Anyone close to him," she amends, and I'm not sure if it's meant to broaden my thinking or because she doesn't like to be called his woman. And I damn sure can't reveal myself to her until I'm certain she hasn't actually formed a loyalty to Michael that supersedes her love for her sister.

"What about you?" she asks. "What's your story?"

I arch a brow. "Are you interviewing me now?"

"The death wish thing," she says. "I'd like to know you're not a loose cannon about to blow up in my face."

My lips quirk. "I'm not."

"Prove it. What's your story?"

It's my opening to connect me to her sister. "I'm ex-FBI."

Her eyes widen and her delicate little throat bobs. "FBI?"

"Is that a problem?" I ask, when I hope instead it's a solution, and her out of this.

"No," she says quickly, giving me the wrong answer, but the only one possible considering she doesn't know me as anyone but a man Alvarez has hired. "Why would that be a problem?"

"You look shocked."

"Michael doesn't radiate toward law enforcement inside his inner circle, and I would think the reverse would be true for you as well. You're working for a criminal."

"And you're sleeping with a criminal."

Her spine stiffens, her expression turning thunderous. "And you're an asshole."

Her reaction is fierce and real, but once again, I can't be sure where that reaction originates. Guilt? Fear? A feeling of being trapped? I hope like hell it's one or all of those, not defensiveness because she really is into this life and Michael Alvarez. If that is a real part of this equation, or even if she's developed Stockholm syndrome, which would complicate the hell out of this, it doesn't matter. I still want to save her.

No. I'm going to save her, whether she likes it or not, but if it's against her will, it's going to gut Kara and become a blow to the entire Walker clan, who have become my family. Who am I kidding? This isn't just personal for the Walker clan. It's personal for me and that makes it dangerous.

I stand and she scoots to the edge of the chair, almost as if she wants to grab me and keep me from escaping, but instead presses her hands to her legs. "Are you leaving?"

"I'm going to talk to Juan."

"And?"

"And what, Myla?" I ask, sounding short. I feel it, too, considering I expected Juan's head games, not hers, and I think she might be playing me.

"Are you going to take the job?" she asks, and there is just a hint of urgency in her voice that I'm not sure she intends.

I stare at her—a beat...two—trying to figure out her motives. "Do you want me to take the job?"

"Yes actually," she says quickly. "I do."

"Why?" I ask.

"Does it matter?"

"Yes. It matters."

"Because now I know you."

"Neither of us know each other any more than we did a few minutes ago when you said we didn't."

"I know you well enough to know I want you to take the job."

"Why?" I repeat, hoping like hell it's the FBI-Kara connection. The doorbell rings. "Why, Myla?" I press, looking for a hint of something, anything that tells me she's looking for help.

"The devil you know," she says softly.

"Some call Alvarez the devil."

"Yes. They do."

"Do you?"

"Everyone does," she replies, doubling down on the comment, and when I want to demand that she explain, that she give me just a little more, the knocking thunders ten times faster and louder, followed by a doorbell.

My lips thin. "Obviously Juan is an impatient man, which is not a virtue." Ready to get rid of him, and get back to the work ahead of me with Myla, I start to move away, but never get the chance.

"Wait," she says, grabbing my hand, and suddenly she is standing in front of me—close, really damn close—and there is this dart of electricity between us that is like a shot in the arm. It's unexpected when perhaps it shouldn't be, after a year of looking for her. A year of hearing stories about her. A year of those green eyes that are just as vulnerable in this moment as they were on the video tape, which only makes me want to keep her alive more.

I lift our now joined hands between us. "If there are cameras in here," I warn softly, "you'll get us both killed."

"You were sitting—"

"Too close, but I did it, not you."

She pales, looking visibly shaken. "Oh God," she murmurs. "You're right. I'm so sorry." She sits back down, proving she knows the danger this world represents and I sense the fear in her. But does she welcome it? I know people who do. Certainly those with Stockholm syndrome forget who and what they are, and even what normal feels like.

"Open up!" Juan shouts. "Open up now!" I turn on my heel, intending to go deal with the piece of shit, when I hear, "Wait," again, and the plea in that word stops me in my steps.

Pausing, I face her, hoping some grand confession will follow that tells me she's still on our side. Instead, she asks, "What are you going to do?"

"I haven't decided," I say, when of course I'm taking the damn job and I hope like hell she wants me to for the right reasons. Because she does want me to take it. That much is clear.

I turn and start walking again, my stride long as I head toward the door that jerks and hits the resistance of the deadbolt I've latched.

"Open the fuck up, Kyle," Juan growls.

"Impatient much, Juan?" I demand. "Let go so I can unlock it."

He does as I say and I pull my gun, opening the door and shoving it at his chest at the same moment he does the same with his, to me. "What are you trying to pull?" he demands.

"I wasn't aware that conducting the interview you invited me to was pulling anything."

"And yet you dead bolted the door and pulled a gun on me."

"If this was a test, which I suspect it was, I assumed you'd want to know that I actually thought of things like locking the door and that I was smart enough to open it with my weapon pulled."

His teeth grind together, eyes glinting hard. "What took so long?"

"Holy fuck, man. I barely got the woman to speak to me until five minutes ago. You didn't tell her shit about the man who's supposed to be protecting her."

"That's your job. Put the gun down."

"Not a moment before yours is down."

"On three," he says, sounding and looking exceedingly irritated.

"One, two, three."

I give him a beat of movement before I lower my weapon, both of us re-holstering at the same time. "I'll be needing a down payment," I say, playing the game.

"Let's go inside and step into a private room."

I back into the hallway, letting him go first, and he stupidly strides forward as if he owns the world, when all I see is a man who, once again, freely places me at his back. No wonder Alvarez needs to hire help. Shutting the door, I lock it to maintain the façade of it being about safety, when I'd really like to pin him against the wall, and beat the shit out of him. If that wouldn't blow my chance of getting Myla out of here alive, by her own free will or not, while still rescuing the women in Alvarez's sex trade operation, I would. I fantasize instead about a moment not far down the road. One where I either make him do that bleeding I'd wished for earlier, or at least, help the FBI cuff him and take him to a steel cell with all kinds of new friends to welcome him by bending him over in all kinds of intimate ways.

He cuts right and into a bedroom, far away from Myla, which I assume is the point. "Shut the door," he orders, but I've already done it, joining him in the mini living area to the left of the door and past a desk, where he sits on the couch, no doubt to downplay the full twelve inch difference in our heights.

I give him an even playing field, that would only be even if I was the man I say I am, claiming the chair to his left and he sets a folded sheet of paper on the table. "That's what we expect from you. Either you can deliver it or you can't, but before you read it, know this. Her sister's FBI and disapproves of Myla's choice to be involved with our operation."

Ex-FBI, I silently amend of Kara, wondering if he doesn't know that, or simply chooses not to tell me.

"The entire reason the powers that be want you," he continues, "is that your knowledge and expertise will be useful in protecting her not just from our enemies, but her sister."

This isn't a surprise. In fact, it was part of how we set this up. "You can call the powers that be Alvarez," I say. "Myla does, and as for the situation, I'm a master of staying off the FBI's radar. Does her sister know she's in Dallas?"

"She thinks she's in San Francisco."

"Then we don't have a problem."

"Make sure it stays that way." He reaches into his pocket and hands me a folded sheet of paper, his brown eyes glinting with disdain, I haven't earned, but plan to earn.

I make no move to accept it, already rising to the challenge. "What is it?"

"Additional instructions. The ones that really matter."

I pick up both documents, scanning the details that amount to Myla barely going to the damn bathroom by herself. This is not someone they trust and I say that much. "If she's this much of a risk, why is she about to be on her own?"

"Two motivations. For starters, her business is an excellent place to funnel money, but at the core of this, Alvarez wants to believe she isn't a risk. He wants her to prove herself and he's giving her the freedom to do so."

"But he has doubts," I assume, and despite the fact that it probably kept her alive, I'm really not liking what seems a growing certainty that a kingpin has an attachment to Myla.

"A man like him always has doubts," Juan replies, "and if they're valid, it's your job to find out. That's what he wants from you. Find out. Use your FBI background and outsider persona to get her to turn on him if you can. And consider this your gateway drug to a lot more work and money." He stands and so do I. "I'll leave you with her." He rounds my chair and heads for the hall, while I turn, following in his footsteps, until he pauses at the door, and looks at me. "Trust is earned. I'll have several men on your heels at all times."

"Anyone I don't know could get shot. Make sure they announce themselves."

"Of course, they'll introduce themselves. At least, the ones in your line of sight."

"Why not have them guard her?"

"I told you. You're an outsider who can find out where her loyalty lies. And they'd end up dead, like you will if you fuck her."

He exits the bedroom, disappearing into the hallway. I listen to his footsteps thunder and then soften, the door opening and shutting. I follow in his wake, wasting no time, reaching the lock, and flipping it shut to ensure no introduction takes me by surprise. And Juan was wrong, I think. I won't end up dead if I fuck Myla. I'll end up with my balls in my throat, ripped there by one of the Walker clan. And the very fact that I'm even thinking about that as a problem is a problem in and of itself. One that could get me and her killed.

Chapter Three

KYLE

I start down the hallway and I'm almost to the living area when Myla appears in the archway separating me from the living area. "You took the job," she says softly, standing her ground as I stop in front of her.

"Yes, I took the job, and we're going to talk about why you wanted that to happen, but just not now. Not until I secure the room." I step around her, that sweet floral scent of her perfume following me all the way to the desk in the corner of the living area, where I grab the phone receiver and punch in the number to the bell desk.

"I need to speak to Les," I state, and the very fact that I'm still smelling flowers, and thinking of dark hair and green eyes, tells me how much Myla affects me.

"He's not available," the female attendant on the line replies.

"Tell him it's Kyle," I reply. "The one in the Mustang."

"Oh yes, sir." I hear a complete change of her tone telling me money talks to Les. "He's expecting you. Wait just one moment."

I start to turn and check on Myla, but already I hear, "This is Les."

"I need you to personally bring my bags here to my room," I instruct. "I assume you can see where I'm calling from."

"Yes sir. The private wing. I'll be right up."

I end the call and turn to find Myla standing in front of me, no more than two steps away. "Secure the room?" she asks, folding her arms protectively in front of her. "What does that mean? Is there a threat of some sort?"

"No active threat," I assure her, "but considering you're Michael Alvarez's woman—"

"Please don't call me that."

"Are you saying you aren't his woman?"

"I'm saying you make me sound like a possession." She doesn't give me a chance to declare its accuracy, already moving back to her prior worry. "Why do you need to secure the room?"

"From this point forward, I'll be securing every room you enter, as long as you're under my protection."

"Juan's people checked out the room."

"Juan's people aren't responsible for your safety or mine." And then because I can't have her alerting anyone about what comes next, I step closer to her, our legs nearly touching, my voice a mere murmur. "I'm going to sweep for recording devices and get rid of them. Then we're going to have that talk we mentioned."

I back away, but she grabs my arm. "No," she hisses, her fingers gripping my jacket sleeve, our eyes colliding, the spark of some unnamed something I've sensed between us spiking hard and fast.

I arch a brow. "No?"

"Don't cross them."

Her voice is barely audible, but I respond to the panic I sense in her, my hand settling on her shoulder. "You wanted me to take this job," I remind her.

"And I want you to consider who you're working for."

"I know what I'm doing," I promise. "And I need you to trust me to protect you." I pause, our gazes colliding, the air between us heavy. "Trust me."

"Trust you? I don't know you."

"That's not what you said earlier."

"I don't know you," she repeats, pulling her hand back as if she's just been burned.

But I don't let her escape, my fingers snagging her waist, my hand remaining firmly at her shoulder. "You will," I assure her, "and when you do, you won't feel the fear I see in your eyes when I'm with you. Of that, I can promise you." I release her, taking a step back, and she turns to walk away but not before I see the wash of unreadable emotion over her face, which has me wishing I could grab her and pull her to me and promise her things I don't even know if she wants to hear.

But I can't and I don't, because even if we weren't being recorded, nothing I can say or do at this point changes the fact that she doesn't know or trust me. The truth is, no matter what fear or panic she's shown me, no matter how much hate she has for Juan, I can't count on the Myla that

Kara remembers still truly existing. I can't even count on the spark I feel between her and I, indicating she's not in love with Alvarez, but loyal to him, be it real or because she has Stockholm syndrome, which in and of itself could make her irrational and dangerous to both of us. And right now, I have to focus on drawing lines in the sand with the Alvarez clan, and creating a free zone for her and I to communicate.

Reaching into my pocket, I remove a small electronic box, flipping the device on. It begins to beep and I turn in the direction it guides me, letting it lead me back to the desk. Reaching for the phone, I flip it over and remove the pencil head-shaped microchip I find there that could easily be mistaken for a battery. Resetting the scanner, I turn toward the room again, and find Myla now facing me, a question in her eyes. I hold up the chip between my fingers, showing it to her. Her chest slowly rises, her gaze lifting skyward, her reaction clearly indicating that she is not pleased, though I'm not sure if it's about the room being bugged, or about me removing the recording devices.

Whatever the case, I slip the microchip into my shirt pocket, and resume my search, locating two more devices. By this time, Myla is sitting on the couch watching my search, her expression emotionless, as I switch gears to begin a sweep of the air vents, and pretty much every nook or cranny where a camera might be hidden. "This room's clean," I announce, now certain that my two up close and personal encounters with Myla, though easily played off as attempts to test her loyalty to Alvarez, have not been recorded. I point to the master suite. Is that yours?"

"Yes," she confirms. "That's mine and…" She seems to reconsider whatever she is going to say, before repeating,

"It's mine."

"We'll inspect it last and end with a bang," I say. Not giving her time to argue, I walk to the opposite side of the room and enter the dining area, where I find a single chip. Exiting back into the living area, Myla is back to staring out the window, and I can only hope she's wistfully imagining escape, which I can give her, not my demise. I leave her there, heading down the hallway, where I search an office, a bathroom, and two more bedrooms, collecting only three more devices. I've just reached the junior suite by the door where I'd met with Juan, which is a perfect location for me to set up my room, and an electronic monitoring center, when the doorbell rings. I flip the "off" button on my scanner, stick it in my pocket, and step into the hallway, finding Myla hovering several feet away, her expression stark.

"It's my luggage," I assure her. "You heard me call for it." She nods, but she doesn't look convinced. In fact, she looks pretty damn certain that we're both about to have a gun pointed at our heads, which I find doubtful, but not out of the question.

Giving us both a little peace of mind, I slide my jacket back, exposing the Glock at my ribcage. "If it's Juan," I comment, "I say that I shoot him."

She doesn't laugh. "What if it really is him?" she says worriedly.

"It's not."

"You can't know that."

"Even if it is, I have several big guns and I know how to use them."

Her eyes spark. "You think it's that easy?"

I sober quickly, and don't even hesitate to shackle her

elbow and walk her to me. "I do not think dealing with Juan is easy," I assure her. "But I can handle him and I'm not going to let you get hurt. I promise."

She pulls away from me, as if my touch is fire, and I'm not sure if that's good or bad. "You can't make that promise," she says, "and you know it."

"I can and I am." Another knock sounds and I turn my attention to the door, calling out, "Who is it?" and receiving an immediate reply of, "Les, from the bell desk, sir." I refocus on Myla. "See? Everything is okay."

"For now," she concedes. "But he'll be here soon."

I'm not sure if she means Alvarez or Juan, but either way, I can't leave Les waiting. I flip the lock and then erring on the side of caution, crack it open, confirming Les is indeed alone. Opening the door, I greet him, and step into the hallway to help him deal with my half a dozen equipment-heavy bags. By the time I've returned, Myla is walking toward the living area.

Eager to get back to my work before Juan does indeed show up, I help Les gather the remainder of my bags, deposit them in my room, and then walk him to the exit, where I palm him a hundred dollar bill. "I'll be here with Myla on an extended stay," I explain. "I need a man on my side and I'll be generous in exchange for loyalty. There will be five of those a day for you."

He glances at the cash, and then at me, approval etched in his stare. "Consider it all yours. What do you need?"

"For now, just give me a heads up on any visitors coming my way, and that needs to happen even when you're off shift. We'll work through further details later."

"Consider it done. How should I contact you?"

We exchange cellphone numbers before he departs and I flip the lock back into place. With Myla still MIA, I quickly remove my scanner from my pocket again, turning it back on, and then locating one last recording device inside my temporary room. Ready to search her room, I head back into the hallway, but just as I'm about to enter the living room, she once again steps into my path. "I know you really think—" she begins.

"Not yet," I warn softly, indicating my shirt pocket, where the live chips are still present. Her eyes go wide with understanding, and I motion behind her. "Your room."

She inhales and flattens her back against the wall, staring ahead and not looking at me. "Next time it won't be Les at the door," she warns softly, her gaze averted.

"I have a plan," I assure her. "More than one big gun and my own set of rules."

Her gaze jerks to mine. "You already said that."

"You needed to hear it again. And no one hired me, or wanted me here, because they thought I was a "yes" man, and I suspect your motive for wanting me hired was the same. Am I right?"

"I can't speak for them."

"No. But you can speak for yourself when I'm done in your room and you will." And with that promise, I move on, crossing the living area again and entering the high-end glitz and glamour of a master suite, decked out in pale blues and fancy artwork.

Pausing a few steps inside the doorway, I scan for potential camera locations, a full living area framed by a wall of windows, to the right of the bed, a dresser with a flat screen TV above it to my right, directly across from a king-sized bed. And that bed, is what holds my attention, tormenting me. For a few brutal moments, I consider the moment Alvarez shows up here, and walks her toward this room, with the intent of shutting the door behind him. I'll want to stop him. I'll want to *kill* him, but if I do, I jeopardize the rescue of every woman caught up in his sex trafficking ring.

The air shifts slightly, and I sense, rather than see, Myla enter the room, her presence jolting me back to the present. I step into action, following the beeping sound to the nightstand closest to the wall of windows framing the room, and remove a chip from the lamp by the bed. Myla says nothing, just stands in the entryway, watching me move through the room, removing chips, and surveying the curtains, furnishings, and movable objects for video equipment. My search leads me to the elephant statue sitting on the cabinet holding the flat screen television, and pointed directly at the bed, which doesn't fit the décor. A quick inspection and I confirm there's a camera inside which means that sick fuck Alvarez was going to watch her sleep. Or maybe it was Juan, in which case I will shoot the bastard.

Fantasizing about how many ways I can kill Alvarez and Juan, and justify doing it myself to Blake, I scoop up the elephant, and walk across the room toward what I assume to be a bathroom. Flipping on the light, I enter a room so white it's blinding, the giant tub on the other side of the bathroom clearly meant to help justify the ten-thousand dollar a night fee I estimate it must cost to stay here.

Setting the statue down on the counter, I pull the plug in the sink, turn on the water and set the elephant inside before removing   the chips from my pocket and tossing them in with it.

"You lied," Myla accuses me, appearing in the doorway.

I turn off the water and face her. "What exactly did I lie about?"

"Not having a death wish for you or me." She glances at the sink and then back at me, her green eyes sharp with certainty. "Any moment, all hell is going to be let loose."

"Good thing I know exactly how to tuck the devil back into his box," I say. "You don't like Juan, Myla. Let me make him go away."

"You can't," she insists, no hesitation in her.

"I assure you, I can." I narrow my eyes on her, trying to read her psyche. "But tell me. Is it just Juan you're afraid of or is it Alvarez, too?

"He paid you to protect me, not hurt me."

"That's not an answer. Are you afraid of Alvarez?"

"You can't defy him and get away with it."

"Again. Not an answer so I'll take that as a yes."

"I didn't say that."

"You didn't have to."

"You are making mistakes you can't take back."

"Being a pushover with these people would be my mistake," I say. "I told you. They didn't hire me to be a "yes" man, and I don't get the impression you've survived in this world by being a wilting flower, either. So why would I?"

"I know my limits," she says, "and you clearly don't."

"And I'm setting my limits while changing yours for the better."

My cellphone starts ringing and she swipes her long, dark brown hair behind her ear. "That's going to be Juan."

"What did he do to you?"

"What he did or didn't do to me isn't what's important. It's what he'll do to us both if you don't answer your phone that matters."

In this case, I'm not sure if the "he" she references is Juan or Alvarez, but I reach into my pocket, grab my phone and hit the answer button. "Yes," I say as my greeting. "I removed the listening devices, and the camera, because she knew they were here, thus I'll never test her loyalty when they're around."

Myla's eyes go wide with shock that quickly shifts to disapproval that, while illogical to me, is not in doubt. It's real. It's a live charge and she whirls around to leave, and not sure what she will do to save herself from whatever perceived threat she feels from me or anyone else, I shackle her arm, maneuver her around, and place myself in the archway to prevent her departure. "The powers that be—" Juan begins.

"You mean Alvarez," I state, while Myla's expression tightens and she turns away from me, putting several steps between us.

"You don't need to name him," Juan states, a reprimand in his words, while Myla sits on the edge of the tiled ledge surrounding the giant tub. "He doesn't like to be named," he adds.

"Tell Alvarez to call me," I reply to spite him, while Myla squeezes her eyes shut, as if she wants to block out everything I'm doing. I wonder what else she's blocked out just to survive this past year and if she knows she's done it.

"You deal with me," Juan snaps. "And I'm sending a team up to re-install the devices, and if you don't like it—"

"If you want to know if she's loyal," I say, leaning against the sink, and placing Myla in profile. "She has to think you aren't looking. She has to believe you aren't watching."

"Knowing we're watching keeps her loyal. Where is she now?"

"In her room," I say, "and pissed at me because she's afraid she'll be blamed for my actions."

"She should be afraid," he replies. "You should be afraid, too."

"Fear isn't loyalty. Fear is a motive to run. You need to know what she'll do when she thinks you're not looking. Do you really want to tell Alvarez that her fear equals her loyalty and then let her burn him later?"

"It's you I'm worried about burning us."

"And yet you're paying me a million dollars for eight weeks of work."

"We are paying you a million dollars," he agrees. "And we expect compliance in exchange."

"Compliance isn't success, and my failure comes with consequences that I'm not willing to pay. I won't operate with my hands tied. If that's what you want, then this isn't the job for me."

"Take her to dinner while we re-install the room devices," he bites out, the reply telling me Alvarez won't be happy if I quit.

"I told her that Alvarez ordered the removal of all devices," I counter.

"You did what?" He all but growls into the phone. "You are pushing my limits, but this changes nothing. In fact, this is good. She'll never know we've re-installed the equipment."

"She knew they were here the first time," I lie. "She's smart. Don't let her be smarter than you. Alvarez needs to tell her he removed them because he trusts her, then, and only then, will you find out if she rises to the challenge or runs for the hills."

He doesn't immediately answer, remarkably silent considering his big mouth, before he says, "I'll be in touch."

"Make it fast," I say, "because time is money that I won't waste."

"I said, I'll be in touch," he snaps, ending the call, and the moment I lower the phone, Myla is standing in front of me, green fire in her eyes.

"First and foremost," she says, "do not speak for me. Telling Juan that I knew about the equipment and didn't tell Michael is bad for me. It means I knew and didn't tell Michael."

"Why is that a problem?"

"It matters," is her only reply. "They're paying you a million dollars to be here with me?"

"Yes. They are. Clearly you mean a lot to Michael Alvarez."

"Silence means a lot to Michael Alvarez," she counters, inferring she isn't what's important, but she's already moved on. "Were you actually hired to protect me or test my loyalty?"

"Both."

"If you're testing me, then why would you tell me that?"

"Because if you fail their test," I say, sliding my phone back in my pocket, "then so do I."

Disappointment flares in her eyes, and quickly shifts to anger. "So this is self-serving."

"This is what you call mutually beneficial. We both stay alive."

"You assume I'm going to betray him," she says,

guarding herself as any survivor would.

"How long have you been with him?" I ask, despite knowing the answer.

"Why does that have to do with anything?"

"How long?" I push.

"A year."

"Then you know him well enough to know that his definition of betrayal and yours might be different. And his is the only definition that matters. I'm not leaving this up to his interpretation."

She inhales and takes a step backward, leaning on the wall directly across from me, several beats passing before she asks, "Why did he choose you over someone else?"

"My FBI background."

"Because of my sister," she says, her voice turning raspy.

"Yes," I confirm. "Because they think I'm the right person to keep you away from her."

"Well then, you're going to impress them because I have no intention of contacting my sister now or ever," she declares, her fingers curling into her palms. "She thinks I'm dead. I'm not going to give her any reason to start a new mission to find me again."

"Because she won't approve of Alvarez?"

"Of course she doesn't approve. She's FBI. Or...I guess you are too, and it doesn't matter to you, but it would to her." She hesitates. "Do you know her?"

There are equal parts hope and fear in that question, and I know that this is a moment of truth or lies that I will have to live with later, a decision thankfully delayed when a phone starts ringing in her pocket. She reaches inside her dress pants, removing it, but all too aware of the potential of Stockholm syndrome controlling her actions, I close the space between us and catch her wrist before she can answer the call. "Are you crazy?" she demands, her eyes and voice sparking with anger. "That's going to be Michael, and the last thing either of us wants right now, I promise you, is for me to ignore him."

"Tread cautiously," I warn. "He wants to trust you and I've given you the resources to ensure he does. Understand?"

"Yes. I understand, so let me go before he starts thinking the wrong thing." I want to know what the "wrong thing" is, but right now the content of her conversation with Alvarez is all that matters. Her phone stops ringing. "Damn it," she hisses. "That's bad. Let me call him back."

"He'll call back," I say, "and we need to get our facts in line."

"I heard the call with Juan. I know what to say."

"You tell him that I told you that I was instructed to remove the recording devices."

"I know," she insists, and her phone starts to ring again. "I have to take his call."

I study her for several more beats, assuring myself we're on the same page, before I release her and when I expect her to quickly answer the call, she doesn't. Instead, her gaze drops to her phone, and she stares down at it. One second passes. Two. "Answer it," I urge softly, instinctively settling my hand on her waist. "You can handle this." For the briefest of moments, that "something" that keeps passing between us is there again, a magnet pulling us together.

It jolts her. I see it in her eyes, and she reacts, cutting her stare, to murmur, "I hope you're right," before with a trembling hand, she answers the call. "Hello," she says, pushing around me to exit the bathroom and enter the bedroom. Seeing this as an opportunity to assess her relationship with Alvarez, I stay where I'm at, listening and observing, in search of the true heart of Myla. "Sorry," I hear her say. "I had to run to the bathroom and left it on the bed. Yes. I know. I was just a minute." There are beats of silence, then, "Of course I knew you monitored me. I didn't know it was a secret, but I do wish that you knew that wasn't necessary. Not with me, Michael."

It's exactly the right thing to say to feed the narrative I've set up. She wants his trust. He can give it to her and with it, enough freedom for me to walk her out of here without gunfire, but then there is silence. And more silence, and without seeing her face, I can't know if that's trouble I need to be ready to handle. Standing, I exit the bathroom, bringing the bedroom into view, finding her sitting on the couch, her body angled away from me, the phone at her ear, as if she's trying to shut me out. I lean on the wall, listening, waiting. And watching.

"He's fine," she finally says. "He's better than Juan. You know how I feel about Juan." She hesitates. "I want you to trust me. You can trust me. I know it's hard for you to believe it anyway, but you won't be sorry for this."

The sincerity in her voice grinds along my nerve endings with such force, it damn near crushes bones. Maybe she's gotten really good at faking it with this man. Or maybe she's actually come to care for him, even if it's Stockholm syndrome, or simply her mind's way of letting her survive. But if I assume she's just surviving, when she might really be in love with Alvarez, the people who care about her, and that I care about, could end up dead.

"I will," she promises. "Yes. I'm very excited about my meetings tomorrow and about how this helps you, too." There is more silence. Then, "Yes. Goodnight." She ends the call and stands, whirling around to face me, steel in her eyes. "You're playing with fire. You're missing the big picture and you need to get a view right now."

"It sounded to me like the call went well."

"A call means nothing," she says. "It's a temporary reprieve for both of us but we're in the same hotel room around the clock for weeks. Those recording devices made sure he didn't have to use his imagination about what's happening when we're alone. The minute he decides we're sleeping together, we're dead." Somehow we've moved to the middle of the room, standing toe-to-toe again, as if a magnetic pull wants us together, and she realizes it at the same moment as me. I see it in her eyes. Feel it in the shift in the air. "This is dangerous," she whispers, and it's clear she's talking about us.

"But I'm not," I promise her, "and on some level you knew that, or you wouldn't have pushed me to take this job."

"I don't know what I thought. I don't know what I think now, but Michael's possessive. The longer you're with me and unmonitored, the more he'll read into who and what we are."

"Do you really want him to read into every interaction we have?"

"No, but…maybe you taking this job was a mistake."

"Nothing about this feels like a mistake," I assure her, letting her read whatever she wants into it. "You need protection and I'm going to do whatever it takes to ensure you stay safe. So yes. I'm close and if I have to get closer, I will."

"What part of "you're going to get us killed," do you not understand?"

"No one is dying that I don't kill or let die."

"No one lives that Michael Alvarez wants dead," she counters, her eyes narrowing, realization of some sort filling her face. "You're not afraid." She sucks in air and then lets it out, before calmly asking, "This is part of the test, isn't it?"

"I'm the one who told you about the test in the first place."

"What better way to make me trust you and then try to convince me to turn on Michael?"

"No," I say, my voice hard steel. "That is not what is happening here. I'm not setting you up."

"But I can't know that, now can I?" She takes several steps backwards. "Please go."

"I'm not setting you up," I repeat, my voice as solid as the wall I can feel between us now that she reinforces by once again folding her arms in front of her. "Myla—"

"I need you to leave and please shut the door behind you."

The urge to refuse, and to demand she trust me, is instant, but I have to force myself to repeat the golden rule of undercover work: Earning trust is critical. Earning trust takes time you won't want to give it. And finally, assuming you have it too soon, can get you and everyone else killed. Accepting these things, knowing they are about survival, I inhale, and with Herculean effort, force myself to walk to the doorway, pausing under the archway without turning.

"I explained my motives and they stand. I'm looking out for only two people. You and me and no one else."

Exiting into the living area, I pull the door shut behind

me, accepting the divide she's demanded, but not for long. In fact, as I walk away, something is clawing at me, warning me that I'm missing something. I stop walking, fighting the urge to return to Myla, every instinct I've honed over the years telling me to pull Myla close and keep her there, and do it really damn fast.

Chapter Four

KYLE

Twelve months of looking for Myla... That I've found her hits me as I walk to the spare bedroom by the front door, and I come to the realization just inside the entryway, my fists pressed to the wall, my head low between my shoulders. "Twelve months," I repeat softly, the timeline surreal. "Twelve months and I found her." Twelve months of knowing in my gut that she wasn't dead, and living with an intense drive to find her.

No. It was an intense need, like I was supposed to be the one who saved her. But I haven't. Not yet.

Now I need to think through a way to make that happen. I replay my interactions with Myla, looking for her motives, her alliances that I might have to fight. My first focus is on the very real fear in her eyes, but I quickly dismiss that as a conclusive way to evaluate where she is with Alvarez.

Lord only knows that I understand how you can condition yourself to feel, and even embrace fear, as a way of being reminded that you're alive. It can be a high you start craving and even needing. So I move on, remembering the shared looks between myself and Myla, so intense that she'd called us "dangerous." I come to one conclusion. If she is truly seduced by this life, or by Michael Alvarez, even by way of being brainwashed, there is no way the attraction between us—and there is an attraction between us—could have been this hot and instant. Out of the blue, her statement about Kara replays in my head: *I have no intention of contacting my sister now or ever.* Those words deliver a jolt of reality and a rationale as to why she's seemingly loyal to a kingpin.

Shit. I push off the wall, and run my hand over the newly forming stubble on my jaw. I'm speculating, but I have damn good instincts, along with a year of studying all things Myla. I would bet money that Myla believes Alvarez will hurt Kara if she does anything but show undying devotion to him. And the thing is, I believe she's right, a problem Royce and I never talked about because we simply didn't think finding Myla would be this easy, if at all. Cursing softly at what could be an imminent threat to Kara, I push off the wall and start unpacking my equipment, with the goal of securing the room and setting up private communication I can use to contact Royce.

A few minutes later, I've unpacked, set up three MacBook Pros on the desk, and claimed the chair in front of them, two of the dozen disposable phones I have with me charging next to me. I then move on to a quick hack of the hotel computer system, pulling up views inside and outside the building, though irritatingly nothing for this floor, where you'd think high profile clients would dictate monitoring. Once I have eyes on every spot I can manage, and I've confirmed nothing is needing attention at the moment, I reach for a phone, but hesitate as I glance at the door I don't want to shut.

I leave the phone where it's plugged in, and instead return to my keyboard, opting to activate a private messaging system to ping Royce and type: The assignment starts now. I'm in the private wing of the hotel for several months.

Royce: Who are you protecting?

Caution prevails, out of fear Kara and Blake are with him and I type: Are you alone?

Royce: Yes. Can you call me?

I really need to have a real conversation with him, but concerned the exterior hallway outside the room might be bugged, I'm stuck right where I'm at, with Myla in potential hearing distance. Standing, I scan the area and head to the bathroom, stepping inside to muffle the sound, but still managing to maintain a view of the hallway before punching in Royce's number.

"Talk to me," he demands, answering almost instantly.

"I will," I say, "but softly. I'm not in as private of a location as I like. However, I'm in the private wing of the hotel, where they want me to work for the next eight weeks."

"Protecting who?"

"Myla," I breathe out, keeping my voice low. "I'm protecting fucking Myla." Even saying those words is surreal.

"You have to be shitting me." He sounds as disbelieving as I felt when I first saw her. "You have Myla?"

"I do. She's still his woman, but in my professional opinion, she's surviving and protecting Kara only."

"Holy fuck. Of course, Kara would be his leverage against her, and so would any other family she had, if they existed. Is she suffering from Stockholm syndrome?"

"Considering how quickly she gravitated toward me, I don't think so, but she's scared. I think she might panic if she finds out I'm connected to Kara and I'm not sure how she'll react. But my gut instinct is to get her out of here quickly, even if I don't tell her what's going on before we extract her."

"If we do that, then we force her, Kara, and Blake into hiding for the rest of their lives if we aren't careful. Hell. We might force ourselves there."

"Then we have to do a turnaround on him. Let's make him think she's dead."

"He could kill you for that."

"I can handle me. Let's get a plan that gets her out of here safely and I'll frame my exit plan. And if that means I need to get out of the country for a while to ensure I don't lead Alvarez to the team, so be it."

"We aren't throwing you into a black hole."

"Someone will need to acclimate Myla to a new life. It makes sense for me to disappear with her, at least for a while. And…" I consider a moment. "Kara leaving the country right now, at the same time Myla disappears, might be suspicious and bring attention to her."

A beat passes before Royce concedes, "You're right. I'll talk to Luke and between us, we'll come up with a plan for handling Blake and Kara."

"If you tell them—"

"They'll want to be involved," he says. "I know that, but I'll be damned if I want to lie to them anymore than I know you do. Let me talk to Luke."

"Don't tell Blake and Kara anything until you talk to me."

"Agreed. I'll get with Asher and Jacob tonight, and we'll put together several extraction options, but I can tell you, we're going to need more information. Who is around you both? What is she doing in the next eight weeks?"

"I won't know those things for a few days."

"What can you tell me?"

I update him on the little I know. The business I kick myself for knowing nothing about when I should. Juan. And finally the recording devices and camera I removed. "Myla is terrified of Alvarez creating a worse version of what he can't see on film."

"Maybe he'll have to come see for himself," Royce says.

"Exactly," I say. "But that means we need to be ready for him immediately, and at this point, I can't be sure Myla would leave of her own free will, should we decide to extract her. And Royce, man. I don't know if I can let him touch her again."

"I get it, man. I haven't met her like you have, but I feel like I know her. I feel the same. But if you move too fast—"

"All the women he's forced into his sex trade operation are lost unless she can help us get to them. I know. Stay the course as long as I can."

"And if you reveal yourself to her too soon, and you're wrong about her—"

"I might end up dead. I got it. Not the outcome I'm looking for, but if it's my judgment that I have to extract her without her prior agreement, I'll make it."

"Understood and we'll be right there with you." He

pauses a moment. "It's eight-fifteen. We'll have eyes on you, but give me a verbal every ten to twelve hours so I know you're safe. If you hit thirteen, I'm going to assume you have a problem. And try to contact me at a time and place where we can discuss plans."

"Copy that," I say.

We end the call and I flip over the phone, remove the chip and destroy it, before my gaze lands on the empty hallway, but I don't see the empty space. I see that year-old security footage, and Myla's green eyes looking into the camera, with a plea for help in their depths that I fully intend to answer.

• • •

MYLA

Time seems to stand still as I pace the master suite, trying to get my head around everything that has happened in the past hour, and how it impacts my plans, if Kyle will impact them in a good or bad way, if at all. Whichever it might be, Kyle is a reminder that Michael trusts no one, not even me, completely, and I cannot ever forget that.

Dragging my hand through my hair, I ignore the bed, and walk to the window framing the living area in the far right corner of the room, staring out at the Dallas skyline without really seeing it. Instead, I think of the one year, two months, and four days I've been with Michael Alvarez. That's how long it took for him to allow me any freedom and even that is a façade. And now, Kyle is here, and the very fact that he's not Juan is a huge relief, but I don't know his motives, and he's just…I don't know what he is, besides really overwhelming. And intense. And appealing in ways that make him very, very dangerous, especially since he has this crazy way of making me feel safe just by existing, but he could be part of this trap Michael is setting for me.

Blinking, I try to focus on the skyline, the twinkle of city lights touching the now dark horizon, but my mind drifts. *He wants to trust you*, Kyle had said of Michael. He's right. He does, and though he's resistant to really do it, this is a big step that I've struggled to make with him. This is a good thing that helps me become the new me, so why does it feels so damn dirty? Why do I still feel so damn dirty? I press my hand to my face, the blood rushing in my temples. I'm going to drive myself crazy if I stand here much longer. I need to do something. I need out of this room.

Crossing to the dresser, I open a drawer, pausing a moment with the memory of the statue that had sat on top and held a camera. Were the cameras meant to stay or were they were part of a setup and a game? Because if they were real, and Kyle saved me from them, that means Juan would have watched me dress and undress. Was Michael really going to let that happen?

It's a horrible thought, considering Juan is not like everyone else to Michael. I think he would have let it happen. Juan has to go and maybe, just maybe, no matter what Kyle's role in all of this, he's the one who can make that happen.

Encouraged by that idea, I remove a pair of black workout leggings, a black tank top and sports bra, as well as socks, before walking to the giant closet by the bathroom, and flipping on the light. Quickly changing, I pull a black hoodie off a hanger, slip it on, and stuff my phone in the pocket. Somehow, I end up staring at myself in the mirror behind the door, trying to remember a time when I'd bought my own clothes, reveling in every item I'd saved and craved until it was mine. I don't even know that person anymore, and my sister, Kara, wouldn't know this one I am now. And she can't ever know this me, nor am I stupid enough to forget that, though the very fact that Kyle was asked to keep me away from her says that Michael isn't sure of that fact.

Knots form in my belly, where my hand presses, then balls into a fist. I need him to know that I'm with him and loyal. About to drive myself crazy all over again, I exit the closet, and don't give myself time to think about the crazy butterflies Kyle's presence seems to have given me, or about his hot, probing stares, all of which could be a planned seduction. I sure as heck don't let myself think about the way he clearly analyzes my every thought and motive. I push onward and I don't stop walking until I'm at the bedroom door and pulling it open, exiting into the living area, where I find him absent. Deciding he must be in one of the many bedrooms, most likely by the door, where he would know if I tried to leave, I hurry down the hallway and pass open doors, where he is not. Finally, I reach the last door, and I hear what I think is fingers hitting a keyboard.

Inhaling against a sudden rush of nerves, I step to the doorway, lingering just outside the room, and knock on the wall. In a blink, Kyle is standing in front of me, big and just so darn masculine, that musky, spicy scent of him exploding in my nostrils.

"Is everything okay?" he asks, his blond hair sexily messed up, his green eyes sharply alert, and guaranteed to see too much.

"Aside from no one trusting me and me not trusting

them, everything is peachy. I just need to take a run. It's stress management for me. I know you get dragged where I go, but—"

"Give me a minute to change," he says. "And come in. I have security equipment I set up that I want to show you." He widens the door and backs up, but I hold my footing, nervous about entering his bedroom, when Michael would be furious over such an action.

"I'm not going to bite," he says. "At least not now."

My gaze jerks to his, where I find mischief and laughter. "It's not funny," I chide.

"Perhaps not," he says, "but the way your cheeks are heating is absolutely adorable and not at all what I expect from the woman at Michael Alvarez's side." He doesn't give me time to digest that observation, let alone respond, before he's moved on. "And yes. This room is where I plan to sleep, simply because it's also our new security center." He firms his voice to a command. "Come inside." He disappears into the room, assuming my compliance. I could refuse, but somehow, I just don't.

I step beyond the doorway, finding him waiting on me a few steps back, his room a reversed direction, smaller version of my own, only his dresser and TV are on the right wall, and his sitting area is much smaller. "Our new security system," he says, indicating three MacBook Pros sitting on the desk directly in front of his bed. "I want to show you how to operate it."

My brow furrows. He wants to show me how to operate it? This new premise that includes me knowing what's going on around me is something that has me eagerly joining him at the desk. "Okay," he says, leaning down to punch a button on computer number one, and displaying a visual for my view.

"Is that the hotel lobby?" I ask, surprised.

"It is," he says, and then, hitting the "Tab" key, he shows me how to change the view to several other locations. "It's that easy to see every location I have live." He straightens. "Unfortunately this is just what I could hack—"

"Hack?" I ask, turning to face him. "You hacked the hotel security system?"

"I did," he confirms, glancing over at me, "and are you really sounding panicked about that, considering all Michael Alvarez does in his life?"

"I...well...I'm the one here in the hotel, not him."

"Exactly," he says. "You're the one I'm protecting, and I told you I'll do what is necessary to keep you safe. Unfortunately, the hotel doesn't have cameras on our floor, which is an important view for me and you. I'll have to install equipment tomorrow."

"What if you get caught hacking or installing whatever you want to install?"

"I paid the right people to make sure I don't."

"Right," I say. "Of course you did."

"I told you," he adds. "I have a plan. I always have a plan." He softens his voice. "And that plan looks out for my interests, not his, and my interests, are your interests."

"I can't—"

"Know that," he supplies. "Of course you can't. Trust takes time."

"Trust," I say, my throat going a little dry. "That word is..."

"Is what?" he prods, his green eyes hooded, but

somehow probing.

Frighteningly impossible, like he's frighteningly appealing in too many ways to count, but I settle for a reply of, "Difficult," and eager to change the subject, I motion to the desk. "What are the other computers for?"

"One of them is for you," he surprises me by saying. "You'll have the exact same views. And the third is my personal device."

I turn to face him. "Why are you including me?"

"I'd tell you that it's to earn your trust, which wouldn't be untrue, but safety is about awareness. You need to know who and what is normal and right around you at all times. I'm also going to install an encrypted text message program on your computer and phone that you can use to communicate with me. We can use it to talk, should we need to." He glances down at me again. "Eventually, maybe you'll believe it's really safe to say anything to me through that connection or in person."

"Doubtful," I confess.

"I'm persuasive," he assures me with a wink that would really truly get his eyes gouged out if Alvarez saw it, which tells me there aren't any cameras I don't know about. At least, not in here. "Let me grab my clothes and get changed," he adds, reaching up and loosening his tie. "Feel free to sit down and play around with the security feed."

"You don't have to work out with me."

"I'm working out with you," he insists, already walking to the suitcase on the bed, where he begins shrugging out of his jacket. "Have you tried out the gym here?"

"Not yet," I say, leaning against the desk, my hands pressed to the wooden surface while my mouth goes a little dry at the way his white shirt hugs a broad, muscular chest. "I just got here this morning."

"Considering the size of the private wing we're in," he says, flipping open his bag, "I'm surprised there isn't a treadmill in one of the rooms. I'm sure we can have one delivered."

"I like the weights in the gym," I say. "Of course, we're in a hotel. They might not have much to offer."

"There's a great gym a few miles from here," he says, shutting his case, and tossing a hoodie on top. "If this one doesn't make the grade, we can go there." He grabs a stack of clothes and walks into the bathroom directly behind him, but doesn't shut the door.

I stare after him, repeating the word "we", that is oddly right and still so very wrong. This has to be a test, because there is no other reason, or way, that Michael would allow me to be in such intimate quarters with anyone. Unless... he's that afraid of my sister, and he really feels Kyle is the answer to keep her away. That has to be it. This is all about Kara, and the idea that Michael's this focused on her is unsettling. Or maybe it's not a focus on her, but rather on me. On trusting me far less than I thought he did, which means I have to tiptoe with every step I take. I face the desk, my hands settling on the back of the leather chair. Maybe Kyle is telling the truth. Kyle told me Michael's worried about Kara, which I believe. So was he telling me the truth when he said he's not setting me up? Maybe he really is more worried about Michael reading more into his actions, or mine, than he is about Michael assuming actions in the absence of video, which leaves me conflicted. I don't want to be filmed, but I know better than anyone how Michael's creative mind can paint a person an enemy. But it's my enemies I'm most worried about right now. Who is Kyle and what are his motives?

My attention lands on the computer Kyle had said was for personal use, which would certainly hold some sort of clue to him as a person as well as his motives for being here. Not giving myself time to chicken out, I reach down and try to power it to life, only to have a password protector pop up. "Sorry to disappoint, sweetheart," I hear from behind me, whirling around to find him looking hot and hard in gray sweats, a gray t-shirt, with his gun and shoulder holster over the top. "It's password protected." He snatches up his hoodie from the bed, pulls it over his holster, and crosses to stand directly in in front of me. "And I require at least one naked romp in the sheets before I give out my personal passwords. And since you seem to think that would get us killed—"

"It *would* get us killed," I say, and then it hits me that I've inferred I might otherwise. "Not that I would betray Michael. I just…"

"Right. You wouldn't. I get it." He's not smiling. In fact, he seems rather displeased before adding, "I guess you have to ask before you use my computer, then."

"I just wanted to know what you were saying about me," I say, wondering how any one man can exude the amount of heat he is right now. "And what your motives are."

"I told you. I control what Michael Alvarez knows about you and me, and no one else. Are you ready?"

"Yes," I say, but I don't move, my mind returning to the hacking skills he's claimed, and truthfully, I'm curious about this man. So very curious. "Can you hack my phone and my computer?"

"Yes."

"Will you?"

"Yes." He motions to the door. "Ready?"

"Why would you admit that?"

"Because it's what I do. I hack. And I'm damn good at it. You can't spend months with me and not figure that out, unless I don't want you to figure it out."

"Why not hide it from me?"

"Because believe it or not, I want your trust, and I won't get that without being honest."

"Why?"

"Why what, sweetheart?"

"Don't call me that or it—"

"Will get me killed?" he asks, arching a brow.

"Us killed."

"Are you going to tell?"

"No."

"Then unless it offends you, and since you feel like a "sweetheart" to me, when no one else has in a long time, I don't see the problem. Does it offend you?"

"I…if it did, the fact that you just asked if it does makes it not."

"Well then, problem solved. Let's go to the gym, sweetheart."

"You really don't have to work out with me." I eye his gun. "And how are you going to workout in that anyway?"

"It will suck but it's easier to get to than an ankle holster."

"Easier is you not working out with me."

"Of course it is," he replies, zipping up his hoodie to hide his weapon. "But I'm supposed to be the badass who beats everyone up and protects you. I can't do that eating donuts and binge watching Dexter, though I do like me some donuts and Dexter, sweetheart."

"You don't have to do that, either."

"Do what?"

"Make jokes and try to make me comfortable."

"I wasn't aware that I was supposed to try to make you comfortable or uncomfortable. I'm just being me and I happen to like donuts and Dexter. Do you?"

"Do I what?"

"Like donuts and Dexter."

"Éclairs are heaven and I've never watched Dexter."

He looks appalled. "Did you just say that you've never watched Dexter?"

I laugh. "No. I'm not into serial killers."

"He's not like your average serial killer."

"Any serial killer is a serial killer is a serial killer."

"That's where you're wrong. He a vigilante with a code. You can't appreciate it until you watch it."

"Killers make me uncomfortable," I say, and the fact that Michael is one, has me quickly adding, "I won't watch it."

He studies me a moment. "Do you like cartel movies?"

"Not at all and I know you're surmising things about me right now."

"I am surmising, and I imagine you think you know what."

"That I am illogical in all I do."

"No," he says solemnly. "I do not assess you as illogical, in any way, shape or form."

"Then what do you think about me?"

"I think there is far more to your story than meets the

eye and those are the kind of stories that intrigue me. So. You intrigue me."

"I think you're flirting with me."

"Am I?"

"Are you?"

"I'm just being the me I am with you."

"Because they paid you to be."

"No. But you said it and I know the truth. You can't know that. Not yet."

"But I will?"

"Yes."

"Promise?"

"Yes Myla, I promise, but even that means nothing right now." His cell rings and he pulls it from his pocket, glancing at the screen. "Per the hotel staffer I have on payroll," he says, slipping his phone back into his pocket, "a couple of Juan's goons are on their way up here," Kyle tells me, slipping his phone back into his pocket.

"Is Juan with them?"

"No. Juan is not with them but I find it curious that the reason for their visit is less important to hear, than confirmation that Juan isn't with them."

I blanch but recover quickly. "He's difficult. You've seen that. Sometimes, I wish I had a warning bell for that man."

"You don't need a bell. You have me. What did he do to you?"

Now I need space, and I take a step backwards, hitting the desk. His eyes narrow, understanding in their depths that tell me, I've shown my hand. "What about the last sixty seconds made you want to run?

"I wasn't running. I just...he's...." He arches a brow.

"He makes me uncomfortable."

"Did he touch you?"

"What?"

"*Did he touch you?*"

"Why are we talking about Juan?"

"That's a fucking "yes". Did you tell Alvarez?"

"I didn't say he—"

"We both know he did. Did you tell Alvarez?"

"Juan said that if I did, he'd make it look like it was all me and he's Michael's half-brother and—"

"Wait. Juan's his half-brother?"

"Yes and Michael trusts him like he trusts no one else, me included, obviously. Is this where you ask me—"

"No. I'm not going to ask. Juan wants your fear and that is exactly what I see it in your eyes. Alvarez sees it too, and he knows he'll never truly own you, as long as it exists. Be glad I took out the cameras. It would have shown even more on the film."

"It's what doesn't show that I fear right now. What's left to his imagination." There's a knock on the door. "How do you know they aren't coming to get rid of you?"

"I'm not easy to get rid of, sweetheart. Especially when I decide I have a reason to stay around. And I have."

"And that reason is?"

"The same one that made me take the job. You."

Chapter Five

MYLA

"You took the job for me?" I ask, stunned by that declaration, and the many things I could read into that possibility dart through my mind.

"You asked me to take it."

"I did, but you don't know me, so why would anything I ask matter?"

"I choose my jobs based on who I'm protecting, not who's paying the bill."

"And you chose me," I say, and it's not a question. He did, and I want to be happy, but I am not in a position to accept what I don't understand. "Why?"

"Because you aren't one of them."

"And yet you took a meeting thinking I might be one of them?"

"And you just answered that without denying that

I'm right."

I blanch at my mistake and then try to recover. "Different doesn't mean I don't belong."

He arches a brow. "Doesn't it?"

"Is this a test?"

"No," he says. "It's not a test. It's simply my answer. You wanted to know why I took the job. I took it because you're different than them, and if I had any doubt of that, I would have declined the job."

"Then why even take the appointment?"

"A million dollars is always a reason to consider a job. It's not, however, a reason to take one."

A knock sounds on the door again, thundering louder this time, and I jolt, once again hugging myself, when I know better than to show a visible reaction. It says I'm on edge. It says I'm withdrawn, but I justify it because Kyle is new to me. Michael would, in fact, expect me to be nervous with any stranger, most especially one this close to me. And since my gaze somehow collided with Kyle's green one, there is no question that he's noticed, even before he says, "It's okay. They won't be here long."

"We hope," I say. "We don't know why they're here."

"I told Juan if I saw anyone in my line of sight that hadn't introduced themselves first, I'd shoot them."

"I could have about a million fantasies of you actually doing that," I confess.

"If that's your best idea of a fantasy, we have a problem."

"I didn't say it was the best."

"Is it?"

Me killing a few of them myself, Juan especially, would be better, I think, but I say, "Should we be talking about fantasies?"

Another knock sounds on the door, and he shocks me by shackling my waist. Heat rushes through me as he turns me toward the hallway. "I prefer live action fantasies, so be careful what you wish for." I'm pretty sure he's not talking about killing people, but if he is, he's just made it sexy and guilt-free. "Let's get rid of these assholes and then go to the gym," he adds, gently urging me into the hallway, where I quickly pull away from him, but not without feeling the jolt of cold that is the loss of his hot hands.

He, in turn, walks to the door, unzips his hoodie and settles his hand on the gun that's returned as part of his gym wear. "Who is it?" he calls out.

"Ricardo Martinez," comes a familiar deep voice, one that conjures an image of a heavyset, broody Mexican with lots of muscles and a huge scar down his cheek. "Juan sent me."

"Who's with you?" Kyle asks, the question making it clear that he's one step ahead of Ricardo by knowing, or assuming, he's not alone.

"Marcus Chavez," Ricardo replies, while Kyle immediately shoots me a questioning look.

"Mid-forties, tall, lean but athletic with a mix of perpetual ice and hate in his eyes." I shiver just thinking about it. "He's right up there with Juan in my book."

He narrows his eyes on the "scary" description. "Then he won't be back," he assures me, adding an order of, "Stay inside," before he opens the door, and disappears outside, quickly shutting it behind him.

I'm there in a flash, my hands pressing to the door, my ear as well, but all I can make out are muffled voices that lift here and there, before there are footsteps. Then silence. Then some sort of beeping noise. Then the door opens and I have to double-step backwards not to get hit. "Well?" I ask as he appears.

"They left," he says. "And he won't be back without calling first next time. Will that help you relax a little?"

"Some. Thank you."

"The only thanks I need is for you to stop feeling like you have to hug yourself and hide."

"I…" I release my arms and then press them to my hips, before awkwardly folding them in front of me again, and just as awkwardly owning the action I knowingly keep repeating. "It is what it is."

His eyes soften with his voice. "We'll get there," he says, issuing another promise instead of the commands I've become accustomed to with Michael, and it does this funny thing to my chest and belly that I can't quite name. "I'm here to protect you, sweetheart," he adds. "Really protect you. Deep under all that fear you own, you already know that."

"I don't know what I know right now," I confess, but the truth is that there's an energy and confidence about him that, despite just meeting him, makes me, as I suspect it does many around him, feel safe. "I still can't be sure—"

"That I'm not setting you up?"

"I can't ignore the possibility," I amend. "You have to see that."

"I do see that," he says, "and while I don't like it, caution is smart, and something I'm going to encourage you to have every chance I get. Case in point." He holds up another small chip between his fingers. "This was at the front door. Had I not been cautious, I would have missed it. Let me get rid of it and we can go." He disappears into the bedroom, and I follow him, appearing in the doorway at the same moment he enters the bathroom.

"What did Ricardo want?" I call out.

"To intimidate me," he says, re-appearing and moving in my direction, his strides long, confident, his body lean, hard, and powerful.

"And what happened?" I ask, as he stops directly in front of me. Close. So very close and yet for reasons I can't explain, I don't step away. In fact, I inhale the masculine, autumn and spice scent of him, almost forgetting what I've just asked him, until he replies.

"Ricardo and his puffed-up chest amused me," he says, his lips quirking in a sexy smirk.

Amused is not a word I expect in relation to Ricardo. "Does he know he amused you?"

"Since I told him he did, he should, but that one isn't going to start glowing from his IQ anytime soon. Whatever the case, he's getting rid of Marcus. How do you feel about some asshole named Alfredo?"

I'm stunned and pleased with this new development. "Better," I say, but alarm bells replace my relief. "Why would they agree to that? Marcus is a long-term employee. Why are they doing anything you want?" I try to take a step backwards, and he catches my arm, our gazes colliding, and I feel that connection in every part of me.

"Don't run," he orders softly.

"I'm not running."

"We both know you are," he says, and there is this charge in the air that steals my breath, and seems to radiate heat between us.

"You can't keep touching me," I say, but my voice lacks the certainty it should possess, almost as if I want him to tell me he can, when I can't let that happen.

"They're doing what I want," he says, as if I haven't issued the warning at all, "because I'm the best bodyguard money can buy, and I've convinced them that I'm the one who can protect you and them."

"By keeping me away from my sister," I say, forced to dare down this taboo path in a hunt for his agenda.

"Yes," he says, his eyes, those too green, too observant eyes, narrowing before he releases me, folding his arms in front of that broad, perfect chest of his. "What do you want to ask me?"

A hundred questions, all of which could hint at things I don't want him to know. "I asked my question already."

"No, you didn't."

"Then I don't have a question," I say, and then amend, changing the subject. "Actually I do. What time is it?"

He arches a brow. "What time is it? That's your question."

"Yes. It is. I think I might have seen a note that the gym closes at nine."

He glances at a black Gucci watch with red stitching and then back at me. "It's going on nine now."

I sigh. "No run tonight."

"It's seventy outside despite it being February," he says. "We can take an outdoor run, but be warned. The humidity here in Texas, even this time of year, is a bitch until you're used to it."

"I could take the humidity, but I don't want to deal with any game Juan or Ricardo might play with us. Not tonight."

"I can handle Juan and Ricardo if you want to run."

"Thank you, but no," I say. "I don't want you to have to handle them."

"You're sure?"

"Positive. And honestly, I'm starving. I haven't eaten since about six this morning. I'd have crashed and burned on the treadmill, anyway. Are you up for room service?"

"One hundred percent in," he says, "and we need to talk through your plans for the next few days anyway."

"The menu is probably in the living room," I say, and despite making this suggestion, I'm suddenly, ridiculously nervous about sharing a meal with him.

"The living room it is then, sweetheart," he says, and the "sweetheart" endearment manages to do that funny thing to my belly that I experienced earlier.

Afraid he'll notice, and that I'll fail some test he says he's not giving me, I turn away, entering the hallway, where I walk toward the living area. And I know the moment Kyle is behind me, his presence heavy, but I wouldn't describe it as uncomfortable. In fact, everything about him is a little too comfortable, too automatically familiar and safe, and I remind myself that making everyone feel this way could be his gift, thus rendering them vulnerable. Thus justifying his million-dollar payments.

I hear the sound of his phone ringing from behind me, and I reach the living area, where I cross to the desk and open the drawer to find the menu that I flip open, focusing on the food choices, not the man I hear speaking to someone on a call I can't quite piece together as anything that makes sense. I stop trying. I scan a bunch of fancy dishes that look less than appealing.

"How does it look?" Kyle asks, stepping to my side and

when I face him, I find him standing so near, I'm staring at his chest.

"Good grief," I say, and taking a step backwards, my neck stretching to even make eye contact, I quip, "How tall are you?"

"Six-foot-four and two hundred and twenty pounds."

"And Ricardo's like five-foot-eight," I say, picturing him trying to act tough with Kyle, and finding it quite amusing, "and you're big and intimidating. Maybe I do see why you're getting what you want."

"Intimidating?" He arches a brow. "Is that what I am?"

"You're huge," I say, setting the menu back on the desk. "I'm pretty sure just your size alone would be intimidating to most people."

"I'm not asking about what I am to most people," he says, his tone serious, his expression unreadable. "I'm asking what I am to you."

"You don't intimidate me," I answer truthfully, thinking of the comfort level I feel with him.

"No?"

"No."

"Good," he says, his voice low. "I don't want to intimidate you, Myla."

"Because if I'm scared, you'll never see the real me."

"That's right," he says, "but we'll keep it between us. That way we both win." He doesn't give me time to question that or argue, tapping the menu. "Did you look at the menu?"

"I did," I say, reluctantly letting him move us away from the topic of trust, where we'd been headed. "And it's limited, which kind of stinks since we'll be staying here for a while."

"Luckily we're in my hometown and I can tell you that

we have the best pizza on the planet a few blocks up the road, and they deliver."

"On the planet? That's pretty extreme." I smile. "And I'm sold. Let's get the best pizza on the planet."

"Made to order," he says, grabbing the phone receiver. "What do you want on yours?"

"Pepperoni for me."

"Good choice," he says, punching in the phone number that he's clearly memorized, while I sit down on the sofa, my palms flattening on my legs, nerves fluttering in my belly with a sudden realization. I'm alone with Kyle, and while yes, he's a bit of a drug I can't seem to completely resist, he's also an outsider. The only person who isn't part of Michael's direct entourage that I've been around in a year. Tomorrow I'll be at my new office, with other outsiders. It's taken a year, but slowly, I'm gaining freedom I can't afford to lose.

"Thirty minutes," he says almost instantly, crossing to sit down on the leather chair next to me, his elbows resting on his knees. "Just enough time for us to get that plan together for the immediate future, starting with tomorrow. Where are we going and why?"

"Alvarez Clothing now has offices with a warehouse, business office, and a retail location, inside a high end shopping area. From tomorrow forward, that will be where I work, but we don't open to the public for a month."

"Located where?"

"About a mile away," I say, and then recite the address.

"I know that area," he confirms, "but I'm going to want to go check it out in advance. Is there a set time that you need to be there?"

"Nine for sure. I have meetings with the design manager

and then models coming for interviews at ten.'"

He removes his phone from his pocket and punches in a number before I hear, "I need access to the facility where Myla will be working tomorrow." A pause. "Tonight." Another pause. "I really don't give a shit. I'm protecting her. I also need an emailed list of every staff member who works for the place." A beat and then, "Just use the email we've communicated on in the past." A pause, and then, "I'll be waiting." He ends the call and immediately focuses on me. "Do you know any of the staff you are working with?"

"I've been dealing with a handful of them by phone for a few months."

"I need you to write down their names and everything you know about them."

"Of course," I say, grabbing my sketch pad from where it's resting on the coffee table and flipping it open to one of my favorite formal dress designs. The idea of seeing it come to life tomorrow comes with mixed emotions. I start to flip the page when Kyle reaches over and stops me, his gaze surveying the pencil sketch of a beautiful woman with long, striking hair, wearing my dress, before he looks at me again.

"Did you draw this?" he asks.

"Yes," I say. "I need to envision a person wearing the garment I'm designing."

"Your artistic skill is incredible. You're gifted."

"Oh I…thank you. Actually, a big thank you. Compliments are welcome tonight. The people I'm working with tomorrow have worked with some powerful people in the fashion industry, and I have done nothing before this."

"Surely if they didn't believe in your work, they wouldn't be working for you."

"They work for Michael," I correct, "and we both know he makes things financially advantageous for people to take a job."

"But anyone as experienced as you say these people are would have a reputation to maintain," he argues. "They must like your work."

"I'd like to think they do," I say, appreciating the vote of confidence, which he doesn't have to give me, more than he can know.

"Will your name be on the labels at all?"

"No, but that's okay," I say, and before I can explain why, he's already rejected my answer.

"It's not okay."

"It is," I assure him, and not because this is Michael's decision. "Designing someone else's brand is how a lot of people get started and honestly, they get credit. For instance, Marc Jacobs is renowned for his work at Louis Vuitton."

"Louis Vuitton is not even close to the same as a Michael Alvarez label, for reasons we'll leave unspoken, and I'll leave it at that for the moment."

"For the moment? If you have something to say, then say it."

"I don't want to overwhelm you on my first night here."

"I don't get overwhelmed easily," I assure him, "and frankly, I'd rather have you speak just as freely."

He does one of those several second, intense stares, and then asks, "Your sister's FBI. Your father was FBI."

"And you want to know how I ended up with Michael Alvarez?"

"Yes, but we both know your frank conversation isn't going to be frank on that topic, and you've already given me an answer."

"That you don't like."

"That I don't accept, but like I said, we'll leave it alone tonight. I want to know about you and your design work. How did it become your passion?"

My gaze narrows on him. "Do you really still know nothing about me or are you just trying to see what I will tell you?"

"What you tell me is what I'm interested in."

"So you do know things about me now?"

"Yes. I know many things about you, Myla, but what I don't know is the person beyond the statistics and history."

"You don't need to know those things to protect me," I argue.

"You'd be surprised how knowing you helps me protect you."

"Aren't you supposed to keep a professional distance?"

"What I'm supposed to do is keep you safe," he says, "and you're about to be working in the fashion world, where I'm going to be shadowing you and protecting you. That means every single person around you influences you, and your actions, in some way. Knowing your history helps me predict your actions and reactions to situations around you."

Predicting my actions and reactions isn't exactly what I want anyone doing right now, but it's clear he's going to keep pushing for an answer. "I don't talk about me," I say. "I don't talk about my past."

"Why?"

"Why? Because it's the past."

"The past is a part of the many layers that make us who we are now."

"The past is buried with my family that I know you know were murdered."

"Your sister's alive."

"And thinks I'm dead."

"Myla—" There's a knock on the door, and his jaw clenches with obvious irritation at the timing, while I'm simply worried that Juan or Ricardo have returned. "That can't be the food that fast, can it?"

"The restaurant's literally three blocks down from us," he says, removing his cellphone from his pocket, "but since I paid Les to warn me of all visitors, he's obviously going to require training."

"Or someone stopped him from telling you."

"Don't be paranoid, sweetheart. I have more control than you're giving me credit for."

His cellphone rings in his hand and he eyes the number, "It's Les," he says, and answers the call, and listens a minute before saying, "All visitors mean all visitors." He ends the connection at the same moment more knocking begins. "The pizza," Kyle says, standing, the news delivering a welcome rush of relief. "And I was right," he adds, his lips thinning. "Les is going to require training. Maybe too much." He lifts his chin toward the hallway. "I'll be right back." I push to my feet, turning to watch him disappear. The way he moves is confident, graceful, the control clinging to him like a second skin that is simply who he is, not what he demands. And it's hot. So very, dangerously hot, but even more dangerous is him asking too many questions.

Somehow, I have to make it through tonight without giving this man everything he wants, and I already know he wants too much. The problem is, that despite any worry

I have about Kyle, he makes me want too much, too. He makes me need things I promised myself I'd never need again. He makes me shiver and he makes my body tingle, while my heart races. All those things, and I've only just met him. How am I going to survive two months of this man? But then, I'm pretty sure that's the point in our shared living quarters. I either resist Kyle or I won't survive. He's the apple in the Garden of Eden, and Michael Alvarez is the snake tempting me to take a bite.

Chapter Six

MYLA

Is Kyle a friend or an enemy? That is the question I have on my mind as I watch the apple in my line of sight disappear into the hallway to greet whichever hotel staff member brought us our pizza. A friend is what comes to my mind. He's a friend. But I do not know why my gut says this, when it's said it about no one else in a year.

I don't want to be a fool. I can't be a fool and survive, but a friend would be really well timed right now. An enemy, on the other hand, could be my demise at a time when I'm finally earning freedom with Michael. I cannot forget that Michael is a man of passion. He hates as viciously as he loves, and outside of his odd affection for me, what he loves is money and possession. If ever he feels that I've betrayed him, I have no doubt he will lash out with the wickedness of a finely sharpened sword.

Inhaling, I turn and walk to the shiny, light brown credenza where the flat screen TV sits, and grab several bottles of Ritz Carlton-branded water, lingering there a moment, with my mind awhirl. No one knows what Michael is capable of better than me, and if Kyle is a friend, albeit a capable friend, I still have to protect him. If he's the enemy, I have to stay the hell away from him. And if that's not possible, I have to prepare to destroy him before he destroys me. Destroy him. My God. What has this life made of me? A survivor, I remind myself. I'm surviving, something most in my position could not, and that is nothing to feel guilty about, especially since I have a plan to make it count. And no one, Kyle included, can be allowed to get in the way.

I turn to face the living area again, and I've just set the waters on the coffee table when Kyle reappears, with our food in hand. "Where do you want to eat?" he asks. "In the dining area or here?"

"Here in the living area works for me, if it's okay with you?"

"Comfortable is always better for me," he approves, reclaiming the chair and setting the box down on the table, while I sit down on the couch, cautiously choosing a neutral spot that is close enough to talk to him but not too close for comfort. "We have napkins and paper plates," he adds, "unless you require something fancier than paper?"

"Are you kidding? Paper can be thrown away. Paper is good."

"My thoughts exactly," he says, setting a plate in front of me, his green eyes becoming a shade paler with amusement. "I'm a single guy who doesn't like dishes."

"Have you ever been married?" I ask before I even think

about what I'm asking.

"Never even proposed," he says. "You?"

"Never even close."

"Not even with Alvarez?"

"Michael isn't a marrying kind of man," I say, trying to shift things back to him. "Apparently you aren't either. I mean, how old are you?"

"Thirty-five next month," he says. "And I was in the FBI for a decade, most of which I was always undercover, and unavailable. I wouldn't do that to someone, even if I'd have had time to even meet anyone, which I didn't."

"That's actually honorable," I say, thinking of the many dinner tables with an empty seat for my father. "It was hard on us when my father was undercover."

"It is hard on the families and I swore I'd never have one as long as I was inside the agency." He starts to open the box and pauses. "Damn. I didn't order any drinks."

"I got us waters, but they aren't cold," I say, hating that we were sidetracked before I found out more about his family. "I have diet Pepsi in the fridge but nothing else."

"Water is fine by me," he says, proving once again to be pretty easy to please, and eager to get to the food. "Are you ready for the best pizza of your life?"

"I'm ready," I say, rubbing my hands together, saying to heck with the questions, and deciding to just live in the moment and enjoy a really good pizza. "Bring it on."

He holds up his hands, like he's preparing us both. "I've been traveling so much that it's been years since I got to enjoy this piece of heaven." He lifts the lid and then grimaces. "They burned it. I don't fucking believe they burned it." He drops the lid. "I've been eating at this place since I was a kid and never once have they burned my damn pizza."

"If it's been around that long, maybe they sold out or the owners retired?"

"Impossible," he says, and then amends his words with, "Holy shit. The owner isn't exactly a spring chicken. Maybe I've lost my favorite pizza place." His brow furrows and he reaches into his pocket and punches in a number. "Is Adam there?" He listens a minute and grimaces. "When? Right. Well, it shows. I'm the guy from the Ritz. We just got our pizza and for the first time in twenty years of ordering there, I'm not happy. It's ten degrees of hell it's so burned. When can we get a new one?" He scowls. "You're three blocks away. Yeah. No. Forget it." He ends the call and returns his phone to his pocket. "You were right. Adam retired, and despite getting us our pizza in twenty minutes, he says it will be an hour for a new one."

"You look so disappointed," I say, trying not to laugh, and failing, which earns me a scowl this time. "I'm sorry," I add, forcing a straight face. "Pizza is sacred. I'm joking around, but I get it. I love it. I need it in my life. Let's eat it. It can't be that bad." I flip open the lid and stare down at the black edges of the crust. "Yikes."

"Yeah. It's bad."

"But," I say, holding up a finger. "The cheese and sauce is the best part. Let me get us some forks."

"No need," he says, grabbing the bag. "We have some." He reaches inside, and hands me one, though he doesn't look pleased about it. "It's ridiculous to eat pizza with a fork."

"Hey, hey," I say. "I object to that statement. Really cheesy, saucy pizza is messy and a fork keeps me from embarrassing myself by wearing it."

"Men do not think of such things," he says, puffing up his chest. "That's my Ricardo impression. You like?"

I laugh, imagining Ricardo's mannerisms, and pointing my fork at him. "That was good. You should have been an actor."

"I was an actor. That's exactly what undercover work is, but now," he holds his hands out, "what you see is what you get, and that's exactly what I tell my clients. Unfortunately, your pizza is the same. I promised you the world's best pizza and a man should not go back on a promise. A man says what's he's going to do, and then does it."

"Per my mother, that's actually true, but this wasn't your fault."

"But I'm responsible for what I promise," he says, and suddenly, the air has shifted, thickened, and I'm not sure we're talking about pizza.

And suddenly, I have to force air out of my lungs. "What are we talking about, Kyle?"

"Many things," he says, his eyes lightening again, the serious moment gone without answers. He lifts his fork. "Which is why I have to save face now."

"Save face? Over pizza?"

"Pizza is sacred. You said it yourself."

Now I laugh. "I did say that and it is. So I guess you defiled the pizza process by not using magical powers to know that it would suck tonight." I straighten. "I challenge you. How are you going to save face?"

He deepens his voice. "We will begin a hunt to find the best pizza in the world. A new sampling will occur nightly."

"Nightly? And an extra hour on the treadmill will occur nightly."

"It'll be worth it," he promises.

"On that you're right," I agree. "Pizza is actually one of my favorite things in the world, and honestly, I can't remember the last time I ordered it at all."

"No?"

"Michael is not a pizza guy."

"Another reason to dislike him," he says.

"Another?"

"He's a kingpin, Myla. I won't pretend to like him."

"But you're working for him."

"I'm working for me. Not him. And right now, I'm working for you. We should order a new pizza from someplace else, and let you enjoy it."

"I'm way too hungry to wait," I say, glancing down at the pizza, "and the sauce and cheese really do look good." I pick up a slice and glance at the bottom. "It's not really that bad on the bottom. Just a little brown so you can skip your fork." I take a bite and the cheese and sauce explode in my mouth with delicious results. "It's actually really good, Kyle. Really good."

He looks skeptical, but reaches for a slice and tries it, and nods. "Okay. Well at least they kept the recipe. Maybe I'll buy the damn place just to save it."

"Just like that? You'll just buy it? Are you serious?"

"I actually might. I have a few investments that need to keep growing."

"What kind of investments?"

"Real estate mostly," he says. "It's easy to hire management and just forget about it." He opens his water, gulps a drink and then reaches for a slice. "My security work keeps me busy."

"So you just take random bodyguard jobs?"

"I take random jobs that pay well, and don't require a long-term commitment, but we were talking about you and your sister before the pizza arrived, not me."

So much for fun and laughter. "What's wrong with talking about you?" I ask, taking another bite to ensure I have an excuse to process whatever question he throws at me next.

"Nothing," he surprises me by saying, finishing off a bite of pizza. "You need to trust me and I'll be glad to give you every reason I can to make that happen."

I set the burned crust of my slice down and straighten. "Really?"

"Really," he says, tossing his crust onto a plate. "The sauce is still damn good, right?"

"Very. Sweet and still spicy. I love it." And eager to take advantage of his invitation to ask him questions, I get back to the topic of him. "Why'd you leave the FBI?"

"Quid pro quo," he says softly, a rasp of suggestion in his tone. "You give me something I want and I'll give you something you want."

Is this where he tells me why he really took this job? Or what he's really after? "What do you want?"

"Many things, it seems, but I'll settle for hearing about two sisters who are birds of different feathers."

He's back to Kara, which seems to support his claim that he's been hired to keep her away from me, or me from her, but I want every tidbit of confirmation I can manage. "Tell me again why this is important?"

"Considering the biggest fear Michael Alvarez seems to have is your sister—"

"I get it," I say, considering he's just repeated my thoughts from moments before. "You need to know if she's a problem that could bite you in the ass. She's not. She thinks I'm dead. I told you that."

"She's resourceful and you're no longer underground."

He's right.

"You're right," I concede, and I suddenly want to tell him whatever I can to ensure she doesn't find me. "She *is* very resourceful and if you're the one who's going to make that happen, then you do need to understand the dynamic between us."

"Which is what?"

"Kara and I were really very much alike. Our mother was a highly successful fashion model, who retired to open her own clothing line, and both me and my sister were helping her prepare for the launch when she died."

"But you ended up holding onto her dream, while Kara followed in your father's. It's hard to see the likeness in that."

"Our reactions to the murder of our parents was the great divide. Kara got angry and wanted to fight crime, and I got angry at my father."

"Why were you angry at your father?"

"He was always gone, and when he was around, he wasn't the father I remembered in my younger years. He was a hard person, even mean, and ultimately he ended up getting my mother killed. He almost got us all killed."

"He'd been undercover for years inside a notorious motorcycle club," Kyle says. "I'm sure it affected him. And you were young. I'm sure that made it harder to deal with his transition back to the real world."

"Yes," I say. "And logically as an adult, I believe that

to be true, but at the time, it had a lot to do with how I responded to the murders, and my future. And to Kara. I mean, he brought those criminals to us, and she wanted to join the same agency, and do it all over again."

"She wanted the control, not them," he supplies.

"Staying off their radar was the control I wanted, and she refused," I say, trying not to think about how stupid I sound considering I'm in Michael Alvarez's bed.

"Because of your father, the agency brought down a big portion of their criminal operations. He saved a lot of lives, Myla, and I've looked at your sister's record. She has as well."

"I know and it might seem like I'm not proud of them, but I am. Actually, very proud of them."

"You don't seem like you know or that you are." He lifts his hands. "You're here."

"This wasn't planned. It's complicated."

"In what way?"

"My sister was an FBI agent when I met Michael."

"And you shut her out because she wouldn't accept you being with him."

"No," I say firmly. "That isn't how this happened at all. Not at all. I wouldn't do that, and—" I inhale with the realization that I've raised my voice, and let real emotion into my voice. "She thinks I was killed in a helicopter crash, and I chose to leave it that way."

"You shut Kara out," he repeats.

"Stop saying that. I love my sister. I was mad when she took the FBI job, but that was years ago. We got over it and never, ever did we lose each other in the process."

"Until Michael Alvarez."

"It's not how it seems."

"You let Kara hurt over you."

"Stop pushing me."

"I need to understand. You let her grieve your death. You let Kara hurt. You let her—"

"I know what I did," I hiss, my chest tightening. "I know and—" I stop speaking, my brows furrow with a realization that has me studying him just as hard as he is me. "Wait." I tilt my head to study him. "You called my sister by her name. You called her Kara."

There is a flicker of something in his eyes that is there and gone in a blink, before he asks, "Isn't that her name?"

"Of course it is," I say, "but it was the way you said it, like it was second nature. Like you know her." I turn a bit more toward him, my hand going to the coffee table. "What do you know about my sister?"

He rotates even further, his eyes, those green eyes, looking right at me, not a blink in sight. "I could recite the contents of her file just like yours, but that doesn't tell me anything more about her, any more than it does about you. I need to hear things directly from you. I need to know you, Myla."

Still no blink. Still no hint of him making a confession that perhaps doesn't exist. But he wants more from me. He wants too much, I think again. And maybe me looking for Kara in him, and the way he said her name, is me wanting too much as well. "The bottom line," I say, "is that Kara and I are not estranged. Not even close. She will come after me if she gets the chance and she won't believe I chose Michael Alvarez to be the man in my bed, by choice."

"Did you?"

"I'm here," I say, shutting the pizza box, fighting a wave

of anger at too many things to name that have nothing to do with him. "That should answer that question."

"It doesn't," he says, and I start to stand, afraid he will see something in my eyes that will motivate him to play hero or monster, whichever he might be, but he catches my arm, heat radiating all the way to my shoulder. "But I'm here now, too," he says, his voice soft, but no less absolute.

"I'm not sure if that should make me feel better or scare the shit out me."

"It should scare the shit out of anyone who wants to hurt you. Not out of you."

I have no idea why, but my stomach flutters like I've just had Prince Charming tell me that I'm his princess, which makes me angry at me, not him. I don't do the whole fairytale fantasy thing. Ever. And I sure don't do it now. "I know too little about you to accept that I'm safe with you, and no one else is."

"Good," he surprises me by saying, his eyes lighting with approval. "You shouldn't accept things on my word. You should make me prove it's true."

"Then prove it," I say. "Right here. Right now. Prove to me that I can trust you and that you are who you say you are. Prove to me that you want what you say you want…which actually, what do you want?" My mind races through the conversations we've had. His way of getting what he wants. His past in the FBI. The familiar way he called my sister by her name. "Because I think there is more to your story and I want to know what it is right now."

"Quid pro quo, sweetheart," he repeats. "I'll tell you my secrets, if you tell me yours."

Chapter Seven

MYLA

I blink at his inference that I have secrets, but I do not stumble. "This is about you this time. Prove to me I can trust you."

"Trust doesn't work that way. It's earned. It takes time."

"I don't have time. Why did you leave the FBI?"

"It took a toll."

"What kind of toll?"

"I was burned out."

"No," I say, shaking my head in rejection of a too generic answer. "There's more to it than that. You were FBI and now you're here. Now you work for Michael Alvarez."

"We're repeating, Myla. I told you. I work for me. Alvarez doesn't own me."

"Why are you here?" I whisper, not sure what I am looking for or need him to say.

"You. I'm still here for you."

"That makes no sense."

"You want more?"

"Yes. I want more."

"I'm here because when I first saw you, when I first looked into your eyes, you on the arm of Michael Alvarez made no sense to me. I'm here because I see the fear in your eyes and I don't like it. Do you still want more?"

Yes. "No. Yes. I'm not your business."

"I made you my business."

"I don't know if you are my friend or enemy—"

"Friend. I am your friend."

"Then I don't want you to die. And even if you're my enemy, Kyle, he'll turn on you. You'll be the man that got me into your—" I stop myself before I say bed which would be telling in so many ways, and the look in his eyes says he knows it.

"Into my what, Myla?"

"He'll turn on you, Kyle. Get out while you can."

"I'm not going anywhere, sweetheart." His hands settle on his knees, "Except to go get something I have for you." He stands. "I'll be right back." And then he's walking away, and my fist is balled against my chest, my heart racing so fast I think it might explode from between my ribs. I'm confused. I'm worried. I'm feeling like I'm not alone for the first time in a long time, and that terrifies and excites me in equal portions.

Standing, I gather our trash because I have so much energy and adrenaline and no place to put it. I carry it all to the kitchenette just off the dining room, where I dispose of it all, and by the time I return to the living area, Kyle is returning too, and we both stop mid-way into the room. And we stand there. Just stand there, looking at each other, and I think that in itself, if caught on film, would have destroyed us with Michael. There is something between me and this man, a charge in the air when we are together that can't be created by choice. It's not something any man could create to set a woman up, unless she was just panting over him, and that simply isn't me. But that doesn't mean he's a friend. That doesn't mean he won't use whatever is between us against me.

He crosses toward me and I stand my ground, showing the strength that has allowed me to prosper in Michael Alvarez's world. He stops in front of me, a step away, not touching me, but what scares me is that I want him to touch me. I want that hero I just got mad at myself for wanting, and I want that hero to be him. "Let's sit, sweetheart," he says softly.

"I don't think I want to."

"Yes, you do."

"I don't think I should."

"Of course, you should. Come on." He motions with his head and when his hand just barely brushes my waist, I step away from the instant fire in me, walking back to the couch, where I welcome the support of the cushion. But it seems there is no escaping Kyle in this moment. He joins me and bypasses the chair, sitting down next to me, close enough to be in my personal space.

"Do you know what this is?" he asks, setting a small handgun down in front of me, along with a case and a strap.

"A Sig," I say of the tiny gun. "I used to carry the cheaper Ruger version."

"Used to?"

"Michael won't allow it."

"You're carrying it," he insists. "In your purse or on your person. I prefer on your person." He holds up a strap. "This will allow you to wear it—"

"At the center of my bra. I know. I have a sister who's an FBI agent, remember?"

"Actually she's not."

I blanch. "What?"

"Kara took a leave last year and then eventually resigned."

I suck in air, my chest tightening, before I breathe out. "Where is she now?"

"Married to an ex-ATF agent and working in New York City. You can take comfort in knowing that Ricardo didn't know that. He was told she's active FBI, which means they dismissed her as a problem they think only you can re invent."

"Oh, thank God."

He studies me, his eyes too keen, too knowing. "You're protecting her."

"She's my sister," I say, choking a bit on the word sister, "and I might not want her in my life, but I love her."

"Then we'll keep her away. You have my word because I understand being angry at family, but still caring if you lose them."

"You do?"

"My father was murdered, too."

My chest tightens just a little more. "How?"

"He crossed the line, and played a little too dirty, for his own benefit, not that of the FBI, and in the process he double-crossed the wrong person. He was point blank assassinated."

"My God," I whisper. "How can your story be so like mine?"

"They hired me because they knew I'd have this connection to you and they expected me to use it against you."

"Will you?"

"Never would I ever use my father, who I never even talk about, against anyone."

"Then why did you tell me?"

"Because I want your trust."

"And what will you do if you get it?"

His hand comes down on my leg, intimate, wrong. Right. "When I earn it you won't ask that question."

"I wish you could earn it," I say, and my hand goes to his and I tell myself it's to push him away, but I don't even try.

"I can and I will," he says, leaning in, or maybe I lean in or we both do, but we are close, our faces, our lips, and our breath. "Maybe not tonight or tomorrow, but I'm not going anywhere."

"And then what?"

"And then, everything changes," he promises, and suddenly his lips brush mine, a barely there touch that I feel, oh how I feel it in every part of me, before he pulls back and then he's gone, leaving me swaying and grabbing hold of the cushion.

"Fuck," he curses, standing up and giving me his back, just long enough to run a rough hand through his hair and to face me while I try to calm my racing mind and heart. "That can't happen," he says.

I blink. "What? I didn't try... we didn't..." Confused,

heat and embarrassment assail me and I stand up, rushing toward the bedroom, running this time, but I simply don't care. But I also don't escape. He's there before I make it into the bedroom, stepping in front of me, his hands settling at my waist, branding me, scorching me.

"If we happen now, you'll question why. You will fear that I'm setting you up, and fear is not what I want from you."

"Then what do you want from me?"

"I could tell you trust again, which is true, but right now, in this moment, what I want is you. Every part of you naked, every way I can get you. Beneath me, on top of me, under my tongue, and many other ways."

"You can't say that to me."

"And if I'd given you some generic bullshit answer you wouldn't have believed it, I would have scared you just as much as actually doing what I want."

"I wouldn't have let you."

"We're fire, sweetheart. We both know it. It's inconvenient, but it's undeniable, which means we're going to have to find a way to deal with it because I meant what I said. I'm here. I'm not leaving."

My hands go to his wrist. "Let me go."

"I'll stop touching you, sweetheart, but I'm not letting you go."

He releases me and steps around me, leaving me cold in every place I was hot only moments before. I dart forward into the room and shut the door, but I don't stop there. I rush into the bathroom, and I shut that door too, as if it protects me from him or anything. Then I'm standing at the mirror, though I don't remember moving toward it, and I relive the past in random flashbacks. Me at fifteen, yelling at my father on the eve of his murder. Me and Kara hiding in a closet, huddled together, crying while we prayed the men in our house would go away. Then me and Kara under an umbrella at our parent's graves. The me just over a year ago, in the restaurant the first night I'd met Michael Alvarez. To the moment when he'd sent Ricardo to find me in the bathroom at Shivers, right after I'd been waiting on his table.

Pushing off the door, I open it and gasp to find a man with a long scar down his cheek standing in front of me.

"What are you doing in here?"

"Mr. Alvarez requests your company, which means I'll need your phone, and I'll need to search you."

"What? No. No. I don't agree."

His lips twist evilly. "I don't remember asking."

My heart thunders in my chest, and I consider refusing, but Alvarez is not only a drug lord. He owns this restaurant and he's demanded that I join him for dinner, rather than service his dinner, as is my normal job as a waitress assigned to his private basement dining area. Somehow, I step forward, the brutal stories of drug cartels my father had thought perfect dinnertime conversation, often focusing on female sex slave trafficking, playing in my mind, and a kind of tunnel forms around me. I just have to get through meeting him and get out of here alive and well. I'll call Kara. I won't come back to work.

The man behind me is close, at my heels, and not about to let me escape, and it's pretty clear to me this isn't a good thing. Alvarez had seemed a little too intrigued by me when I'd taken his order, a bit too eager to chat, which makes the moment I reach the steps leading down to the private dining area where he's seated, all the more daunting. Inhaling, I start walking, my heart racing with every step, torture. Too soon, I am at the bottom level, and I find Alvarez alone, sitting at the table…waiting on me.

I blink back to the present and shove aside the memory, and Alvarez with it, my fingers touching my lips the way Kyle's lips had, and in that moment, I am the woman I was that night in the restaurant. The one thrilled with possibilities, romance, and the future. The one who wanted to get kissed like she'd never been kissed. I pull my fingers back and curl them into my palm. That me can't, and doesn't, exist anymore. But it doesn't seem to matter. I can still smell Kyle. I can still feel his mouth brush mine. And I'm feeling things I shouldn't feel. Wanting things I can't have and do not dare even let my mind name. I back up and lean against the wall, balling my fist at my chest, and then it happens. I do what I haven't done in nine months. What I swore I wouldn't do ever again because it's a weakness I can't afford if I want to survive.

I cry.

Chapter Eight

KYLE

Clean shaven and standing at the bathroom mirror, I finish knotting the silver tie, which I've paired with a light gray suit, after all of three hours of sleep, but morning has come with no regrets from the night before. Undercover, you make split second decisions you believe will keep you and others alive. I did exactly that when I told Myla I want her and I have zero regrets about that decision. The fire between us is clear and present, and she's right. It could easily get us killed if we let anyone else have the slightest idea it exists, which is something we'll have to talk about today. It's also a magnet pulling her to me, it's clear to me that I'm going to need to use it to get her the fuck out of here, the Walker clan will just have to deal with it. And she *does* want out. I am certain of that now. She just doesn't know how she can do it and protect Kara, and I have to show her that path, before I tell her who I am, even if that path is me killing Alvarez.

Exiting the bathroom, I walk to the desk in my room and sit down, keying up the security feed, and then shifting to my instant message function to look for updates, finding none. Knowing Royce was catching some shut eye like me, I key in: Asher?

The reply: I'm here.

Short and to the point, about summarizes everything Asher does by choice, but unlike any one else I've ever known, the man is a chameleon who can don leather and boots as easily as he does a suit. Which makes him one hell of an asset.

Me: Anything I need to know before Myla and I leave?

Asher: Royce and Jacob are already monitoring Alvarez Clothing, and waiting on you. We have four of our best contractors on a plane here now. And I'm caffeine and bacon deprived, which is fucking hell. Oh and SFB is parked across the street, and dumb enough to think he's discreet.

Asher gives people nicknames, and "SFB" stands for Shit for Brains, the nickname he gave Juan after watching him for a few hours last night.

Me: We'll be down in half an hour

Asher: Bring coffee. Or bacon. Bring both.

Standing, I rest my hands on the desk, considering any stone unturned, and while I'd hacked the security to get our team into Alvarez Clothing unnoticed last night, I consider running over there myself for a quick preview before I taking Myla there, but quickly rule that out. I can't leave Myla alone, with Juan, who clearly needs to die for touching her, hanging around, ready to demand entry into her room.

Pushing off the desk, I exit and make my way toward the living area, finding Myla's door open. Sounds coming from what I know to be a mini kitchen area off the dining room, lead me in that direction, and I find Myla in the small, rectangular space, staring at a Keurig cup dripping, her long dark hair a sleek shiny wave down her back.

Seeming to sense my presence, she whirls around, the pale pink dress she's wearing hugging every slender curve, which I'd rather be hugging myself, the hem falling just past her knees. "Hi," she says, pointing at the machine, and looking incredibly nervous. "They have a Keurig, but the coffee is just Plain Jane. You might like that, but I like my chocolate coffee. I need to see if I can get it ordered." She grabs some sort of box I think has condiments, and manages to drop it.

I am there immediately, picking it up to hand it to her, the sweet scent of her floral perfume mixing with fresh brewed coffee with surprisingly sexy results. She reaches for it, and I close my hand over hers. "Easy, sweetheart. We're okay. Everything is going to be okay."

"Last night—"

"Was me speaking the truth and after I kissed you—"

"You didn't—"

"Yes," I say, "I did, and not only do I own that action, it was too damn short, and too damn good for us to deny it happened. Or that it won't happen again."

"It can't happen again."

"It will, but not now. Not when you doubt me."

"It's not about doubt. It's about Michael."

That name is the one and only reply she could give me that makes me release her and step backwards. "Right. Michael."

Her lashes lower and she turns to face the counter, pressing her hands to the marble. "I'm his. That's just how it is."

"And yet, you want me."

"I'm his."

I shackle her arm and turn her to face me. "You don't belong to him. No one owns you."

"Let go, Kyle. You're my bodyguard, but that doesn't require touching."

I narrow my eyes on her and find what I'm looking for. Fear. Anger. Confusion. "This won't work."

"What won't work?"

"You can't push me away. There is no door that will shut me out."

"I already did. Door shut." She turns and sets the condiments on the counter, grabbing her cup and trying to get the cream out of the container, and I don't miss how her hand shakes a moment before she drops her sugar packets on the floor.

She squats at the same time I do, and we end up eye-to-eye, the charge between us electric; a punch of pure lust and attraction that sucks up all the air around us, then seems to sway us toward each other. "You're making me crazy," she hisses. "This isn't helping me. It's made me a wreck."

I reach for her elbow and help her to her feet. "Making me the enemy isn't the answer," I say, forcing myself to let her go. "And you have no reason to feel awkward with me. None."

"Last night—"

"I was honest. I've done undercover work for a lot of years, sweetheart. What we hide from instead of control, is what becomes the poison that can destroy us." I scoop up her sugars and tear them open. "How do you like your coffee?"

"You don't have to make my coffee."

"Myla," I say softly. "How do you like your coffee?"

"From Starbucks, but I'll settle for two creams and two Splendas."

I empty the contents of all of the packets and fill her cup, using a stir stick to blend it before tasting it. "Just the way I like it," I say, handing it to her, a challenge in my action. Will she drink from the cup I drank from? "Try it."

She takes the cup from me and considers me a moment, then takes a drink.

"Well?" I ask.

She sets the cup down and rests her hands back on the counter, head low. "What are we doing, Kyle?"

I mimic her position, my shoulder touching hers. "Let's talk about that."

She faces me and explodes the minute I do the same. "Talking won't solve this. I can't share coffee with you and you can't touch me or call me sweetheart. No more. *No more.*"

"That won't be enough."

"It will. It has to be enough." She hesitates, and frowns. "Wait. What does that mean? That won't be enough?"

"The danger isn't in what we say or do. The fire between us wasn't created by me or you. It simply is. It's a living, breathing, life of its own that radiates energy, and it's that energy we have to control."

I expect denial, but she gives me acceptance. "How?" she asks, folding her arms in front of her.

"I'm going to take on a persona of being cold and withdrawn when I'm with you. There won't be conversation between us. There won't be laughter or friendship. No matter what happens, I can't react like the man I am, but only the man they expect me to be with you."

"So I'll hate you like I do Juan."

"Don't act like you hate me. Don't act like I'm anything but that bodyguard who is there, and won't go away."

"Aren't you supposed to be seducing me or something?"

"They want me to prove or disprove your loyalty to Alvarez. I'm going to tell them you're reserved and keeping to yourself, and eager for his phone calls."

"You make it sound easy."

"It will be for you, because I'll set the tone, and sweetheart, that doesn't mean I watch Juan or anyone else treat you like shit. I won't. You're mine to protect, and I will protect you." I glance at the zipper on the front of her dress and then back at her. "Are you wearing the gun?"

"Yes. That's why I picked this dress."

"Good choice. If you need to use it, you use it and let me deal with ensuring there are no consequences."

"I have no idea how you would do that."

"I've been undercover inside operations just as nasty as this one. I know how to manipulate events and come out on top. You're in good hands and not just mine. I have a team that works for me. They've already cleared the facility where you're working and they'll have our backs, but that's absolutely between you and I."

"Of course. Who are they?"

"People I trust. People who you can trust. People I don't want on Alvarez's radar. That's all you need to know."

"And you trust me to not tell him?"

"Quid pro quo on trust, too, Myla. I simply went first.

You now have one of my secrets."

"I'm not sure you really went first. I mean, right now, if you wanted to, you could tell Juan anything about me, and he'd believe you. I'm trusting you not to do that."

"You hope I won't do that. That isn't trust." My cellphone rings, and I reach for it, glancing at the screen. "That's Juan," I say. "Grab your things and let's get out of here." I answer the call. "Good morning, sunshine," I say. "Good to know you get up before noon."

"Shouldn't you be leaving by now?" he asks, while Myla stands in front of me, waiting for the bombshell she always seems to believe is coming.

"I wasn't aware I needed to control her schedule," I reply. "Is there an agenda here? Because if there is, it would be nice if I got a fucking copy of it."

"She has a meeting in thirty minutes."

"Isn't she the boss?" I ask, while Myla walks out of the room, as if she can't take the exchange anymore.

"When the fuck are you leaving?" he asks.

"Is she a prisoner I'm supposed to be guarding, or am I protecting her while she leads her normal life? Because if she's a prisoner, the concept of testing her loyalty is void and what the hell am I doing here?"

"When the fuck are you leaving?"

"When she picks a pair of shoes that she doesn't want to change." He hangs up.

I shake my head and shove my phone in my pocket, and make my way to the hallway where Myla meets me with her purse and briefcase on her shoulder. "If I shoot him, you can clean it up?"

"Easily, though I'd be disappointed I didn't get to do

it. Let me get that." I reach for her briefcase, taking it from her and glancing at the label. "A Louis Vuitton," I say. "An expensive piece of Marc Jacob inspiration."

"Yes," she says, responding to the question I've left in the air. "Michael bought it for me. And yes. It's a five-thousand dollar bag, but I didn't ask for it. I didn't even tell him I liked the brand. It was his pitch for me to be his Marc Jacobs."

"I didn't ask any of that."

"I saw it in your face."

"No one sees anything in my face I don't want them to see," I tell her.

"Then you wanted me to see it and you wanted my answer."

"I let it show," I confirm. "Just in case you wanted to tell me. Clearly you did."

"Now you know." She glances at her watch, also a Louis Vuitton. "I need to get to my meetings. I need to get this over with."

I arch a brow. "That doesn't sound like someone excited about living a dream."

"Please stop analyzing everything I say and do. I'm nervous." She steps around me and heads toward the door, and I'm at the door when she is, pressing my hand to the surface at the same moment hers goes to the knob.

"Myla," I breath out, that sweet scent of hers teasing my nostrils.

"What?" she whispers, without turning.

"Turn around."

"No. I—"

"Turn around."

Her shoulders flex as she inhales, and then rotates, leaning on the door, our bodies close, and it's all I can do to keep my hand on the wood by her head, instead of on her. "Remember our plan."

"You act like a cold-hearted bastard and I act like…I don't notice."

"Like I'm just another one of the assholes around you."

"But you aren't just another one of the assholes, now are you, Kyle?"

"No. I am not."

"When are you going to tell me who you really are?"

"When you tell me who you really are."

"I'll have to figure that out first," she says. "Can we go now?"

I am not pleased by this answer that says she's lost herself while she tried to survive, which is what my father did. It infers that Alvarez has messed with her head more than I wanted to believe. I don't believe she has an allegiance to him, but I need to be certain. I push off the wall, and she turns, opening the door and exiting our suite. Running from the wrong person, and proving that Alvarez has a hand on her even when he's not here. I need to step things up before he shows up and make sure the only hands Myla wants on her are mine.

Chapter Nine

MYLA

I make a beeline down the hallway toward the elevator, trying to gather my thoughts, but Kyle's perfectly fitted gray suit, and cool, way-too-interested green eyes are making that impossible. It's making logic a hard to gather resource, even though logic and a steady handle on everything around me has been my salvation. There is so much adrenaline surging through me, fueling my body where sleep has not, that I can feel my hands and knees trembling. I never tremble. Thus why I spent hours pacing my room last night, trying to understand how Kyle so easily stripped away all my many, carefully erected layers, and then had me crying. Crying of all things! Worse, I have some innate need to trust him and touch him and let him touch me. I mean…the man is pure sex, so what woman wouldn't want him to touch her? That part I get. It's the gut instinct to trust, that I've tried to lend a reason to and I just can't. There is no question in my mind that there is more than meets the eye to Kyle. That he might expose this is true of me as well, though, is the immediate problem I'd thought to address by shutting him out.

But as he joins me, falling into step, the way I feel him in every part of me, the way I know exactly how perfectly that gray suit fits his big, muscular body, pretty much says that plan was destined to fail before it began. I should have taken the lusty thing we have going on into consideration with that plan. Right now, every moment I'm with him, actually, I feel a push and pull between us, the pull fighting to win, and in the morning light, I think this is partially about his connection to my past, to Kara. Add to that the fashion line that forces a collision of the old and new me, and it makes sense that the combination proved volatile last night. But today is a new day. That is over, and I cannot blink or it will be noticed by someone other than Kyle, and that could destroy me, and the plans that have kept me pushing forward.

We round the corner, and without looking at Kyle, I punch the elevator button, relieved when the doors open instantly. He places himself in front of the entrance, his broad shoulders and big, delicious body successfully blocking my entry. "Wait for the next car," he orders, punching the button again.

My brow furrows, and when I'd ask why exactly we're waiting, another car opens and he nods. "This one's fine." He immediately steps toward it, holding the steel doors for me to enter.

Confused, and a bit concerned, by the musical chairs elevator routine, I step into the newly arrived car and head to the left wall, leaning on the hard surface, my hands on the railing behind me. Even as I wonder what just happened, a bit of clarity comes to me in other places. My past coming into the light is what is shaking me up. And why is that when it should be a reminder of why I have to be strong?

Kyle joins me, and as the doors begin to close, I swear the man sucks all the air I was just breathing out of the tiny space. He punches the button for the garage level, and I'm a crazy person because I notice how strong his hands are, how expensive his black Gucci watch is, to which my fashion-adoring mother would have given a thumbs up. He moves then, and when I think he will step away, he places himself in front of me, and all six feet four inches of hot, hard man are a mere lift of a hand from touching me again. One step from making me forget everything I was thinking or might have been about to think, and there lies another part of his power over me and the source of his danger. Just as he consumes the tiny car, and the space we're sharing, leaving room for little else, he does this every moment I'm with him, no matter where we are. He could make me forget, of this I have no doubt. He could make me let down my guard. He could give me an escape I crave, but at what price?

He's also making me crazy by just standing there watching me and I can't take the silence, or the certainty he might see more in it than words. "What was that with the elevator?"

"This one isn't being recorded." He doesn't give me time to reply or assess his answer, softening his voice to softly order, "Talk to me, sweetheart," that endearment becoming exceedingly appealing and far too sexy. "What's going on in your head right now? Because something is. I see it in your face."

I was right. He is seeing things he shouldn't be able to see, because like him, I've learned not to let things show. I've learned to be what I need to be and nothing else. "I thought you weren't going to call me sweetheart?" I ask, deflecting but also concerned.

"When we're alone, everything changes."

My belly flutters with the inference that "alone" comes with sexy, forbidden promises. "What if you slip up and do it when we're around people?"

"I don't slip up."

I believe him, but considering how he impacts me, how easily I feel his every word and action, I'm concerned about me, not him. "What if I do?"

"You won't. You haven't so far, or you would not be standing here right now, and we both know it. Why would you start now?"

"I'm off," I say, not denying what he obviously knows. "I'm all over the place today, and that isn't the demeanor of a person surviving."

"The survivor hasn't gone anywhere. She's right there. Let her out to play. You can handle Alvarez. You can handle these crappy designers today."

"They aren't crappy. They're my idols. People I've admired for years."

"First," he says. "They're just people, who thought the same thing you just expressed about other people, at one point in their careers. And now, they're not only your co-workers, they're your employees and you're their boss."

"I'm not," I say, letting a hint of bitterness into my voice that I do not intend. This was my dream, but now...I hesitate, but say it. "Michael is their boss."

"You *are* their boss," he says pointedly, "and that gives you control we both need you to have. So own it, sweetheart. Own everything you touch today, the way you own Alvarez."

"The control *"we"* need to have?" I ask, and I hate how appealing it is to have a "we" in my life that doesn't include Michael Alvarez.

"We both benefit from your perceived loyalty to Alvarez. We're making sure that's exactly what everyone else sees."

I don't miss yet another inference, this one dangerous, and I cautiously ask, "Because you don't think I'm loyal to him?

"I see more," he confirms. "You know I do."

He does, and with the floors ticking by, I don't have time to try to change that, nor do I think I could anyway. I really don't want to change that with Kyle. What I want is for him to be real and honest, a friend. More so though, I want us both to be alive tomorrow. "You need to know that I can own the job," I say, "but I don't own Michael Alvarez. I don't have that kind of control over him. No one does. You know that, right?"

"What I know is that he doesn't own you and I'm going to make sure *you* know that, too."

"You have watched the Godfather, right?" I ask trying to make him see reason.

"Didn't he die?"

I blanch. "What are you saying?"

"I'm saying that everyone has an expiration date, and it's not our time."

Is he telling me he's here to kill the man in my bed? Is he—*Oh, God.* Is he a Fed? Does he know my sister? Is he helping put her in the line of fire or will he in the future? I try to think back to how he'd replied to my question about knowing her. *I could recite the information in her file...* He'd avoided a direct answer. If he's a Fed, what do I do next? And if I ask him directly, will he tell me?

"Are you FBI, Kyle?"

"Ex, sweetheart. I've you that. You know that."

But the truth is, if he's a master of being undercover, like my father, and even my sister, I might not.

"Ask me what you want to ask me, Myla," he says, clearly aware that I'm chasing real answers.

"Do you know my sister?"

"You already asked me that."

"And you never answered." The elevator dings.

"If you want to ask again, do it tonight, when we're alone," he says, shutting down the topic. The answer feels a little cryptic, but at this point the doors have opened and he's holding them for me. "I had Les park my car near the door so we're in the garage, and while there are no cameras on our level, if you see anyone, assume they might be the enemy."

"I already do," I admit, before I exit the elevator, and enter into the dimly lit space to do the other thing I always do, and immediately scan for danger, and activity I don't find.

Kyle is instantly beside me. "This way," he says, clicking his keychain, the rear lights of the vehicle flashing.

"What kind of car is that?" I ask, noting the sporty, slightly lifted back end, and thick tires.

"I'll pretend you didn't ask that," he says. "Because not knowing what this car is, is an absolute sin against man and metal."

Expectantly, considering all I've been through, I'm laughing, the tension easing from my spine, his way of making pizza and cars life-altering events is actually quite adorably sexy. "It's a Mustang," I say as we stop at the passenger door. "See? I know what it is."

"Not just a Mustang," he amends. "A 2008 Shelby GT500KR Mustang. I should have it parked and protected but that just seemed a waste."

"How much does a car like this cost?"

"You can't put a price tag on a car like this," he says. "I won it in a bidding war."

"So a lot."

"It was worth it." He reaches for the door. "Stay out here a minute." He opens the door, sets my briefcase in the backseat, and then slides into the passenger side of the vehicle before shutting me out and him inside.

The odd action dissolves the final remnants of my laughter, replacing it with a mix of confusion and worry. Is he looking for bombs? Does he think someone wants me dead? That's ridiculous, I chide. If there was a bomb threat, he'd have made me stand back, and if he thought someone was going to grab me, he'd never leave me out here alone. But this thought process is enough to remind me of the many threats around me, not just from inside my new world, but from those who hate Michael, and want to hurt anyone close to him. I'm starting to come up with even more ways to run with my horrid thoughts when the door pops open, with Kyle on the phone. "Right," he says. "Keep an eye on him."

I'm thinking he might actually have left me out here to make a private call when he stands, showing me another of those little recording chips for my viewing. "How did they get into your car?"

He chucks the chip across the garage. "Les is fired."

"As in the doorman?"

"He's the only one who had my spare keys," he confirms, stepping away from the car to allow me to enter this time.

"What are you going to do?"

"I'd like to throttle the bastard, but I won't. At least, not yet. We'll let him think he's still considered a friend, and watch what he does next."

Let him think he's a friend? Considering I've just hoped and prayed for him to be a friend, those words hit me like a freight train. Is that what he's doing with me? I don't think he is. I really don't, but what if my hormones are confusing my instincts? I do not like where this is leading me, and afraid he will read my reaction, I quickly slide in to the car.

But Kyle doesn't allow me shelter. Nor does he immediately shut my door, compelling me to look at him, to confirm what he senses in me, which I know is distrust, but I do not do as he bids. I stare ahead, his unnamed questions and mine once again heavy and hard between us. Finally though, an eternity later, he shuts me inside, and rounds the rear of the Mustang, climbing inside with me, but he doesn't start the engine.

More seconds tick by like hours, until he faces me while I hold steady and face forward. "Look at me," he orders.

"No, I—"

"Look at me, Myla," he repeats, his voice a command, compelling me.

Damn it. I do it. I turn and then we are close, a small space between us, as I blurt out, "Is that what you are doing to me? Pretending to be my friend to see what I do next?"

"No," he says firmly. "It is not and I know on some level you know that, but you refuse to trust your instincts."

"Would you trust you in my position?"

"So you admit that you want to trust me?"

"Of course I want to trust you, but I can't. I won't."

"You can," he promises, and oh how well he does promises. They touch his eyes. They touch his voice. They touch me. "But I've told you that I approve of your caution, and understand it, but sitting here right now, it occurs to me that we haven't discussed the obvious, so let me make this easier on you. Alvarez has some doubt about you or I wouldn't be here."

"He doubts everyone," I argue, before I let him go on.

"Does he pay someone a million dollars to look after them like he did me?"

"No," I say. "He does not."

"Okay then. Because of him hiring me, I'm now in a position to either protect you or destroy you."

"No," I say, rejecting that idea. "No. You can only destroy me if I let you."

"Sweetheart, that's not true. If I wanted to destroy you, I could have already asked for a bonus for making your true self show so quickly and then be done with this. Juan could do the same. Anyone could. You're exposed whether you like it or not, and I'm your buffer."

"If Juan, or whoever, could do as you say, why haven't they?"

"In my book, that means someone either thinks Alvarez is worse to deal with without you by his side, or they're afraid he'll shoot the messenger if they turn on you. But that doesn't mean they won't turn on you." He settles further into his seat. "Whatever the case, we need to go before they come looking for us."

He sticks the key in the ignition and before he can turn it, I say, "Why haven't you turned on me for a fast payday?"

"That was where I was leading you, sweetheart. I haven't and I won't, because like I've said over and over, and will continue to say: I was never here for the money. That's not what I'm about or who I am." He cranks the engine to a deep roar.

I lean against the seat, staring forward, and all I have is what I already knew. Kyle isn't what he seems, but then neither am I, and I'm not sure what that makes my next move, or his.

Chapter Ten

MYLA

It's a short drive and we are at the new Alvarez Clothing location, where a shopping center frames the left side of a two-story red brick warehouse, while the front door is hugged by enough space to hold two hundred cars. "It's very large," I comment as Kyle parks us next to the front door, in a reserved spot, while no more than fifteen vehicles scatter the rest of the lot.

"Not what you expected?"

"We aren't doing mass distribution right now, so no," I say. "It's not what I expected."

"Alvarez is doing plenty of mass distribution, and opportunist that he is—"

"He told me he wouldn't—"

"You talk to him about his business?" he asks, and suddenly he is facing me, looking at me; disapproval in those fierce green eyes.

"No," I say, "but I'm no fool. I know who he is. I know what he does and I don't want to be connected to that."

"You're connected to it as long as you're connected to him."

"He promised me this would be legal."

"Of course he did," he says dryly. "But in case you didn't know, money laundering is not legal, even if the clothing in the warehouse is."

My defenses bristle. "I'm pretty sure you working for him isn't either."

"I'm guarding you, sweetheart. There is nothing illegal about that."

"What else are you doing?" I ask. "Because you still haven't told me who you really are and what you want."

"What am I doing?" he asks, once again avoiding a direct answer. "Getting us the fuck out of the car before Juan nags me again and ends up dead sooner than I plan." He reaches for his door.

I blanch. "Wait. What? Sooner than you plan?"

"He's a dead man walking, of that I can promise you, but right now, he's a buffer between us and Alvarez, so he lives another day. Stay here. I'll come around for you." He gets out of the car.

Okay. New direction here. He can't be FBI. He wouldn't be planning on killing Juan if he was. Would he? Wanting a chance to ask something else, anything else, before I can't, I grab my purse and open my door. Twisting to get out, I find Kyle towering over me, so close I can't stand up, the warm Texas sun lifting his spicy scent in the air, while I've apparently stirred his temper. "What part of "wait" do you not understand?" he demands.

"I can get my own door."

"And get out of the car, just in time for someone to grab you?"

"Oh, I—"

"Oh is right," he says. "You wait when I tell you to wait."

"Right. Asshole mode now in full force."

"You haven't seen asshole yet, sweetheart. This is me keeping you alive."

He's taken me full circle back to my worries in the garage. "Is there a threat to my life I don't know about?"

"You're his woman. Isn't that the only answer you need?"

That jolts me and I react instantly. "Fuck you, Kyle," I say, before I can stop myself. "And move so I can get out."

"That was a test," he says.

"Isn't everything with you?"

"Don't react to anything I say like it matters to you," he warns, taking a step backward and giving me space.

The test was not the test I thought it was, and I feel the blood drain from my cheeks. "Damn it," I murmur, inhaling and shutting my eyes a moment, envisioning myself stepping into the invisible box that I live in when I am her, when I am his woman.

"Myla," Kyle says, and I open my eyes, standing to face him.

"I get it. I failed the test."

"You failed one, but you passed the one that matters."

"What? No, I—"

"Passed."

"What test?"

"Think about it," he says, taking yet another two steps

backwards, aligning himself with the door, but I am thinking about his second test and the meaning hits me. I reacted with honest distaste to him calling me Michael Alvarez's woman, I'd fret that, but really, he was right. If he wants to hang me out to dry, he could do so with little or no, facts.

I inhale a calming breath, that isn't calming at all, but I don't let nerves delay my departure. I step out of the Mustang and walk toward the door, by the time I'm there, Kyle is with me, holding the door. "Don't look at me," he warns softly, and the very fact that he a) needs to tell me this, and b) knows what I will do already, is compelling proof of...I don't know what. But it's big and I'll figure it out later. I have to figure it out.

Entering the glossy white lobby, I observe the pictures of stylish, bright colored clothing painted on glass windows, unbidden, the elation of a dream realized, if only for these few fantasy moments, washes over me. "It's beautiful," I murmur, turning in a circle to take it all in.

"Myla!"

At my name, I face forward and blink the pretty blonde behind an oval stainless steel desk into view, finding her standing up to greet me, her suit dress as white as the leather chairs and couch behind me. It's also mine. Mine. Mine! "It's your creation," she says of my dress, speaking as if she knows me.

I have a rock star kind of moment, like I've made it to the top, and a thrill slides up and down my spine. "Do you love it?" she asks, rounding the desk. "I love it!"

I do love it, but just as unbidden as the misplaced joy I'd felt entering the lobby, I find myself assessing her in an unwelcome way, finding her twenty-something, model-gorgeous, and exactly the kind of woman that would be a target for the cartel for very bad things. All elation is gone and it's all I can do to maintain my smile. "It's stunning on you," I say. "You are beautiful and I am honored to have you wear it."

She beams. "Okay now," she says. "You are officially so very nice." She glances at Kyle as he steps to my side, a tiny hint of admiration in her face, which bugs me. "Hi," she greets, flirtiness in her tone. "Can I help you?"

"No help needed," he says.

Her brows furrow, her admiration starting to turn to discomfort. "But...who are you, please?"

"The bodyguard," he says flatly, and the rush of awkwardness in the room is instant, as is his success at turning her admiration into intimidation, which has me feeling guilty for my hint of jealousy. She is young and he is older, good looking, and overwhelmingly...him. Just him. That's all I have to say or think on the topic.

"I'll let Barbara know that Myla and her bodyguard are present," she says, heading back to the desk, and seeming like she wants a barrier from the awkwardness, she nervously adds, "And my name is Heather if you need anything." She flicks Kyle a look that gets her nothing but a hard stare.

Trying to ease her discomfort, like I have others before her, like I want to do for so many more, I say, "He's Kyle, and a robot actually. He looks very real, right? That's why he's so big. It takes a lot of space to make it look like he has muscles when he doesn't."

She gives him a curious look and Lord help me, she inspects him like I might not be joking. The man has rattled the poor girl and he and I will be chatting about that, very forcefully. "He's very authentic, right?" I ask, holding out my hands as if presenting my specimen and Kyle either doesn't care or play along, just standing there. Finally, she gets it, and bursts out laughing. I laugh, too, while Kyle says, "I need to do a walkthrough of the building with Myla in a secure location."

"Our building is secure, I assure you," comes a female voice and now I have a genuine thrill with no guilt because I am staring at The Barbara Van Gleek, who is sixty, silver haired, and somehow elegantly sexy. She's also been the assistant to some of the biggest names in fashion.

I want to gush. I want to hug her. I want to act like a school girl, but I know, that won't get me respect, which I need at all levels to keep surviving.

"Forgive me, ma'am," Kyle replies, "but my responsibility is to Myla's safety and I will be making that assessment myself."

Barbara purses her pink-painted lips. "Men. They're all the same. They have to be in charge. Well, you're not in charge young man, but if it makes you feel better, do whatever you need to do. I'll take Myla into my office. No. To her office." Her gaze lands on me. "Why am I talking to him and not to our superstar? Come." She holds out her arms. "I must hug the future of fashion."

Oh god. I'm having a mixed moment of fan girl and dream girl, both of whom want this to be real, not a money laundering operation for a drug cartel. And I let myself. Just for these few beats, when time stands still as I'm wrapped in Barbara's arms. I mean, she is hugging me, after all, and she smells like cinnamon of all things, and I really like cinnamon.

She pulls back and looks at me. "You look uncannily like

your mother."

"I do?" I don't give her time to answer because I've never met anyone who knows my mother. "You knew my mother?"

"I did. She was a beauty with quite the eye for design work. Which brings me to the surprise I have for you." She takes my hand, Barbara Van Gleek takes my freaking hand, and leads me down a curvy artsy stone encased path, but there is a sudden, odd fizzle of unease in me, and I don't know why. Where is it coming from? Why am I so on edge that I can feel Kyle behind me, close, connected, and yes, looking out for me? Once again, he makes me feel safe. No. He always makes me feel safe, and despite knowing I am responsible for my own safety, I welcome the sense of not being quite as alone with him around. I revel in the cold steel between my breasts, and it hits me then that even having it, should equal trust in Kyle, a detail so obvious, that I don't know why it hasn't registered.

Our travels, and my fizzle of unease, continue to the right and down another hallway, this one's walls layered with fashion magazine covers as if they are embedded in the stone, I love it, but that fizzle is becoming a bubble. I try to tame it by reminding myself that thanks to Kyle I could shoot any enemy that attacked me if I had to do it, and it's that thought that brings us to a halt at a corner office.

"Your castle, madam," Barbara says, motioning me forward and bowing dramatically.

I smile, but I don't quite feel it, aware this isn't the dream. Aware now that the bubble is a well of emotions over wanting, but not wanting, so many things. I know then that these feelings had been building with today's approach, and I can no longer blame Kyle for last night. I'd been ripe for that cry.

"Go in!" Barbara urges when I still stand in the hallway, aware of Kyle behind me, wishing she was gone, and he was the only one here now. I don't analyze why he's okay. He just is. He's the only one that is or has been for a very long time.

Forcefully, I step forward, entering my new place of work, and when I do, I feel nauseous, not elated, at the perfection of the space. I take it in, try to comprehend it and form the positive reaction it deserves. I mean, it is fabulous. Not only is the desk this stunning, shiny dark wood, the floors are a pale tan contrasted with walls that mimic their color. But what steals my breath, what guts me, are the life-sized fashion shots of my mother lining those walls.

Barbara steps to my side, sliding her arm over my shoulder. "Do you love it?"

"Yes," I whisper, unable to find my voice, that bubble of emotion now in my throat. "Yes, I do. I love it." And truly I do love it, just not what surrounds it. Not what got me here.

She turns me to face her, her hands on my shoulders. "Soon this place will be filled with the visions I am certain she inspired."

"She did. Very much so."

"I see her in your work." She releases me and eyes her watch. "How about a tour in thirty minutes? I moved our meeting back to give you time to be settled, so we start in an hour."

"That's perfect."

"Great," she says, "then make yourself at home and you will note that there is a Keurig right here in your office." She indicates an adorable round glass table in the corner right next to a bookshelf and a cozy looking brown leather chair. "And," she adds "I hear we stocked your favorite chocolate coffee." She turns and stops in her tracks at the sight of Kyle standing in the doorway, his shoulders all but touching the frame. "Is this a safe stop for her?"

"It'll do for now," he concurs, "and I'll need full access to the facility."

"I was told you would," she says, "and there are no deterrents to keep you from looking around anyway."

"Then I can already tell you security changes are coming."

"You won't get any complaints from me about making things safer, but I do not want my staff feeling as if they have something to fear. Understand, Mr.—?"

"Kyle," he says. "Just call me Kyle. And I'm discreet."

She gives him a once over. "Nothing about you says discreet, sir."

He arches a brow and then amends his words to, "Diplomatic."

"That I can accept and live with," she approves.

He gives her an incline of his head and steps just inside the door while she accepts the invitation to depart, quickly crossing the room and disappearing into the hallway. Kyle shuts the door and immediately removes the same box he'd used to scan the hotel for listening devices. I face the largest photo of my mother, her dark hair draping her naked shoulder, a sleek silver formal gown hugging her curves, my heart squeezing with the sight of her. She was beautiful, but she doesn't look like me. She looks like my sister.

Kyle steps to my side. "The office is clean, but I wouldn't

be surprised if that changed tomorrow, when they think I've already cleared it. The same goes for the hotel room."

"That's good," I murmur, only half listening, Kara on my mind. My mother on my mind.

He places himself in front of me, blocking the wall from my view. "Myla, you do know that all of this—"

"Is fake. Yes. I know."

"No. It's not fake. That woman, those women, and the love for your work, that is not fake. Your talent is not fake." He reaches up and caresses my cheek, sending goosebumps down my spine, but this time, his touch is calming in ways I don't try to understand, but welcome. "I need to—" he begins.

"I know," I say.

He hesitates, as if torn about leaving me, before he walks toward the door, and then pauses there, turning to look at the photos of my mother. "She was beautiful," he says. "And you do look like her." He opens the door and exits, shutting me inside as he leaves me with a compliment that means more to me than he knows. Or maybe he does know. Maybe he really does see the me I've successfully blocked everyone else from seeing.

My cellphone starts ringing in my purse, and I know without looking who it is. I dig it out, and answer, "Hi Michael," sounding cheerful, which is just one of my practiced emotions.

"Bella," he murmurs, his voice deep and rich, but oh how I know the way it can whip and cut. The way, quite literally, *he* can whip and cut. "Do you love everything?"

"I do," I say, walking to sit at my desk, a cushy high backed velvet chair my new, but wobbly, throne, my briefcase on my desk where Kyle left it. "The lobby is stunning.

Barbara is as wonderful as I'd hoped." I laugh. "You got me chocolate coffee."

"I know how you love your coffee," he says, his little gifts part of his way of making me his pet. "I hate that I am not there to enjoy this with you, but business must come first."

"Where are you exactly?" I ask, gauging the time I have to enact my plan.

"South America, but I should be home in a week rather than three."

This news twists me and my plans in knots. "That's wonderful," I manage. "Three was forever."

"It would have been an eternity without you otherwise," he says, though I worry his motivation is really about assessing my loyalty and dealing with me. "How do you like your new bodyguard?" He asks.

"He just stares at everyone and he freaked the poor receptionist out. When I joked that he's a robot, his reply was to simply stare her down yet again."

He chuckles, something I always welcome, as it means for that moment he's content, a state of mind we all want him to have. "No personality," he says, "but that's fine. I'm paying him to protect you, not make everyone feel at ease."

"His coldness and constant monitoring is rather suffocating," I say, knowing this will actually make him want to keep Kyle, not the opposite. "I don't like it."

"You always have guards. I always have guards."

"I know, but…is there a threat I don't know about?"

"There's always a threat, but with us separated and you on your own in a new place, the chances of you being targeted are higher."

"Why not use your men?"

"Kyle fits into your fashion industry more discreetly, and he's from Dallas. He knows that area and his references are exceptional." There are voices in the background and he answers in Spanish, which I've pretended not to understand, but do. "Tell him he's dead," he says to the other person. "See how he replies then," he adds, before returning to me, to say, "Negotiations on a deal are heating up. I need to go."

"Okay. Thank you again for all of this."

"The world will know your gift, as we do," he promises, but unlike Kyle's, his are jagged edged, promising to cut me and make me bleed. As is his pause, which is followed with, "You haven't mentioned the photos of your mother."

That fizzle of unease starts up again. "No, I...they choked me up. I feel emotional, so it's hard to talk about them, but they are wonderful. It's such an amazing gesture."

"It's a connection to family that doesn't risk death. It is something I thought you would like."

The fizzle becomes bitter cold ice at what I know to be a threat, and I go into auto-pilot, barely remembering what he says next or what I say. Suddenly, the call is over and I am standing when I had been sitting. *Family that doesn't come with the risk of death.* He was threatening Kara. Wait. My God. I've been a fool. If I am front and center in this fashion business, she will come for me. She will find me. And he knows it. He didn't hire Kyle to keep her away. He hired him to know when she arrives. To know when the time to kill her has arrived. I consider a moment, to wonder if Kyle is involved, and I don't think so. I really don't. But this is my sister's life I'm playing with. I have to find out for sure, because it's time to accept the fact that my plan can't work when she's in danger. I need help.

Chapter Eleven

KYLE

I've barely exited Myla's office when I get a text that reads: Fuck, fuck, fuck. Call me at this number. Blake, of course, because who else uses "fuck" to say good morning, how are you, and what's for dinner? And considering I've known him long enough to decipher three "fucks" as a problem, I start for the lobby and exit to the parking lot, hoping like hell Kara doesn't know about Myla, and is now on her way here. Scanning the parking lot, I head for the Mustang, unlock the door, climb inside. Comfortable that my crew has my car under secure watch, I punch in Blake's temporary number, protocol indicating that it will be blocked, secure, and appear disconnected should anyone else try to use it, as is the case, with all numbers we maintain, once one of us is undercover.

Blake answers his on the first ring. "Holy fuck. You have Myla, and hell no, Kara doesn't know. It's killing me to keep this from her but she wouldn't stay away. But holy fuck. You have Myla."

"I know, man," I say, relieved that he's on board with this, but Kara isn't. "I couldn't believe it when it was her."

"How is she?"

"Being manipulated by dreams and family, but smart and strong enough to use it to survive and protect Kara. But I need to get her the hell out of here."

"Does she know who you are yet?"

"I can't tell her until I can assure her Kara is not only safe, but will stay that way, and that leaves us with two options."

"Alvarez dead, arrested, or thinks Myla is dead, which forces her to hide her entire life."

"I'm not sure he wouldn't reach for her outside a jail cell," I say. "She's too close to him for him to just let her go."

"So we kill him," Blake says, no hesitation, decision made. "Let's talk logistics. Can we get to him?"

"He'll come for Myla," I say. "But I need to bring her into the loop, prepare her for what comes next, and I need to extract as much information from her to destroy the cartel and tear down that sex trade operation now, not later."

"If we get enough from her we might have to bring in the Feds," he says. "And that dirties things up."

He means it makes killing Alvarez more complicated. "He'll be in my face, and I'll be in his."

"Fuck, man. That was supposed to be me. You better enjoy it for me."

"Oh, I will," I say. "I will. But back to Myla. She has tolerated being in that man's bed, doing God knows what, to survive and to protect Kara. If she thinks I've endangered her sister, this will fall apart. I have to be able to convince her that Kara is safe, out of reach, and that she will stay that way until this is over. She's been through hell to protect her sister. If she thinks I'm endangering her, I'm not sure how she'll react."

"I couldn't get Kara on the plane to Italy and I wasn't leaving her here alone."

"What about the Ella case?"

"I have men on the ground chasing what, right now, is iffy lead. If I get something solid, I'll use that to get Kara to Italy. We're in New York."

"You need to get off the radar completely."

"You don't have to tell me that," he says. "I get it. I convinced Kara to go away for a few days with me to Seattle. I've arranged a private plane, and I'll conceal our destination and identities, but I can't keep this from her. I'm going to tell her when we're there, give her some explosion time, and get her head on straight. She needs to get past the emotional aspect of this."

"Make sure she does, man, because I have the same issue here. I can't keep lying to Myla. She knows I'm not what I say I am. I'm going to kill any trust I've started to earn if I don't tell her the truth and fast."

"We leave in an hour," he says. "I'll tell her by morning and I'll tie her to the damn bed until she's reasonable, if I have to."

"That's what I want to hear," I say. "That's what I need to be able to tell Myla."

"Understood." He pauses a moment. "You never gave up on her, man. You were as obsessed with her being alive as Kara. More, even."

"It was a gut feeling."

"It was you doing what I couldn't do and keep Kara sane at the same time. You did this for us. You are a fucking brother, a Walker in every way."

The emotion in his voice punches me in the chest, while mine hits me in the gut. Blake, his brothers, they are the family I never had, and that's why I can't leave this unsaid. "I am your brother," I say. "And this started about you and Kara, but it's become about Myla just as much. No. It is about her to me now."

"Fuck, man, I get where this is going. She's vulnerable and you know that makes her off limits."

My jaw clenches. "I haven't touched her."

"Not yet, but you were warning me where this is going, preparing me so I can prepare Kara. This isn't just another undercover job. This is her sister."

"And I'm the one here. I'm the one undercover, keeping us both alive, and that means I'm going to do whatever I have to do to keep us both alive." And instead of reminding him that he was undercover when he met Kara, I change the subject. "Tell Royce I need those emergency exit strategies now, not later."

"We've already arranged a private jet and the Rosa Airfield is on standby around the clock. Get there and you get out. F Hanger, with Louie. I'll text you his number."

"I know where Rosa is."

"Kyle—"

"I'm going to do what it takes to keep us both alive, and that's not your call," I repeat, and then hang up, immediately reaching for the door, only to have the phone ring again. I answer it and Blake says, "You're fucking right. You do what you have to do. I trust you. We all trust you. Just stay the fuck alive and keep her that way, too."

"I will," I say, and this time when I end the connection, I have one thing on my mind. Getting back to Myla. I step out of the Mustang, automatically scanning the parking lot again, and my gaze lands hard on a black sedan, with equally blacked out tint on the windows. I study it, catching a flicker in the darkness at the driver's side that tells me someone is smoking. I don't like it and I unbutton my jacket, walking toward it, a calm, steady charge; my fingers flexing, and ready to draw my gun. There are shadows behind the glass, movement. Panic. The door starts to open at the same moment I shove it back into place and point my gun at the window. It rolls down, revealing Ricardo, who I happen to know is a prime player in the sex trafficking operation, and a piece of slime I'd happily rid this world of now and forever.

"Put your fucking gun down," he demands.

"I have no way of knowing if you are on Alvarez's watch or working against him. The rules I agreed on with Juan include you telling me when you're here."

"That's not what he said. He said—"

"I don't give a fuck what he said. You identify yourself when you're in my line of sight or not only will I blow your head off next time. I'll enjoy it." I reach for my phone.

"What are you doing?"

"Calling Juan," I say. "I want to know that he knows you're here."

"Fuck." He scrubs his grubby, fat face, and I have a fantasy in my head that includes me shoving it against the steering wheel. No. The glass. Fuck. Both. With a lot of punching in between.

"What do want?" Juan demands, answering the call.

"Is Ricardo outside the factory under your instructions?"

"Yes. Why the fuck else would he be there?"

"Unless he tells me he's here next time, I'll assume he's sidelining for one of Alvarez's enemies, and blow his head off. That goes for anyone I discover who doesn't notify me of their presence."

"You think—" he begins.

I end the call and study Ricardo. "I'm going to lower my gun, and you're going to drive away while I watch. Understand?"

"Yes, you little prick." He rolls the window halfway up and pauses. "Smart to make me leave. I like a man's back."

"I myself," I say, pointing the gun at his temple. "Like his head."

He murmurs something I can't make out in Spanish, and then puts his car in gear, backing up while I step back, holding my gun on the car until he drives away. I scan the parking lot again, and when I'm sure it's clear, then and only then do I holster my weapon, button my jacket and walk toward the building. I enter the lobby to find Heather standing at the glass, looking terrified and like she saw a ghost.

"Should I call the police?"

"Not necessary," I say. "The guy was a gangbanger who picked the wrong parking lot. It's handled."

"Oh. Are you sure?"

"It's handled," I repeat, which is true. For now. At any moment, Alvarez could show up, and right now, I'm not ready for that to happen.

• • •

MYLA

Kyle doesn't return to my office before Barbara finds me for my tour that includes a ton of empty warehouse space. "We seem to be planning big," I comment, surveying the high ceiling surrounded by steel and brick.

"It had been vacant a long while, so we negotiated a really amazing deal," she explains, "but why not plan big? We're going to be big."

I refrain from telling her the growth might not quite be by her preferred method, but maybe she knows. I mean, why is she working for Michael Alvarez? The reality here is that as much as I adore Barbara, I have to face the facts. She has to know what Michael is, and what her exposure could become by working for him. This could be her final hurrah with a big payday, and that makes her loyal to him. Whatever the case, our tour continues and ends in the conference room, which is painted with a mural of New York City, and has a glass conference table, with six people around it, waiting on us.

For the next hour, I listen to the status of production and plans for roll out, and at some point, Kyle appears and silently invites himself to the event by simply claiming a seat at the table. Another hour, and we're still going, and everyone is responsive, excited and full of ideas, a combination that could make my dream perfection, if I could ever see this as my dream. But the bottom line is that a threat against my life, my sister's life, and anyone I dare getting close to, is the manifestation of every nightmare I've imagined since meeting Michael Alvarez.

Come lunchtime, we order in sandwiches, and dive into our marketing campaigns, and no one but me seems to question why Kyle is present, nor does he ask questions or contribute. The staff is just so into the launch, all animated, excited, and eager to please me, as if I am indeed their boss, and I have a fleeting moment in which I decide that once we launch, my death would be difficult to explain, but it's a ridiculous comfort. Michael Alvarez doesn't care about difficult, and he'd just kill my sister and keep me alive anyway. And her safety is what keeps me going, as does the bigger plan I've hatched that gives me a purpose so much larger than fancy clothes, which now seem rather petty and unimportant.

It's in that moment that Kyle's gaze catches mine, and in its depths I see genuine concern, but there is also a promise of protection, and this kind of cool calmness somehow reaches across the table and soothes my frazzled nerves. Suddenly, I am not alone, and while thinking I am not might be dangerous, I can't seem to care. He is here. He makes at least this one afternoon bearable.

It's three o'clock when Barbara finally leads me down a hallway to the design studio, but just as we're about to enter, she's called to the lobby, and I pause at the door to wait on her, which leaves me alone with Kyle. "What's was going on with you in the conference room?" he asks softly, more of that genuine concern in his voice I'd seen in his eyes earlier.

"Nothing that isn't always going on," I assure him, hating this biting emotion in my chest. "I should go on inside." Afraid if I say more, I might lose my necessary composure, and knowing he isn't likely to grab me and delay my departure, I turn away, but he firmly orders, "Stop."

Inhaling, I face him. "Kyle, please I—"

"That nothing was something. I need to know what it is

to protect you."

"It's nothing you can protect me from."

"I can and will protect you, but I need details."

"It's not about danger," I say. "Not really. Michael called. He hit some nerves and I can't seem to shake them."

"What nerves, sweetheart?" he murmurs softly. "Did he threaten you?"

"It's nothing new," I repeat. "He's coming back in a week."

"When was he supposed to come back?"

"Two weeks. But you never know with him. Please let this go right now so I can try to let it go."

He gives me one of those intense, green eyes stares, and then nods. "Okay. But—"

"I know. You're here and I actually really appreciate that." I don't wait for his reaction, instead entering the design room, which is lined with sewing machines, and filled with tables and a good dozen mannequins in random locations. In the center of it all, at the only round table, surrounded by six helpers, is a stunning redhead I know to be fashion designer LeeAnn Orlando. So intent is she and those around her on whatever she is saying, that no one seems to notice my entry. A good minute passes and I'm still standing here. Feeling awkward, I decide to walk around the mannequins, a little thrill with each of my designs, I pass and approve. That is, until I stop in front of what is supposed to be my all-time favorite gown, one that my mother started to design first, only to find it has gone horribly wrong. First of all, it's a pale pink, not the emerald of my mother's eyes, and the waist and bodice are just plain all wrong. I tell myself it doesn't matter. This is all fake. It's not me. It's not a real clothing line, but

I find myself turning around, and irritated to find that that I'm still being ignored.

"Excuse me," I call out, at the same moment Kyle enters the room, assuming guard just inside the door, while LeeAnn continues to keep on with the snub. "Excuse me," I call out a little louder, and this time she glances up, irritation etched on her pretty face, arrogance in her demeanor that says that I am beneath her.

"Yes?" she asks.

"Can I please discuss this design with you?" I ask, indicating the dress.

Reluctance radiates from what has to be every particle of her being, but she crosses the room to stand in front of the mannequin with me. "What can I do for you?"

"I should introduce myself," I say. "I'm—"

"Of course I know who you are."

There is a slap to those words. "Obviously you're no fan."

"I'm a fan of fashion, not people."

"Well then this dress is not the fashion statement intended. The waist, bodice and color are off."

"The color is set to the season of release, which is summer. The bodice and waist had to be adjusted to be workable."

"I've made this dress myself. The bodice and waist were just fine, and I want the green I requested."

She rolls her eyes. "Look, Myla. I know you think you're in charge, but there is a reason Michael hired me."

Michael. She called him Michael. I am stunned when I should not be, and in fact, I'd celebrate any affair between them if I wasn't clear on her role now. She is how this label would exist without me. She makes me disposable, but I do not dare blink. "And Michael put me in charge," I say, my well-honed survival skills kicking in. "Which is why I won't waste his time involving him in this. Now, if we can't come to terms on this dress, but most importantly, my role here versus yours, then I will make it clear to him that I'm interviewing new designers. Think about it overnight and we'll chat tomorrow morning." I don't give her time to reply, crossing the room, leaving the gauntlet on the ground, the shattering of my admiration for one of my idols, with it.

Kyle is, of course, watching my approach without reaction, when I know he's heard the exchange. His expression is unreadable, his stare hooded, the door opening beside him as Barbara appears. "The models are beginning to arrive," she says eagerly. "Come. We're in the room off the reception area." She waves me forward and disappears again.

I glance at Kyle. "Models," I say. "You should enjoy this part of the day."

"The only woman I'm watching is you," he assures me, a hint of something warm slipping into his tone.

I swallow hard, not sure why, but in that moment, I feel vulnerable with this man, exposed in ways I have never been with Michael Alvarez, and my defenses rise. "I guess that's what you get paid the big bucks for," I spout, and it's not only out-of-character snideness, but I regret it the moment I say it.

He doesn't like it either, the glint in his eyes a telltale sign that says he wants to reply, but it is gone an instant later, and so am I. Exiting into the hallway, heading toward the lobby. I'm almost there, when I stop and face him. "I'm sorry."

"What?" he asks.

"About what I just said," I explain, and realizing I've already brought too much attention to us, I enter the lobby. "Where am I going?" I ask Heather.

She smiles and motions me toward a door, but her face freezes as her attention shifts to Kyle. Poor thing. Michael is right on one thing. His normal crew would not work out here. Kyle might be intimidating big, quiet, and good looking, but those guys look like they will corner you alone at any moment. And they will, I think, my gut twisting with a memory I cannot allow to surface right now.

Stopping at the door, I turn to Kyle, lowering my voice for his ears only. "Heather can't take you standing by her desk the entire time I'm in here. You have to come inside."

His lips quirk ever so slightly and he gives me a nod before we enter the room, me first, and we find a row of five chairs in front of some sort of a red carpet I assume is meant to be the runway. Barbara motions me forward to join her, then points for both me and Kyle to sit. "This is your runway show," she says, handing me her clipboard. "Names. Agencies. Stats. Are you ready?"

"Yes," I say, feeling excited all over again, and hating how easily that keeps happening, but the thrill is gone the instant the first girl enters the room and starts strutting her stuff. She's gorgeous. She's perfect. She's everything Heather is at that receptionist desk, which is perfect for the slave trade operation Juan and Ricardo recruit for every chance they get. I need to get her out of here. I mark her card with a negative. Three more girls walk for us, and I do the same. I'm starting to feel sick. I can't hire models. I have to find a way out of this.

Barbara waits until I've declined girl number five

before standing in front of my chair, hands on hips. "What isn't clicking?"

"I don't know," I say, and afraid just coming here is putting the girls on the wrong radar, I change direction. "Maybe I should look through the agency books before we have more come out?"

"We have ten more lined up," she says, "and we need to shoot the campaign in the next three weeks to make the launch publication dates for the top five fashion magazines."

Top five fashion magazines. My designs. My dream. But these girls are potentially in hell. I'm back to this being a nightmare. "I'm sure I'll find someone," I lie. I'm not going to find anyone. I'm not going to let this happen.

"We need three girls for the plan you approved earlier."

"Yes, I meant three."

"Maybe if I leave you alone." She glances at Kyle. "What are your thoughts?"

"I'm just waiting for one of them to pull a gun so I can shoot them," he says, in a completely dry tone.

I gape at him and Barbara chuckles, waving a finger at him. "You have a sense of humor you hide beneath that robot shell after all." She glances at me. "I'm going to send another in."

I nod and she walks away, and the minute the door shuts, Kyle leans forward, elbows on his knees. "What's going on, sweetheart?"

"Same as always," I whisper, but I don't look at him, because that bubble has started again, and it's a big one, a really, really big one. "I think I'm going to talk to them about a more iconic kind of campaign. A decadent cherry, though I have no idea how cherries mean clothing. I will figure it out."

"Myla—"

The door opens again and another woman is walking the floor, but I'm not really seeing her, and Kyle isn't watching her either. He's watching me. He's seeing too much. He knows I don't want to be here, and there is no way I can deny that any longer. I don't want to be here. I barely make it through the rest of the girls. Finally it's over, and Barbara is ridiculously sweet about me declining them all.

"We can look at model books tomorrow," she says, "and have another round sent over. It's only Monday. We have all week to get this nailed down. We just need to do it by Friday."

"That sounds good," I say, when it doesn't at all.

The next few minutes become a blur. I grab my purse and briefcase and Kyle is forever by my side. We exit the building and he holds the door for me. Once we're inside the Mustang, sealed into the safe zone of being alone, he doesn't turn on the car. "What happened in there?"

"A lot," I say, turning to look at him. "I'm not going to pretend it didn't, because you know it did."

"Tell me."

"Not now and maybe not ever. I'm not making a decision about trusting you right now in this moment. I need to get on a treadmill. I need to clear my head. I need to leave here now."

"Then we go," he says, cranking the engine, and putting us in reverse. And oh, how I wish I could go in reverse and turn back time. If only I hadn't taken that waitress job. If only I hadn't gone to San Francisco for a job in fashion. But I can't go back and I have to face facts. Michael threatened

Kara. He sees her as a lingering threat he wants addressed. He absolutely will kill her if I don't find a way to contain her. He will kill her if I run. He will use those models for his sex trafficking if I'm here or if I'm gone. He has to be stopped. And I've fought too hard and long to fail now. I need a revised plan.

And at the core of that plan I have to consider the man sitting next to me being either my only ally or my worst enemy.

Chapter Twelve

MYLA

Once we're on the highway, I sink back into the leather of the Mustang's seat, and my mind is searching for answers, instead finding the past. I'm back where this all started. In the restaurant, and seated at a table across from Michael Alvarez. At first, having dinner with him hadn't been all that bad. He'd been suave, charming even. He'd asked about my dreams, and for reasons I don't know, I told him about my design work. We'd laughed about food, television, and politics, and he'd seemed so very human. He'd told me about his restaurants, the conversation so comfortable that I'd started to think he wasn't the kingpin I thought he was.

When dinner was over, he'd invited me to his hotel room for drinks. I'd quickly declined and he hadn't pushed, but there was something in his eyes I should have known was trouble. Still, he didn't push himself on me or even ask to see me again. I'd left Kara a message, but afraid of scaring her, I hadn't told her why. Just that I needed her to call me. That decision had been the stupidest of my life. Had I told her why, maybe she would have sent help while I was still in the city. But I didn't and hours later, my life forever changed.

I exit the restaurant, into a chilly San Francisco evening, huddling down into my jacket, when a fancy black sports car pulls up next to me. The door pops open and much to my shock, Michael Alvarez is inside. "Get in," he orders.

"I'm meeting a friend," I say, but suddenly the man I now know as Ricardo is by my side.

"He said, get in," he repeats, and when I look up I find two more men leaning on a car to my left, and watching me. My heart is racing. I have to get in. I don't want to get in.

"Bella," he says, calling me "beautiful" in Spanish, but my gut tells me to pretend I don't understand. I decide in that moment to be whatever he wants me to be, to survive until I can call Kara.

I slide into the car, and give him a shy smile I pray looks real. "I guess my friend can wait. What does bella mean?"

His lips curve, his eyes possessive as he brushes hair from my cheek, and chills of absolute terror slide down my spine.

I blink back to the present and Kyle is pulling the Mustang into the parking garage of the Ritz, but my mind drags me to one last horrible moment, forcing my lashes to lower. *I am in his hotel room. The room is elegant, large, and thankfully the living area is separate from the bedroom that I don't want to see, but fear I will. I take a step toward a chair to join him, but he holds up a hand. "I want to see all that ivory skin naked. Get naked for me, Myla."*

I blanch. "Now? Here?

His lips curve slightly, his eyes darkening. "Now. Here."

I have a moment of pure panic, and I want to turn and run, but logic reminds me that he is a drug lord, a man who murders without question. I cannot decline. And there is a gut feeling inside me that says if I act as if I want to, he will kill me.

I play coy, like he's the only person I would do this for. Another instinct, I just grab on to. "I don't normally...I feel very nervous."

"Don't be nervous. I will be gentle."

My gaze snaps open and Kyle has pulled us into a parking spot. And still, the image of me standing naked in front of Alvarez, my hands tied, just before he did things to me, a vision I wish I could forget slams into my mind. Then there is another, of Juan, in the back of a car, that should be worse, but it's not. Michael Alvarez is always worse. Struggling to catch my breath, I reach for the door and open it, grabbing my purse and briefcase, and exiting the car, my heart racing. Still, I scan for watchful eyes I don't find, and start walking, making a beeline for the elevator in sight.

Kyle catches me halfway there, his hand coming down on my arm, turning me to face him. "Easy, sweetheart. You're telling the world you're upset, when you need to just tell me."

"There's nothing to tell. I just need to run. I need to get out of my own head. And I know that kind of sucks for you because you have to follow me around, but—"

"It doesn't. We'll run, but what just upset you?"

"Nothing running won't solve. I promise. It always fixes things for me. It takes the edge off. It lets me think. It's my drug."

He gives me a steady look and then nods. "I get it. I understand what it's like to be deep undercover and beat up by it. And we both know you're being beat up."

"I'm stressed. That is not undercover."

"You might as well be, and we both know it." But he doesn't push for more, releasing me. "Let's go run."

Gladly accepting the reprieve, I start walking, impatiently punching the elevator button once at the doors, and relieved when they open instantly. He catches the door, allowing me to enter, and then he's inside with me, smelling all spicy and manly, and consuming the space around me. Michael Alvarez does that too, but it's different. It's like an attack you can't escape, while Kyle's presence is a promise that being with him is too good to even want to try to escape. And his silence on the ride is a promise that he really does understand what I'm feeling and that now is not the time for questions and answers.

Once on our floor, more of the same silence from the elevator settles between us, and somehow our steps are in unison, like he's somehow feeding off my emotions. Like he's telling me I'm not alone, or maybe I just want that to be his message. But alone has served me well. Trusting no one has protected me and my sister. It's kept me alive. I am at a crossroads though, and he is standing in the center and there is nothing about him right now that says he plans to do anything but stay there.

The moment we're in the hotel room—no, my prison—I enter the hallway, and call over my shoulder, "I'm going to change," without looking back. I need to deal with all the adrenaline and emotions colliding inside me. If I can just take the edge off, I'll have real thoughts. Real solutions. A new plan.

Shutting the door, I toss my purse and briefcase on the ground beside it, and walk to the closet, gathering my workout clothes and unzipping the front of my dress. That's when I catch the image in the mirror with the gun between my breasts. My gaze lingers on the thick steel, and for the first time in my life, I imagine really killing someone. I want to kill him. And he would have only himself to blame if I did, because he caged me. Pushed me. Didn't think about me being my father's daughter, which, considering all I've been through, means being a survivor. I am not giving up.

I unstrap the weapon and set it on the shelf running around one side of the tiny space and dress in black leggings before pulling a pink tank top over a sports bra, where my gun should be returned. Instead, I fold my dress, set it on the shelf, and then hide the gun in the folds of the material, out of the sight of anyone who might be nosing around. I walk to the bathroom, and somehow manage to tie my long brown hair back without looking at myself in disgust for even feeling what I feel right now. Every single one of the girls that were pushed in the sex trade have it brutally, horribly worse than me. And now I need that run ten times more.

Exiting the bathroom, I cross the bedroom and open the door, finding Kyle in the living area, his scanner in his hand, his hot, hard body hugged by a snug white t-shirt and black sweats. "I'm ready," I say, and even to my own ears, my voice sounds strained. "Are you ready?"

"I need to sweep your room and we can go."

"Don't you just have to do it again when we get back? I mean, every time we leave, this issue exists, right?"

"Every time," he agrees, setting down the device. "And yes. This can wait."

"Thank you," I say, already crossing to the hallway, traveling toward the door, ready to escape, but just as I reach the doorway, I have a thought, and I face him. And damn it, he's so close to me that my hand lands on his rock-solid chest, heat radiating up my arm and across my chest. "I'm sorry," I say, but when I try to pull my hand back, he holds onto it, and I'm struck by the fact that I feel no fear. He doesn't scare me. In fact, he draws me to him, arouses parts of me I thought would never feel anything again. And he's done it now, after I've mentally relived hell with Michael Alvarez. I don't understand how that is possible or why, when he slowly releases my hand, when my fingers slide away from him, that I just want to touch him again.

"I left my gun," I say. "I thought you should know that."

"I have mine and you have me."

"I have you," I repeat.

"Yes," he says firmly. "You do."

He's right. Now, I have to decide what I'm going to do with him, or what I think he intends to do with me. I turn and grab the door, exiting to the hallway and I don't stop until I'm in the elevator. Kyle is right there with me, both of us in the center of the car, neither of us moving away from each other. And I have this crazy realization that when my hand was on his chest, I was thinking of nothing but him. It was a welcome escape and suddenly, I want to touch him now, but the doors open, saving me from my insanity.

I dart forward, hurrying to the gym door. Thankfully, there is just a keycard and no sign in, and in a matter of two minutes, I'm on a treadmill, Kyle claiming the one beside me. I start running, and push up the speed, pushing my body with it. My mind starts working. I start replaying my plans in my head. My past. My decisions. For forty minutes I do this and I still can't get my mind around what comes next. Somehow, I shift my thoughts to every moment I've spent with Kyle, which feels like many, when I've only just met him. He's close to me. I'm going to let him get closer. He's either my friend or my enemy, and I have a sudden realization that comes with a lot of self-hate. I know what I have been missing.

I step off the belt and hit the "stop" button and turn to find Kyle, who does the same. "We need to go to the room and talk right now."

He grabs his towel. "Lead the way."

• • •

KYLE

I have no idea what Myla is about to tell me but the minute I open the hotel room door, she's inside. Entering after her, I shut the door and lock it, only to find her dashing down the hallway toward her room. Considering the urgency of her need to talk to me, I need to pursue, but I force myself to dial Asher. "There's been no one in our room to create an issue with bugs, right?"

"You're clear."

That's all I need to hear. I pursue Myla, pursue her, rounding the corner just in time to find her disappearing inside her room, but she doesn't shut the door. Considering that an invitation, I head right in as she exits the closet and points her gun at me.

"Do you know why I didn't take the gun with me to the gym?" she demands.

"I'm guessing because you wanted to shoot me," I say,

"given you appear to be considering it now."

"Not you. Them. Him. I hate them all. I hate them so much. And I need you to tell them that. Get your payday. Get this over with."

I officially have no clue where this came from or where it's going, but I toss the scanner on the bed and step closer to her. "Stop," she orders.

"I'm not going to tell anyone that you hate them."

"You are going to tell them, or I swear to you, I will shoot you. And I'm desperate enough to do it."

"Put the gun down, Myla. I'm going to help you. I'm here to help you."

She squats and slides a make-up compact toward me. "Under the lid, there's a list. I need you to call your FBI friends and give them that list. Then call and tell Juan I hate Alvarez and that I'm plotting to kill him."

I don't move, waiting until she stands to ask, "What's the list?"

"Locations where he's holding the women he's kidnapped for his sex trade operation. I have them all. I know I do. And I need to know something good came out of this. I need to save them before he kills me. Or at least know they will be saved."

"And we will save them. Together."

"By you calling your friends now."

I take a step toward her. "Give me the gun, Myla."

She takes a step backward. "I will shoot you, Kyle."

"Please don't," I say, "because, sweetheart, I'm highly efficient, but I happen to believe I can do a lot more to help if I'm not bleeding. And we both know, I'm not the one you want to shoot, anyway."

"I'm going to do what I have to do to save my sister and those women."

"This isn't what you have to do." I move quickly then, take two broad steps, and stand in front of her, my hand wrapped around hers and the gun. "Shoot me or let go of the gun."

"And if I let go?"

"I hold onto you. I help you."

"Give me a reason to believe that. Call in the list."

I move then, taking the gun from her in a skilled movement I've used dozens of times, then disarm the weapon and drop it on the ground. My hands are on her waist, and I have her against the wall before she can barely blink, my legs shackling hers.

"Damn you, Kyle," she hisses, her fingers closing around my jacket. "Why can't you just call in the list and then take your payday?"

"Because you are not a payday to me," I say. "And because I have to choose who we tell about anything to do with Alvarez carefully. One bad agent, one leak of this to Alvarez, and we're dead, and so are those women."

"Oh. Oh, God." Her lashes lower and lift, her fist balling at her chest. "I...I didn't think of that at all. I listened to my father's stories. I'm smarter than this. I had to be smarter than this to survive this long. I should have thought of that."

"I'm going to help you," I promise. "But right now, I need you to talk to me. Tell me what set you off tonight, so I know what's coming at us."

"What happened was my realization that this fashion business is just going to lure Kara to me. The minute she sees the name "Alvarez" with "fashion", she'll think of me, and I don't know why I didn't put that together before. He knows that. She's always been a liability to him. He'll use this as an excuse to kill her and justify it to me. "

"And you thought getting killed yourself somehow stopped that from happening how?"

"Then he won't have a reason to kill her."

What feels like years of cold, hard ice around my heart melts with the sacrifice in those words, and I cup her face. "Sweetheart. You aren't going to die and neither is your sister. I won't let that happen. And Alvarez will never touch you again. You have my word."

"You can't stop him. At any moment, he could walk through the door and then I'm his all over again."

"He won't be walking in, and if he does, he won't be walking out."

"It's not that simple, or I would have killed him a long time ago," she says, her fingers curling on my chest. "If he dies, those women will be moved and Juan takes over."

"Not if he's dead. And we'll work this out. And we will get out."

"I can't leave. He'll go straight to Kara."

"Not if he thinks you're dead."

"You can do that?"

"Yes. I can do that and I will."

"Because why? Who are you? And I mean really. Who are you?"

My gut tells me that if I tell her right now, in this moment, it will not be well-received. "A friend," I say, my gaze lowering to her lush mouth and lifting. "And the man who wants to kiss you. Really kiss you. Can I kiss you, Myla?"

"You're asking?"

"Yes. I'm asking. After all you've been through—"

"He hasn't destroyed me. He hasn't beaten me and I don't like that you think he has."

"I don't think he's beaten you."

"He hasn't," she insists. "I'm not giving him that power and damn it, you better not either by treating me like I'm broken and fragile. So kiss me if you're going to kiss me or let me go, if you don't want—"

I cup the back of her head, and slant my mouth over hers, my tongue sliding against hers, stroking, caressing, and the taste of her, one part hunger I welcome, but the other part, the torment, I intend to drive away. I deepen the kiss, my hand pressing beneath her tank top, finding warm, soft skin. My fingers splay over her rib cage, while my mind reminds me that no matter how big she talks, she wants this escape for a reason. She has been abused, used, hurt.

I tear my mouth from hers, my breathing and hers ragged, my hands settling at her waist. "Myla—"

"Don't do this," she pleads, "Don't be the kind of hero I don't need. Give me something good to remember the next time he touches me, something that gets me through it."

"I told you," I grind out. "He will never touch you again."

"You underestimate him."

"You underestimate me," I assure her. "You want to forget? Let's forget."

"Don't treat me like—"

I tangle my fingers in her hair and drag her gaze to mine. "Is that too gentle?"

"It is until you kiss me again," she challenges, and so I do, holding nothing back. My tongue stroking, taking, demanding, and she rewards me by giving me no fear, but rather a soft moan, and a whisper of "Kyle," when I nip her lip.

"That's what I want," I say. "My name on your tongue, not his. My tongue on your body, not his."

"That's what I want too," she dares, and when she adds, "very much," there is this sense of her claiming something outside of a world she'd accepted but hated that empowers me, to help her go there, be there. I reach down and pull her tank top over her head, tossing it away. And she is not shy, timid or scared. She tugs my shirt up, but my shoulder strap and weapon, hold it in place. I'm far from detoured though, unhooking her sports bra and dragging it down her arms, my gaze raking over her high full breasts and pebbled pink nipples. And the minute our gazes collide, the fire between us ignites, and we are kissing again, my hand flattening over her back, melting her naked breasts to my chest.

She tries a new approach to getting me naked, shoving at my jacket and I shrug it over my shoulders, letting it fall to the ground, but when her hand goes for the clasp on my shoulder strap, my reaction is automatic. I grab her hand and stop her. "What are you doing?"

"I can't get your shirt off while your gun is on," she says, and then gives me an unhappy look. "Did you think that I was going for your weapon?"

"Programming," I say. "Protect your weapon, always. And you aren't the only one with a bad relationship baggage."

"I can accept that and understand it, but now it's my turn to say quid pro quo. I'm opening the door to trusting you. You need to do the same and trust me."

She's right. A hand for a hand. I let mine fall away now, leaving hers at my strap, a move from my gun. She closes her hand over the butt of my gun, daring me to challenge her, her chin lifting, gaze meeting mine as she says, "If you were him—"

My hands slide around her neck, dragging her mouth to mine. "Obviously I need to fuck you fast and hard before I go slow and sexy, just to get him the hell out of this room." I kiss her, a deep, demanding, stroke of tongue on tongue, I end with a challenge. "Do you want me or my gun?"

"You," she whispers, her hand sliding away from my weapon. "I want you."

"That's the right answer," I say, stepping back from her to remove my shoulder strap and set it on the ground. "Take your shoes off," I order, ripping my own shirt over my head.

Her eyes travel my chest and jerk to my face. "My shoes? I thought you'd say take my panties off, not my shoes, but okay." She kicks them off, while I do the same of mine, and then, one by one, playfully throws them across the room.

I shackle her hips, walking her to me. "I want to be the one to take your panties off, sweetheart," I say, reaching around her and pulling the tie from her hair, the silky strands waving around her shoulders.

"Too late," she says. "I was teasing about the panties. I don't actually wear them with these workout pants."

I arch a brow. "That's unexpected."

"Not really. You wouldn't like it if things went the wrong places either."

I laugh, at the adorable confession, my already hard cock just got harder, as my palms caress up and down her hips. "Then I'll *finish* undressing you."

"Does that mean I can finish undressing you?"

"If I finish getting undressed, then I'll be inside you."

"And that's a problem why?"

"It's not a problem at all, but we do need to talk about—"

"Protection," she supplies, her hands flattening on my chest. "I'm on the pill, and thankfully he still uses condoms because he's that paranoid someone is trying to kill him." Her gaze drops to my chest." And he kept me to himself. The Juan thing wasn't actual—"

I cup her face. "You do not have to tell me this."

"I just suddenly feel like you might think I'm a walking, talking STD. Juan didn't do that part and never once with Michael without a condom. And I was never given drugs."

"I want you to talk to me Myla, I want to know who you are and what you've been through, but I *hate* that you feel the need to say these things to me right now, in this moment. That you don't know I see *you*, not him. It tells me you feel damaged, or tainted, when he is the one who is damaged and tainted."

"I am—"

"No. You are not and all I was thinking about when I brought this up, was protecting you, and me being inside you. But in the midst of this, is still good news. When he's gone, and he will be, you can wash him away." I caress her cheek. "I want to be the man that washes him away for you. Will you let me be him?"

"Yes. Please. Be him, Kyle. Now. Tonight."

"Then I'm going to make you remember what it's like to not know what comes next and yet, know that it will be pleasure. Just pleasure. I'm going to turn you to face the wall."

"Are you telling me, and then waiting for a reply to find out if I'm going to panic? Or say no?"

"Everything isn't a test, Myla. This is just you and me. It's pleasure. It's getting to know each other's bodies and as for "no". You can say "no" to anything with me, now and always." I don't wait this time. I turn her, pressing her hands to the hard surface, mine on top of hers, my body framing her smaller, softer one. "What do you feel when I do this?"

"I'm not afraid."

"I didn't say you were afraid. I asked, what do you feel?"

"Warm all over."

My hand goes to her belly. "Do you know what I want? I want to hold you like this, and have total trust."

"I do trust you."

"No. No you don't and you can't because trust takes time, but I'm going to make sure that we have that time." I sweep the silky strands of her dark brown hair off her shoulder, lightly nipping the delicate skin, then licking the offended area. "What are you thinking now?" I ask, my hands leaving hers and cupping her breasts.

"How good you feel. How different."

Different *from him*. Fucking Alvarez is still here. I turn her back around to face me, hands returning to her waist. "Sweetheart. No man likes to be compared to another. I'm here. You're here. Just us."

"I know," she whispers. "I do."

"I'll believe you when I stop tasting him on your lips," I say, my fingers slicing into her hair, my tongue licking into her mouth, tasting her hunger, her reserve that I reject, my cheek sliding to hers. "He's still here," I murmur, "but I'm going to fuck him away, and then I swear to you, I'm going to fuck him up so badly, he'll cease to exist." My lips find hers, caressing lightly, lingering. "He doesn't get to be here tonight."

Her fingers sink into my shoulders, her body swaying into mine. "I want him gone," she breaths out. "You have no idea how much I want him gone."

"I do know," I say, leaning back to let her see the truth in my eyes. "I do understand what it's like to pretend to be someone else to survive, but you don't have to do that with me." My fingers curve around her neck, tugging her mouth back to mine. "I'm going to make you feel exposed and show you how damn sexy vulnerability can be when you're with me, when you're safe. When all that matters to the other person, to me, is your pleasure, not mine." And with that promise, I kiss her, my tongue licking into her mouth, in a silky, hot demand, meant to be a prelude to all the places I intend to lick, kiss, and tease.

Chapter Thirteen

MYLA

Vulnerable. Exposed. These are things Michael Alvarez tried to make me, over and over and over again, but all he achieved was embarrassment, anger, and when I'd found a way to no longer feel fear, hate. Kyle promises these things now, but from him they are different. From him they taste like passion and promise. They taste like seduction. He kisses me like he's savoring me, with slow, sexy strokes of his tongue, a taut need in him that says I'm his next breath he cannot live without. I feel like he is mine. I feel like I need him, like he is what I've needed for a very long time.

My fingers flex where they have splayed over his chest, and I lean into the long lines of his hard body, losing myself in the moment, in this man who has taken me by storm, and seems to be everything I need and want. He moans, a low, sexy sound I feel in my sex, in my nipples, just as I feel his hands cup my backside, melding our bodies together, our hips, his thick erection now pressing against my belly. Heat radiates through my body, a deep ache forming in my sex.

He tears his mouth from mine, staring down at me. "God, woman. What are you doing to me?" I can't think to even answer. He's already on one knee in front of me, inching down the band to my leggings, exposing my belly where he plants a kiss. And that simple press of lips to skin, so nearly innocent, is somehow intensely erotic, and yes, tender. He is so very tender with me, and that stark contrast to what I know, and even who he is with those around him, is so incredibly sexy.

"Kyle," I whisper, not even sure why.

He glances up at me, orange fire in his green eyes. "I'm here and I'm not going anywhere, Myla. You need to know that."

"Why?" I ask, and it's a simple question, a one word question, but it has so many layers, so many complicated layers.

"Why? Because I'm addicted to you, Myla. Crazy, insane, addicted to you, I want you to be just as addicted to me."

He wants me to be addicted to him, which is all about my desire, my need, my choices and not his, though he's made it clear that he wants me in a way that manages to be both alpha and sensitive, at the same time. He can't know how much that combination works for me, matters to me, but I won't tell him. I really can't. Not when he's inched my pants a tiny bit further down, just above the V of my body, and his lips and tongue are traveling that line—left, right, center—and all I can think of is, where will that delicious mouth of his go next? A shiver rolls through me, my sex achy, and oh so very wet.

"I want to be your addiction, Myla," he repeats, inching to my side, his teeth scraping my hip. "I want you to think about what I'll do to you next at times when I'm not doing it." His tongue flickers against the tiny spot of his gentle bite, his hand flattening over my belly, to slide under my pants and push them further down, his palm resting over my sex without touching it. And the other hand now on my bare backside, almost as if he's about to spank me. A thought that should terrify me, considering some of the torture I've been put through, but I'm aroused. So incredibly aroused.

But he doesn't spank me. He caress, he squeezes, he caresses again and then he says, "You have a gorgeous ass, Myla," in this sandpaper rough voice, I feel everywhere, inside and out.

I laugh, or whatever that sound is that slips from my lips. I don't know what it is, or why it comes from my lips. Then I actually try to speak. "Kyle I—"

He cups my sex, fingers teasing the now sensitive, slick heat of my arousal. "I fucking love how wet you are for me." He moves then, in front of me again, his hands caressing my pants all the way to the floor before he lifts me and gets rid of them.

"Turn and face the wall for me again, sweetheart," he orders softly, and only then do I realize that I'm holding his shoulders, leaning into him, not away from him, a detail that would seem normal to most. But to me, it's a stunning sign of instinctual trust, especially when I thought I would never trust a man with my body again.

And that scares me. It makes me fear in that moment that I am wrong about him, and right to be guarded. Thus I do not turn. I ask, "Is this the vulnerable part? Your control, not mine?"

I expect some intense, manly demand, but his lips curve in a sexy, almost playful, smile. "Sweetheart," he says. "This is the "I want to see your amazing fucking ass" thing. And kiss it. And touch it. And there might be teeth. Now, if that's a problem—"

I surprise myself and laugh for real this time, which is really quite stunning to me on all levels. "I have no idea how you just made me laugh."

"It's a gift," he says. "Right along with picking the perfect pizza, though I have yet to prove that as true."

"*It is* a gift, actually," I say, "because I don't…I haven't laughed ever during a moment like this."

"There are many first times ahead of us, Myla," he promises. "Turn around, sweetheart."

There is this silky tenderness to his voice that tightens my nipples and my sex, but also my chest. Emotions well up inside me, I don't quite know or understand, and suddenly, giving him my back works for me. I inhale and do as he says, but instead of him just leaving me naked and uncomfortably facing the other way, he is suddenly on his feet, his big body once again enveloping mine, hard and powerful, his hands finding mine and pressing them to the wall. His alluringly spicy scent consuming me, seducing me. "I want you to keep your hands on the wall for me," he instructs. "Don't touch me. Let me touch you."

"I want to touch you," I confess. "Very badly."

"And I want you to," he says, "but right now, this is about you, not me." His fingers flex at my hips, then caress down and over my backside, his mouth finding my shoulder at the same moment he cups my cheeks. Those teeth he'd promised to use, nipping the very edge of my back, and then trailing down my right arm. He shifts then, moving to stand at my hip, one hand possessively at my belly, the other on one of my butt cheeks. "I love how you smell," he says, his breath a warm trickle on my cheek. "Like honey and sugar."

"Amber," I whisper, of the one thing from my past life I'd managed to keep. "It reminds me of the past."

"It makes me want to lick you everywhere," he murmurs, his voice taking on that gravelly quality again. "Can I lick you everywhere?"

"Only if I can lick you everywhere," I say, loving that I feel free enough to say that to him, and more so, that I mean it. I want to lick every last inch of this man.

He leans in, bringing his mouth a breath from mine. "I can't wait," he says, sealing that promise with a deep, sultry slide of his tongue that has us both groaning when he pulls back, his forehead at the side of my head. "Did I mention you're addictive?" he asks, his fingers just barely teasing one of my nipples, his other hand squeezing my backside again. "So fucking addictive." He plucks the nipple, sending darts of pleasure straight to my sex.

I arch slightly forward, panting as he continues the assault on my senses, tightening his grip on that stiff peak and tugging before gently caressing it again. This soft, hard, gentle, rough thing he does is driving me wild and my hands move further up the wall, allowing me to brace myself. He, in turn, moves further down my body, one of his hands finding my belly and then lower. And lower. His fingers slide back into the V of my sex, just barely flicking my clit before finding the wet seam between my legs, and stroking.

My lashes lower, his touch grounding me in the moment, in pleasure. His fingers slide inside me, and at some point he has gone to his knees, his mouth, his teeth, at my hip. Still, those fingers dip deeper, the waves of tingling sensations managing to reach from my sex to my nipples and back down again.

And then he is gone, no longer touching me, leaving me gasping and weak in the knees. I want to turn, to call him back, but I never get the chance. He's already in front of me, his back against the wall I've been holding, and I have no idea how or when, but he's naked, the thick ridge of his erection at my hips, my hands now on his broad shoulders.

"No more barriers between us," he declares softly, cupping my face and tilting my mouth to his. "And now, I need to taste you." He kisses me, a deep, hungry kiss, before picking me up, my legs wrapping his hips as he adds, "All of you," and carries me across the room, not to the bed, but to the living area in the corner, in front of the wall of windows.

He sits me on the couch, going down on one knee in front of me. My knees come together, and he leaves them that way, kissing them, licking them, and when he looks at me, when I see how much he wants me, I can barely breathe. Because he isn't just taking me. He isn't just making demands. He slowly inches my legs apart. Slowly caresses a path up my thighs, his body edging between them, his hands pressing my hands behind me, onto the cushion, and his mouth finds my nipple, caressing it. Licking it. Suckling it. And then he does it again with the other one. He is seducing me, and I have never been seduced. I lose everything. Time. Anger. Fear. There is just his mouth on my mouth. His mouth on my nipples, and finally, his mouth lingering just above my sex in a warm promise of pleasure.

He laps at my clit, and on some level I am aware that I am angled backwards, my hands all that are holding me up, that he has control, but somehow that doesn't matter. That doesn't cause fear. He suckles my nub, and my sex clenches hard. I am just so ready, so close to release, that when he starts licking me and his fingers slide inside me, I am panting, my face lifting to the ceiling, eyes tightly closed. There is no holding back. I stiffen, my muscles spasm, my body outright quaking with the intensity of my release. And when it's over, my arms give way, but somehow, Kyle's hands between my shoulder blades catch me, holding me up so I do not fall. And for a moment, or ten, he just holds me like that, breathing with me, seemingly unconcerned for his own pleasure.

"Kyle," I whisper, a question in his name though I do not even know what it is.

"I'm here," he repeats. "And I'm going to keep saying that, and showing you that, until you believe it." He moves, sitting beside me and before I know his intent, he's pulled me across his lap, the thick ridge of his erection at my belly and between us.

"I have never wanted to be inside anyone as badly as I do you right now," he says, his hands bracketing my hips.

"Yes," I whisper. "Yes please."

"Hang onto me," he orders, placing my hands on his shoulders, while he lifts me, shifting us, his shaft is pressing inside me, stretching me, filling me, until I have all of him, and somehow never enough of him, our foreheads coming together.

"Are you okay?" he asks.

I laugh. "I'm pretty okay right now."

"Are you sure? Because I'm really fucking hard."

The things he says, the way he is himself, no matter what, no matter when, has me giving another soft, choked laugh. "Is that supposed to be a bad thing?" I ask for the second time tonight.

"I don't want to hurt you."

He doesn't want to hurt me. "You aren't hurting me, Kyle. You feel…"

He molds me to him, cupping the back of my head, breathing with me, when sometimes lately, I haven't felt I could breathe at all. "How do I feel, *Myla?*" The way he says my name, like *I matter*, like *he cares*, stirs all kinds of crazy, emotional, feelings I don't try to understand. I just let myself feel them and him. "How do I feel, Myla," he repeats.

"Better than I thought anything ever would again."

He kisses me then, or I kiss him. I really don't know. We just kiss, if there is such a thing as "just kissing" a man like Kyle, who is so very overwhelmingly, perfectly male. And somewhere in the midst of that kiss, we shift our hips, moving just a little, testing out how we feel together. And we feel amazing. Really, *really* amazing. He presses me down against him and then thrusts. I gasp into his mouth. He swallows it with another kiss and the deep, drugging swipe of his tongue, cupping my breast as he does. And then we are doing this slow, sultry sway, body against body. Holding onto each other as we do, like we don't want to let go. I don't want to let go. I want more. And he wants more. It's in the way we move, grind, drive, and thrust. This is the fast and hard. This is the urgency that has been building from what seems like the moment we met. And I don't think about

anything but him. I sit up. I ride him and I revel in the way
his gaze strokes hotly over my breasts, my body.

"Fuck, Myla," he murmurs, a groan in the depths of my
name, his hand sliding between my shoulder blades, molding
me closer, our heads together, a wet, sultry slide to the way
we move that takes me right back to the edge.

"Kyle, I—" I spasm around him, and he makes this
deep, guttural sound, followed by a hard thrust, and he is
shaking with me, the warmth of his release filling me.

Seconds pass, and our bodies still, his easing against
the cushion, mine against him. "Holy fuck, woman. You
undo me."

Again, he makes me want to laugh and smile, but that
stupid bubble of emotion has returned, taking control. Tears
actually form in my eyes, and I stay huddled against him,
afraid I might really totally lose it. He must know, because his
fingers flex at my back. "Myla," he says, softly. "Sweetheart.
Did I hurt you?"

"No," I reply. "It was…it was…." I press my cheek
to his, not even sure what to say, or how to say it. "It was
really good, Kyle." It's not enough, but I can't get to more
right now.

"Can you look at me?"

"Not yet."

He cups my head. "Okay. Then just lay there."

That tenderness is what is my undoing. Tears slip down
my cheeks and I must let out a sob, because he gives a low
curse, and then settles me on my back, and there is no way to
escape those green eyes of his, so knowing, and staring down
at me. Nor is there any way to escape the trust I've put in
him. And I think that is part of my reaction, and these damn

tears. Have I trusted the wrong person? Will my confession get my sister killed? Have I let myself be vulnerable and exposed in the ways that count, the ways that have nothing to do with my body, and chosen wrong? I suddenly need space and to breathe.

"I need a towel," I announce, and when he doesn't react, I add urgency. "I need a towel, Kyle. I'm going to mess up the couch."

"You're crying," he says, his thumbs wiping away my tears. "That's what I'm worried about."

"I'm okay. I'm better. I stopped." I hope and I push for that space I need. "But the couch. I'm worried about the couch. What if we stain it and it's noticed? *I need* a towel."

Something flickers in his eyes, and he draws a breath before he is standing, walking away from me. I sit up, the stickiness of the intimacy I have shared with this man symbolic of the trust I have given him, while the way he stands a few feet away, his shoulders bunched, hand on his head, tells me he is tormented by something. Maybe it's my tears. Maybe it's a truth he doesn't want to speak. My mind starts to race. Could he be FBI and they have a plan that will endanger Kara? Even get her killed? Could he really work for Alvarez, and now, both myself and Kara will be thrown into the sex trade?

He grabs his sweats and pulls them on, snagging his t-shirt, but instead of putting it on, he heads to the bathroom and returns with a towel. In a blink, he's tossed his shirt at the end of the couch, pressed the towel between my legs, and he's pulled us both back down on the coach, shifting us so we're side by side, facing each other.

"I can't believe you just put your shirt between my legs,"

I say, nor can I believe how easily having him touch me again eases my worries, when it shouldn't. Answers. Facts. Those things should be what I need, but it seems *he* is what I need.

"It was closer than a towel," he says, grabbing a pillow that he stuffs under our heads, his hand settling at my hip. "Tell me what I did wrong so I won't do it again."

What did he do wrong? I'm worried about a lie he might be telling me, and his torment is about hurting me? My heart squeezes with this knowledge, my fingers curling on his jaw. "Nothing," I promise. "You did nothing wrong. You did everything right. I don't know what is wrong with me. I've faced hell, found this zone I survive inside, and for a solid nine months I've been without the weakness of tears. And yet, I cried last night and I cried now."

He strokes hair from my eyes. "You cried last night?"

"Melted down like there was no tomorrow," I admit, "and blamed you, but I know now that it was about my sister. This whole fashion thing is bringing back the past that I'd suppressed to survive. But I have no idea what right now was all about."

"I do," he says, covering my hand with his and pulling it between us. "I let you be you and you dared to be you. There's a reason you weren't that person with Alvarez. In character, we're shielded, protected. When we're ourselves—"

"We're exposed and vulnerable," I supply, understanding now.

"Yes," he confirms. "That is when we are exposed and vulnerable. I made the mistake of forgetting that one time and I ended up in the hospital."

"Who was she?" I ask.

"Ah yes. She was a woman all right. I was young, and on

my second undercover job. She was working for the bastard I was trying to take down, and wanted out. I thought I was in love, but I don't know what the hell I was, actually, and it doesn't matter. In the end, he threatened her family, and she chose them instead of letting me save us all. I ended up with a bullet in my back."

"Where is she now?"

"He killed her."

I am unsurprised, digesting this as data, not emotion, as I have learned to do with everything in the Alvarez world. "Did you kill him?"

"I arrested him."

My hand flattens over his chest, understanding in my touch. "But you wanted to."

"No," he says. "He wasn't worth the price to my soul."

"But Alvarez is?"

"Killing Michael Alvarez would be doing the world a favor." He says the words with such fierceness, such guttural meaning, that I know his hate for Alvarez runs deep. And I do not miss the way his heart thunders beneath my palm.

This moment drives home what I know already. He isn't who he says he is, and I say that to him. "You aren't who you say you are," I say. "And the not knowing is killing me."

There is a subtle tightening of his body, the air suddenly thicker, before he rolls me to my back, his big body trapping mine. "Myla—"

"Just say it," I say, grabbing his shoulders, my fingers against the knotted muscle there. "Tell me," I demand, and then softer. "Please. Who are you and what are you after?"

"*You.* I was always here for *you.*"

Chapter Fourteen

KYLE

I didn't plan to be naked and on top of Myla when I tell her who I am, but every instinct I own says that if I shut her down now, she will shut me out.

"Are you FBI?" Myla asks, trying to fill in the blanks I haven't, which is exactly what I don't want her doing. "Because if you are," she continues, "I gave you the list of the Alvarez locations. I can't help you more than that, or I'll get Kara killed. You know that."

"I'm not FBI, Myla. I've told you that."

"Are you loyal to Alvarez then?"

"You know better," I say. "I know you do."

"Kara," she supplies, going to the only logical next place. "She sent you."

And there it is. "I didn't tell Kara I was coming here," I say, not ready to tell her Kara found out anyway.

"But you know her."

"She's a friend. Her husband, Blake Walker, is my boss at Walker Security, the company I work for, and also my best friend. We were in the AFT together. The Ex-FBI thing is a cover story."

"Damn it," she hisses. "I should have known. I did know. You're going to get her killed." She shoves ineffectually at my chest, her legs pushing against mine. "Let me up, Kyle," she demands. "I have to figure out how to save her before you get her killed."

"She's safe, Myla. Blake took her to Washington and has her locked in a hotel room until this is over."

"So does she or does she not know I'm alive?"

"She doesn't, but Blake's telling her tonight."

"No. No, you can't let him tell her."

"She knows Alvarez is alive. She figured out I'm undercover in his operation and showed up here yesterday."

"Here? Right here?"

"Yes. We quickly got her out of Texas, but if she starts feeling out of the loop, she'll come back. The best way to keep her safe is to keep her informed."

"Kara won't stand down if she knows I'm alive. You can't know her and not know that."

"Kara knows how to stay alive and she wants you alive," I say. "She won't do anything to endanger any of us. And Blake won't let her out of that hotel room if he thinks any differently. Look. Sweetheart, I can make sense out of any question you have if you let me. The question is, can I let you up to talk without us having a problem?"

"Yes. We can. Please let me up."

"And I can do this without you going for the gun and

shooting me for real this time?"

"I'll shoot if my sister ends up dead."

"Well, then, I'm safe, because that's not going to happen." I ease off of her, and help her sit, snagging my shirt from the end of the couch and pulling it over her head. She shoves her hands through the sleeves, immediately facing forward, her feet on the floor, her arms folding in front of herself, everything about her body language defensive, withdrawn. Forcing myself to give her space, I move away from her, but I don't let her escape fully, choosing to sit on the coffee table directly in front on her.

"I would never risk Kara's life," I promise her. "I need you to know that. I love her like a sister. And her husband, Blake, he and his entire family are family to me."

"Why didn't you just tell me the truth?"

"For starters, I was taken off guard that you were here at all. I had no way of knowing you were the person I was guarding. Once I did, I had no way of knowing, if you were really aligned with Alvarez, or even brainwashed to support him, which is not uncommon in captive situations. Once I knew you weren't, it was clear that you'd sacrificed yourself to protect Kara. It also became clear to me that she could truly be in danger. I damn sure wasn't going to tell you who I was until I knew she was safe. I wanted you to have that peace of mind and frankly, I wasn't sure what you'd do to protect her if I hadn't."

"And she really is safe?"

"One hundred percent. Like I said. Blake took her to Seattle, and he has a plane on standby to get her out of the country if needed. There's also a plane on standby a few miles away to do the same for us."

"There is?"

"Yes. There is."

Her chest rises and falls, a thunderstorm of emotions raging in her green eyes before they gloss over. "I can't believe this is really happening." Her hands cover her face for several seconds before they flatten on the couch at her hips, her arms no longer sheltering her body, her eyes, still glistening, searching my face. "You're really one of the good guys?"

"I'm no Boy Scout, sweetheart. Call me an "almost" Boy Scout, but yes. I like to think I'm one of the good guys." I dare to lean forward and settle my hands on her knees, relieved when she doesn't push them away. "You've done an amazing job of taking care of yourself and your sister," I say, true admiration in my voice, which I hope she hears. "I've seen trained agents crack under lesser circumstances. But now, I'm going to get you out of here. And those women Alvarez kidnapped, who you're worried about. We're going to get them, too. That's always been the plan."

"You are? We can?" She grabs my hand, the walls of moments before fully falling away. "What plan? Can you tell me?"

"I'll tell you everything you want to know and probably more, but let's move to the other room where I can check the security footage." I sit up and reach into my pocket, pulling out my phone.

"What are you doing?" Myla asks, grabbing my hand. "You aren't calling Kara, right?"

"No," I say. "I'm not calling Kara. I don't know if she knows you're alive yet, and even if I did, we won't talk to Kara until you want to talk to Kara."

Relief visibly washes over her. "Thank you," she says, but she doesn't let go of my hand. "I'm just not ready. I need to hear your plans first. I need to know more than I do right now."

"Understood." I glance down at her hand holding mine, and then back up. "If you let me go, I'll order the pizza I was about to order and we can move to the other room."

Her eyes go wide. "Pizza? That was the call you were going to make?"

"Why wouldn't I?"

"I don't know. I mean, you just told me that you know my sister."

"And...that makes us both less hungry?"

"No," she says. "It just seems like an odd thing to think about right now."

"Being an "almost" Boy Scout takes energy," I reply, leaving out the part where I'm pushing her back into a sense of normal activities, which theoretically, helps create the sense of well-being and safety I want her to feel. "You are hungry, right?"

"Actually," she says, sounding surprised. "Yes. Now that I know Kara is safe, food does sound good." Her eyes light on mine, her hand falling away. "It better be good this time," she teases.

Pleased my plan is working, I wink. "The *almost* best pizza in the world this time," I promise, following with a mock salute. "Scout's honor." I punch in the number to my second favorite pizza joint in Dallas, order, and then stick my phone in my pocket. "Now we move to my room where the cameras are." I stand and take her with me, my plan to move from a smile to laughter, in full effect. "Let me give you a ride."

Her brow furrows. "What?"

I scoop her up and throw her over my shoulder, her yelp sounding as my hand settles on her naked, gorgeous ass. "What are you doing?" she demands. "I can walk."

"Negative," I say, already exiting the living area. "A Scout can never let a woman walk on her own."

"You said you aren't a scout," she reminds me.

"You inspired me to be a better man."

"And you're crazy," she declares, but apparently she likes crazy, because I am rewarded with the sound of her sweet, feminine laughter, which I hope like hell wipes away at least some of her tears and fears.

"So I've been told," I say, entering the bedroom, and setting her down in front of the bed, catching her waist as she sways.

"Wow," she murmurs, laughing again. "The blood rushed to my head." She regains her balance, yanking the loose tie from her hair, and looking so damn hot that I just want to pull that shirt over her head and feel her close. But I don't. Not now. Now when I know she needs answers, and I want her to have them.

"You look good in my shirt, Myla," I say, Blake's warnings I'd dismissed about her vulnerability charging into my mind. "Maybe too good."

"Too good?" she asks.

"Yes," I say. "I don't get involved with someone I'm protecting, and while I don't at this moment regret that, if you do later, I will. I don't want to take advantage of your—"

"Fragile state?" she supplies. "I'm not fragile and I don't want to be treated like it. If you start going in that direction, you and I are going to have problems." She flattens her hand on my chest, softening her voice. "You will not be one of my regrets, unless I end up getting you killed. I couldn't live with that, just so you know. You aren't allowed to die."

I cover her hand with mine. "I will say this over and over if you need to hear it. No one is dying that I don't kill or want dead."

"And I will welcome every time you say it, but let's keep things real. You can't know that."

"But my gun can." I pull her hand to mine and kiss it. "It's a big gun too, sweetheart, and I have about a dozen just as big with me."

"A dozen? That's a lot of guns."

"We're dealing with a lot of assholes, which is also why we need to check the security feed before the pizza gets here." I release her and grab the chair at the desk, turning it in her direction. "Take this one. I'll go grab another one."

"Great," she says, claiming the chair. "Thank you."

Thank you. Great. Smiles. Laughter. Amazed at how grounded and sweet she's remained through all of this, I grab a t-shirt and head for the hallway, pulling it over my head as I walk to the office, where I grab an extra chair. Returning to the bedroom, I sit down next to Myla, tapping the computer in front of her to life, a password screen popping up.

"I locked them down while we were gone today," I explain. "We don't want prying eyes where they don't belong. "2011thedaylight" is the password, all small letters."

"Got it," she says, keying in the code, and almost instantly adding, "It's live. I can see the camera feed."

"Excellent," I say, already bringing my personal computer to life. "Now we can witness our pizza delivery up close and personal." I open an instant message box. "And now, we talk to our team outside the hotel."

"Who are they exactly?" she asks.

"The new family you've inherited from your sister," I say, "and I'll just tell you right now, they will absolutely overwhelm the fuck out of you, but always with good intentions."

"Overwhelm how?"

"Family protects family," I say. "They live together and they bleed together." I make a few keystrokes, ensuring the chatroom is secure. "And at this moment in time, we should be talking to Asher." I turn the screen slightly, letting her see what I type: Checking in. All secure here. Pizza on the way. Anything I need to know about?

The reply is instant: Asher here. Aside from Jacob talking my ear off, it's ridiculously quiet right now. No assholes to hate on or hurt. Interior footage clear. Exterior footage clear.

"In other words," I say, glancing at Myla. "Jacob is, as usual, saying absolutely nothing, and Asher is bored out of his fucking mind."

I type my reply: Heads up. We have a pizza delivery coming.

Asher: Did you order us one?

I type: Get your own.

Asher's reply is instant: Fucker.

Myla laughs. "So much love, I can't stand it."

"Families give that special kind of love," I say, then type: I'm off until morning check in.

Asher replies with: Copy that. Enjoy the pizza. We won't.

Myla laughs again, and while I hate to tamp down on her

lighter mood, I key up the security video from the night of the helicopter crash, with good reason. She needs to know she was never forgotten or alone, and she isn't now.

"I want you to see this," I say, turning the screen toward her. "This is what convinced me you were alive and every time I doubted that, I watched again." I punch the play button and the short security video begins to roll, ending with a close up of her eyes. I hit a freeze frame, then zoom in on her face. "That look," I say, "is why I'm here. I've watched this footage a million times, and it always got to me. I know you're telling whoever was watching that nothing was as it seemed. I know you were pleading for help."

She faces me, looking confused, her gaze searching mine. "How could you know what I was thinking and feeling when we'd never met?"

"I don't know," I answer honestly. "Maybe it was all the years of reading people when I was undercover. Maybe it was just something in your eyes that spoke to me, but whatever the case, and what's important is that I did know. I kept looking until I found you."

"But you said Kara doesn't know I'm alive."

"She doesn't." I look at my watch, noting the nine o'clock hour. "Or she might soon, but not until tonight. Once I knew Alvarez was alive, though, I knew it would only be a matter of time before Kara found out. That's when I got back up."

"But not Kara?"

"I still didn't know you were alive," I say, "And I didn't want to create false hope in her. She was devastated after the crash and your supposed death. And I mean inconsolable, Myla. Blake was her lifeline, and eventually, he made the decision to pull her away from anything to do with Alvarez."

"And my sister agreed to that?" she says, sounding wounded, and then seeming to catch herself, she adds, "I can't believe I just let the idea of her moving on and surviving hurt me when keeping her away from me and safe was my goal."

"You felt alone a long time, Myla," I say. "It's normal to feel what you just felt. And Kara didn't give up on you. She thought you were dead."

"I know she did," she says. "And I'm glad she backed off, but yes. The idea of her not looking for me illogically hurts. You didn't give up."

"Had I told her even in passing that I believed you were alive, she wouldn't have either. And Kara and Blake are too personally involved with Alvarez to hunt him safely. He kidnapped you and killed Blake's ex-fiancé. They'd both gone rogue and undercover in his operation when they met."

"Wait. Kara was undercover in Alvarez's operation?"

"Yes," I confirm. "Right after you went missing. Blake even got his chance to kill Alvarez. He held a gun to his head and Kara talked him out of pulling the trigger. And that was about you. She was convinced he had you, keeping you alive, and if he was gone, you would be, too. Unfortunately, he escaped, ironically, faking his death then as well."

"When was this?"

"A year ago."

She inhales and lets it out. "Kara was right. He has an odd fascination with me that kept me alive. Had they killed him then, I'd be...I don't want to think about what I'd be or where I'd be. Maybe I'd be one of those other girls, strung out on heroin and with a different man every hour. Maybe

I'd be dead."

"Without you, we wouldn't have a chance to save these women. That's an amazing, brave thing you've done."

"I've been clinging to the idea of saving them," she confesses. "It's become what I think of as "my plan", and that plan became life for me. It kept me going."

My fingers brush her cheek. "That was a damn good reason to keep going, sweetheart. You are—"

Our doorbell rings, and my head jerks up, while Myla surprises me by turning instinctively to the computer, and tabbing to a shot of our front door, where Les is now holding our pizza. "What the fuck is he up to?" I murmur, already on my feet and walking to a suitcase, where I remove a Glock.

"You need a gun for Les?"

"He's supposed to call before he comes up," I say, "and as far as I'm concerned, any surprise that shows up at our door could be sent by Alvarez."

Myla's eyes go wide. "Oh God. My phone." She pops to her feet." What if Michael called and I didn't answer? Maybe he sent Les to check on me."

"They'd send someone other than Les," I say, though I'm not ruling this out as a problem underway. "Go clean up our mess and hide your gun."

She's already out the door while I follow, my gun in hand, as I step to the door.

Chapter Fifteen

KYLE

"Who is it?" I call out at the door, not about to let Les, or anyone know about my camera, or my team watching the hotel.

"Les, sir. I was coming up anyway so I thought—"

I open the door and show the little prick my gun. "This is what "you thought" gets you."

His eyes go wide, but there is no fear, which tells me he isn't what he seems. "Oh, sir," he begins. "I—"

"Save it," I say, shoving the gun in my waistband and taking the pizzas. "Earn your paycheck, Les. Follow instructions." I step back inside, shut the door and slide the lock back into place, before re-entering the bedroom, where I deposit the pizzas on the bed, and pull my phone from my pocket, punching in Asher's number.

"A phone call is never good," he says when he answers.

"Les brought our pizza up without calling me," I say. "Watch him."

"Copy that," he says, and I end the connection, heading to the hallway and toward Myla's bedroom, praying like hell we don't have an Alvarez problem.

Rounding the corner to the living area, I'm about to enter Myla's bedroom when she appears in the doorway, the scanner in her hand. "You said clean up our mess," she explains. "I was kind of freaked out that I didn't let you scan my room." She indicates the machine. "It didn't beep at all. That's good right?"

"That's damn good," I agree, taking it from her. "I called Asher to confirm no one had entered the room since I scanned it, but just for peace of mind, I'll double check it all." She steps aside and I enter the bedroom, calling over my shoulder. "Any missed phone calls?"

"No," she says, moving to the sitting area on the far side of the bed by the windows, and sitting down on the couch. "We got lucky," she says, watching me move around the room, "because he's insanely possessive. And he's back in a week. Honestly, he could be back any day. He's big on changing his plans, to throw off his enemies."

"Which is why we have a plane waiting on us," I assure her, relieved as the scanner remains silent. "Where is he supposed to be now?"

"Honduras."

"I'll have our team see if we can find him, but don't get your hopes up," I say. "He's slippery or we'd have had him by now."

"You won't find him," she assures me, proving her hopes aren't even close to being up. "He's a master at not getting caught."

"And yet, we're going to catch him," I assure her, walking into the bathroom, giving it a quick silent scan. Turning off the power, I re-enter the bedroom. "We're clear."

"Thank God," she says, the compact she'd thrown at me earlier now in her hand. "What happened with Les?"

"I haven't decided what that impromptu visit was about yet," I say, "so my answer is to be determined." I cross to stand in front of her. "In other words, it's pizza and movie night, and he's the show."

• • •

Forty-five minutes later, Myla and I are sitting at the desk, having finished a damn good pizza, the empty box on the floor beside us, the computers pushed out of our way, but the security feed is live for the viewing. We've also finished watching Les huddle up with Juan in the hotel restaurant. "I guess we now know who he's working with," Myla says, twirling the compact in her hands, the way she has off and on since she finished eating. "And they can't know you're watching them."

"I have a feeling I know what Les was up to," I say, standing and grabbing our trash. "I'm going to dump this at the door, and check out my theory." I round the desk and enter the hallway, opening the door to set our trash outside, before running a hand over the surface by the doorbell, and bingo. I have a recording device. I start to remove it, and decide better of it, re-entering the room and flipping the locks.

"He stuck a recording device by the doorbell," I say,

reclaiming my seat beside Myla, grabbing a footstool and setting it between us, both of us leaning back in our chairs and putting it to use. "I left it where it is. I want them to think that I think Les is more of an ally than he is and we can stage a little conversation they overhear in the morning."

"What kind of conversation?"

"One that includes you disliking the way I'm suffocating you, but I'm going to think on exactly what I want them to hear." She's twirling that compact again, nervous I think, or anxious, and I get to the point. "What do you want to know? Ask your questions."

She straightens, setting the compact on the desk, and getting right to it. "You said Walker Security is run by three brothers?"

"Right. Royce, who's ex-FBI, Luke, who's ex-Navy SEAL, and Blake, who's ex-ATF. Royce is in charge because, well, Royce decided he's in charge. He's gruff, direct, and thinks he's always right, but he gets away with it, because he usually is. He's also one of the best agents the agency ever saw and one of the best men I've ever known. "

"And Luke?"

"The calm one. Steady Eddie and the peacekeeper in the family."

"I'm afraid to ask what that means about Blake, if Luke's the calm one."

"Blake's the wild one, for sure. He likes things fast, hard, and wild. He's also solely responsible for my overuse of the word "Fuck", considering he uses it like it's a common vowel."

That earns me a small smile. "That bad?"

"Yeah. That bad. To a friend, Blake greets you with,

"How the fuck are you?" and to an enemy it's, "I'm going to fuck up your already ugly fucking face". Though giving credit where it's due, Kara has tamed his usage by a good twenty percent on at least Monday and Friday."

She full-out laughs this time, and there's a delicate little musical quality to that, as illogical as it might be, has me imagining her naked body arching toward me, right before my mouth came down on her. "And he's you best friend?" she asks, snapping me back to the present, where I'd like to repeat that fantasy in flesh and blood.

"For a decade," I say, "and on more than one occasion, Blake was the one who pulled me back to the real world when I came out of deep cover. He was also the one who knew how badly I needed to end that cycle."

"Why?" she asks. "What was it doing to you?"

"Well I sure as fuck wasn't turning into my father, but Blake scared the hell out of me, and convinced me I was."

She picks up the compact again, this time holding it close to her palm. "You still resent your father."

"Yeah," I openly admit. "Probably too much, which in hindsight is why I never would have ended up like him. But I'm glad I made the change."

"And that change means what? What exactly does Walker Security do?"

"Aside from being contracted consultants for most of the major airports around the country, whatever the hell we want, which is half the appeal. Right now, a handful of us, including your sister, are working a missing person's case that started in the States and seems to be leading to Italy."

"Oh wow. That's interesting. Who's the missing person?"

"A woman named Ella. She eloped and then disappeared.

Her best friend Sara, and her husband Chris, are paying for the search. She's a lucky girl. They've thrown a lot of money and resources into finding her, and I hear we got a lead on her yesterday, which I hope pans out."

Her expression tightens. "Michael makes sure the women he kidnaps have no one to look for them."

"But you had Kara, who was an FBI agent at the time."

"I wasn't a planned abduction. I went to San Francisco for a job that fell through and took a job waiting tables at one of his restaurants to pay the bills. He came in and took a liking to me." She holds up the compact. "I want to show you the data I collected." She faces the desk and opens the compact, removing the center disc that holds powder, to reveal several tightly folded pieces of paper.

I twist my chair around and join her. "How in the hell did you find out that could be removed?" I ask, starting to unfold one of the sheets, while she does another.

"I dropped it one day. I'm just hoping the information I gathered is enough to save at least some of the women."

"Let's see what we have," I say, flattening out the page I've just straightened, and scanning a half dozen addresses to include cities and states, as well as if each is a recruiting site, or what she calls "holding camps" or "staging areas", as well as very detailed notes about how and when she knew those locations to be open. "How did you get this information?"

"A lot of eavesdropping and sneaking into places I wasn't supposed to be."

I turn her to face me, my hands on the arms of her chair. "That was stupid and brave."

"I'm not sure if I should say thank you or fuck you," she says. "It's not like I thought I was going to survive."

That comment punches me in the chest. "Yes you did, or you wouldn't have kept fighting and you wouldn't have created the best damn opportunity anyone has ever had to take down the Alvarez operation."

"You really think we can?"

"If these locations check out—"

"They will," she says. "I kept tabs on them. Those are all active, though there were many others that shut down. "

"Then the sooner we get a plan together for an organized raid of these locations, the better. I'd like to get this over to Royce now, but once I do—"

"He'll want to talk to me," she supplies. "That's fine, but please tell me that he understands what my sister won't. If I don't stay until Alvarez shows back up, we will save no one."

"We're all fully aware that just pulling you out of here does not achieve any of our goals, including making you and Kara safer."

"You better be right about him, but okay. Send it to him, because doing nothing isn't saving anyone's life."

That's all I need to hear to go into action. I turn to the scanner I've set up on the desk, and insert the documents, pulling them up on my disc drive before I recall the secure chat room I created last night. "Can't other people see you online?" Myla asks.

"It's set up with special firewalls that can't be hacked," I explain. "The same kind that terrorists use to avoid being listened in on." I dial Royce, who answers with a, "What's wrong?"

"I'm sending you some documents from Myla. And Royce. Hold onto your chair, man. She's given us a comprehensive list of all the places and ways Alvarez recruits women for the sex trade operation."

"How comprehensive?" he asks, showing no other reaction.

"Dozens of locations."

"I'm heading to my computer, but I'm going to have to compare these locations to the FBI database and do some research before I weigh in on this. How good do you feel about this?"

"Very," I say, frowning as Myla stands and leaves the room, when I was certain she'd want to know what was happening.

"I'm at my computer," he states. "Can you speak freely?"

"With caution," I say, anticipating what comes next. "And before you ask. Yes. She knows who I am, but you should know that she gave me this list, before she knew."

"I'm confused. Why would she do that?"

"She wanted me to take it to the FBI after she pissed off Alvarez, got herself killed, and ensured her sister was no longer important to him."

"Holy hell. We need to get her out of there now."

"You yourself told me why that's not an option."

"We'll make him think she's dead."

"That won't help rescue the women in captivity," I say. "She's not going to let that happen."

"But if she's suicidal—"

"She's not," I say. "She's selfless, the way most agents should be and are not. There's a difference."

"That's your professional opinion?"

"Yes," I confirm. "That's my professional opinion."

"She sounds pretty damn affected by all of this to me."

"No more so than I was every time I was under as long

as she has been, Royce. Does Kara know she's alive yet?"

"I haven't heard from Blake." I'm not sure if that's good or bad news and seeming to read my mind, Royce adds, "They both know what's on the line. Kara will not repeat yesterday."

"I hope not, because this is about more than Myla getting rattled. Myla is convinced that Alvarez sees Kara as a threat, and now that Myla's out in the open, he plans to kill Kara, just to be done with her."

"Why does she think this?"

"Aside from him all but telling her?"

"That's enough," he says. "I'll give Blake and Kara a heads up."

"What happened to the Ella case in Italy?"

"We have a possible sighting of Ella, but nothing solid," he says. "Blake sent our contractors to check it out."

"Send Blake and Kara."

"I'll try, but Myla is Kara's sister. It's going to be a hard sell to get her out of the country."

"Fuck," I say, scrubbing the newly formed stubble on my jaw. "And I'm about to make that sale harder too by getting Blake involved. I need a hacker. The only one I know better than me."

"What do you want him to do?"

"Tell him to look for Alvarez in Honduras, returning to the States in a week."

"I'll get him on it. Anything else?"

"Aside from getting Myla out of here," I say. "Nothing. I'm sending the files." I end the connection, and hold down my Siri button, "Clear call log, Siri." And the instant I hear, "Clearing call log," I slide my phone into my pocket.

Refocusing on the chat room, I send the documents, confirm receipt, and concerned about Myla's extended absence, I push away from the desk to go on the hunt for her. Stepping into her open bedroom, I find her sitting on the ground, the couch of her sitting area at her back, her sketchpad on the coffee table, her long dark hair draping her pale face and my t-shirt. My t-shirt. I could get used to this woman in my clothes, in my life. Hell, I feel like I've had her there already, and I have to remember I'm new to her, even if she isn't new to me.

Seeming to sense my presence, she glances up. "Hey," she says, nothing about her demeanor suggesting that she's upset. "All done with Royce, I guess?"

"I am," I confirm, crossing to sit on the couch next to her, catching a glimpse of a drawing she's begun. "Why'd you leave?"

She twists around to face me more fully. "He was going to ask you questions about me, like how mentally stable I am and other things I didn't want to hear and you couldn't answer when I was there." She taps her pencil on the pad. "And I have to do what I can do to help and right now, that's keeping those models away from Ricardo and Juan, which means I need an advertising idea that doesn't require models."

"You said yourself that they only pick women who have no one to look for them," I remind her. "Don't put guilt on yourself you don't deserve."

"A model would be highly sought after in some of the more elite world's Michael sets up." She swallows hard. "He has levels of girls. Gold, silver, platinum. Some are worth more risk."

"How do you know all of this?"

"They think I can't speak Spanish," she surprises me by saying. "It's how I got a lot of the information I gave you."

"That's impressive, sweetheart," I say. "You'd make a damn good agent."

"Thanks but no thanks on that," she says, flattening her hand on the pad, seeming to want, and even need, to focus on the ad campaign. "I'm thinking of something like a really cool multi-color wire mannequin, with a dress hanging on it. The slogan would be: We design. You make the style. What do you think?"

"I think it's brilliant, even if you weren't trying to get away from models."

"Brilliant," she says, but she doesn't look convinced. "I guess we'll see if they're as kind as you. I just need to put it on paper and make it look good." She turns to the table and starts drawing, losing herself in what she's doing, unaware that I get up and go get my computer. Or when I return and sit down next to her, and begin looking for Alvarez myself.

And I leave her that absorbed in her work, watching with interest as her creation comes to life. Because I know what survival looks like. It's needing to do something, anything, to make a difference. It's convincing yourself you'll be here tomorrow to survive another day. It's me promising her we'll get out of here alive, and meaning it. Because if I don't mean it, we won't survive.

And Myla is a master of this type of survival, even if she doesn't know it. She finds a place to put what she doesn't think she can handle, knowing when to seal the little cracks she feels surfacing. She did it when she exited the room when Royce and I were talking. She did it by grounding herself in what she calls "the plan", not in defeat and misery. She did it when she refused to talk to Kara. Because she knows, and I see, that Kara is her strength and her weakness. The problem is that Alvarez clearly sees that, too. Which has a bad feeling forming in my gut. If Alvarez really is targeting Kara, how and why did Juan think Kara wasn't ex-FBI? Something doesn't add up, and I don't like how it feels.

Chapter Sixteen

MYLA

It's the first day in fourteen months that I wake without a monster either in my bed or in my head. I blink awake to the first dawn of a new, better day, immediately aware of the heavy weight at my back, an arm draped over my waist, warmth filling me. Kyle. I smile with the memories of him carrying me to his room again last night, and of how I'd ended up in my current state of absolute nakedness.

He'd set me down in front of the bed, dragging the shirt off of me, his shirt, his hands all over my body, his big, hard body pressing me into the mattress. His shirt had come off next, followed by his sweatpants. There had been kissing, licking, touching. But when he'd told me to turn over, I'd refused. I close my eyes now, reliving it.

"No," I said. "Not this time. This time I get to do the touching. This time I get to kiss you." My hand flattens on his chest. "Lay

on your back."

"No," he says. "You—"

I lean up and silence him with a press of my lips to his, my hand on his cheek, lingering there several beats before I pull back and let him see the truth of my words in my eyes. "I have not touched anyone because I wanted to touch them in a very long time. And I want to touch you."

His gaze darkens, his fingers flexing into my backside that he's now cupping. "Myla," he whispers, my name a hot rasp of pure heat and passion, and when his mouth closes over mine, his tongue stroking deeply, I taste the lust in him, and it is the most amazing feeling to have that arouse me, not repel me. With him, I am human again. I am a woman again. I am me again.

He rolls to his back, taking me with him and I do not hesitate to meld my naked breasts to his chest, nor does he hesitate to cup my breast, to pinch my nipple. I kiss his neck, his shoulders, his lips. I kiss my way down to that deliciously ripped stomach of his, loving the way his hand goes to my head, but doesn't push, tangle or hurt. It's about arousal, about need, not sharing, not taking. And when I slide lower and take his cock in my hand and lick that salty proof of his arousal at the tip, the way his body stiffens, the way he makes this low, almost growl, has me wet and achy in ways I have not ached in oh so long, if ever.

"Good morning."

Kyle's deep, gravelly voice at my ear snaps me back to the present, his hand flattening on my belly. "Morning," I whisper, and he shifts my hips, his obviously hard cock settling in the crux below my backside, where I am already wet with my memories.

His hands slide lower, fingers resting just above my clit without moving. "Do you—"

"Yes please," I say, sounding breathless, feeling breathless, his fingers sliding lower, stroking my sex, and the instant he feels how ready I am, he makes another of those low, hot sounds he makes.

He pulls my legs toward my belly, arching around me, dragging his shaft up and down my sex, back and forth until he is pressing inside me, so damn hard it almost hurts, but oh so good. And once he's there, his hand cups my breast, his lips find my ear. "You make waking up really damn hot, sweetheart."

I don't get to respond. I don't know how I would if I could. Because he's moving, stroking me with his cock in these long, slow, seductive moves, that steal away words and thoughts. There is just the two of us, our bodies joined, our breathing filling the air. And his hand travels my body, between my legs, teasing my clit, driving me wild. The hot burn in my belly gets hotter, my sex tighter, and I arch backwards into him, with the climb to that sweet spot that is on me in an instant. But what makes it even sweeter, is his low groan and the way we shudder and shake together. The way our bodies ease together. The way he slowly inches my legs downward so that they align with his, but doesn't pull away.

"I don't even have words for how much I liked that," he says.

"Yeah?"

"Yeah."

"Me too."

"Yeah?"

I laugh. "Yeah."

He brushes hair from my face and kisses my temple.

"Don't move," he orders. "I'll grab you a towel." He pulls out of me, and I inhale, letting out a contented breath, my mind going back to last night and his worries about me feeling regrets over him and us. And my promise that I have none, which I didn't think he quite believed.

Kyle rounds the bed, pulling the blanket off of me, his dark blond hair a sexy rumpled mess, his green eyes warm with amber as they travel my body. His touch is gentle as he presses the towel he holds between my legs. "Good morning again," he says again, helping me sit.

"Good morning," I say, my cheeks heating and I am suddenly, impossibly shy with this man, in ways that defy all the humiliating things I've been through that should make that impossible.

"Are you hungry?"

"Yes," I say. The idea of sharing breakfast with him is comfortable and right in ways that take me back to last night. "But first. Can we talk about regrets?"

He goes very still. "What about them?"

"I could die before this is over and—"

"You're not going to die."

"Don't say that. I appreciate you trying to make me feel safe and you do. More than I have in a long time, but let's just be real for a minute. As long as we're here, inside this world, there is an active threat for both of us, but that wasn't even my point. My point is that you were worried about me regretting us. I want to make sure you know that I really meant it, Kyle. You saved me from dying with the taste of that man on my lips."

His eyes soften, and he pulls me to him, brushing hair from my face. "Myla," he breathes out, and there is emotion in his voice I can't quite name…torment, maybe? I do not know but I want to find out, but I never get to try. It's at that moment that my cellphone starts to ring, the sound ripping through me, a knife that bleeds reality, because it can only be one person. "No," I whisper, my hands grabbing onto Kyle's shoulders. "I don't want to do this." I push back from him. "I have to do this. I can. I will."

"Deep breath," Kyle says, reaching for my phone. "You can do this. You know how to do this." He hands me the cellphone.

"Don't watch me," I say. "It'll make me think he knows you're here."

"Understood," he says. "I'll make us coffee." He releases me, leaving me cold where I was just hot, pushing off the bed, naked and perfect. "Answer the call, Myla," he says, grabbing his sweats to pull them on.

"Right," I say, inhaling and then I swipe to answer. "Good morning," I greet Alvarez, turning to sit on the edge of the bed, and glancing at the clock by the bed that reads six am. "You're very early this morning."

"I have a flight this morning," he says, while Kyle exits into the hallway. "You took so long to answer," he adds, "but you sound wide awake."

"I am awake and excited to start my day," I say, cheerfully. "I was in the kitchen making coffee. This place is huge, Michael. It was like going to the corner coffee shop. It's at least as large as the apartment in Denver you took me to last month."

"But is it acceptable? Does it please you?"

"It's beautiful with an amazing city view," I say, relishing his affection for the tiny bit of safety it represents.

"But does it please you?"

"Of course, it pleases me. It's just very empty. Are you able to join me sooner than next week?"

"Unfortunately, bella, I am not. I'm on a plane now actually, flying out today to an unexpected meeting for intense negotiations." I do not miss how he leaves out the name of this "unexpected location". "If it's possible, I'll fly you to me for the weekend, even if it's only for a night."

"Please try to come here," I say, aware that my traveling to him would allow me to find out where he is, but should he get spooked, it might mean I disappear as well.

"You do not wish to come to me?"

"I really want you to see the designs I've shown you on paper in realized form and I honestly don't want to leave right before the launch. I want it to go perfectly."

He is quiet several thoughtful beats, in which I know he is questioning me, but then, this too is nothing new. He questions everyone, even me, and I know this spurs his need to dominate me, even punish me. "I would like to see your designs," he finally says. "Take pictures of yourself in the dresses today and send them to me."

"Yes," I say. "That would be fun."

"And the lingerie you're wearing beneath them. I'll send a photographer to your office."

My throat almost closes and I delicately clear my throat. "I can't do that at work," I say and almost choking on the words, I add, "Can they come here this weekend? If you're here, you can watch. If not, I can make you wish you'd come."

"Ah, bella," he says. "I will not make it to see you this way until the weekend. You can do this. I will send the photographer. I'll arrange it. Now, I must go." He lowers his voice and says something absolutely raunchy and disgusting to me in Spanish, before the line goes dead.

Grinding my teeth, I set the phone on the nightstand, my stupid hand trembling as I do, but I do not let myself sit here, where I will think and destroy myself. I stand up, the towel falling to the floor, the cold air rushing over my skin, and I am naked in so many ways right now that it's impossible to comprehend. Suddenly, I just need a shirt to put on. I need Kyle's shirt, and I twist around, noting the suitcase on the other side of the bed, by the living area rushing in that direction. Rolling it away from the couch, I lay it down, and settle on my knees, unzipping it and flipping open the lid, but instead of clothes, I find that arsenal of guns Kyle mentioned.

Inhaling, I reach for one of them, welcoming the cold, steel comfort a weapon will surely deliver. I choose a big one that requires two hands, one worthy of killing Michael Alvarez, the weight blissful in my hands, against my belly.

"Holy Mother of Jesus," Kyle says from the doorway, setting the cups in his hands on the desk, his eyes wide. "This is one of the most confusing, erotic, disturbing—did I mention erotic?—sights I've ever seen."

Only then do I fully register the fact that I'm holding a gun with my naked breasts on full display, my teeth scraping my bottom lip. "I was looking for a shirt."

"Understood," he says. "I always confuse shirts and guns, too. I'll get you a shirt." He walks to the closet to the right of the door, disappearing inside.

I set the gun back down and shut the case, standing and crossing the room to meet Kyle as he returns, a shirt in hand that he helps me pull over my head. "Thanks," I say. "I was cold and just…naked."

His hands come down on my shoulders and he pulls me to him. "What happened, sweetheart?" he asks, his voice soft, soothing, but somehow just the right kind of strong.

"He's at some kind of airport," I say, trying not to think about the photo shoot, and how many ways he could use those photos against me. "He's leaving Honduras for another meeting."

"As in right now?"

"Yes. He said he was on a plane getting ready to leave, but he normally uses private airstrips."

"Is he coming here?"

"He said he wasn't, but he could be," I say. "There is no way to be sure with him."

"Fuck," he murmurs. "I had better make some calls and try to find out." He kisses my forehead. "Are you okay?"

"I'm fine," I lie, hoping I convince us both that I am. "Make the calls, Kyle. Do what you need to do."

He hesitates but releases me, already pulling his phone from his pocket, motioning toward two cups he's set on the desk. "Don't drink that. It's insanely strong. I didn't test it until I was walking back to the room."

"I can make more," I say, welcoming something to do. "How do you like it?"

"Half cream and lots of sugar," he says, and I start to walk away as he catches my arm. "I know you aren't fine, so I'm not going to ask if you are."

"I am," I insist. "Really."

"No, you're not," he says, "but I'm going to fix that. I promise." He releases me and I all but run into the hallway, not sure why I'm this rattled. Kyle is here and amazing. My sister is safe, and yet one phone call from Michael and I am unsteady, rattled to the core. I bypass the kitchen, choosing the bedroom instead, and the minute I see my neatly made bed, survival instincts kick in. I cross the room, tear away the blankets and then just for good measure, roll around in it a few times. Satisfied it looks slept in, I walk to the bathroom, brush my hair and teeth, but at no time do I look in the mirror, and I know why. The old me is surfacing, and I don't want to see her. She can't be here. She is too weak. She can't survive. And I am going to survive.

I start to exit the bathroom when memories assail me. Me tied to a bed for hours on end. Michael using me like I'm some sort of doll, jacking off over and over, sometimes on me. Fucking other women he let touch me. I hate him. I hate him so much. I blink and I'm staring at myself in the mirror and I'm right. The old me is here, but she isn't weak. She is angry. She wants to kill him. I shove off the counter I've somehow leaned over. I am going to kill him before this is over.

• • •

KYLE

My first call when Myla leaves the room is to Royce, who needs to be ready for Alvarez to show up at any moment. My second is to Blake. "Tell me you have someone for me on Alvarez," I say when he answers.

"Fuck no," he says. "Kara and I've been up all night trying to find him. He's a ghost and fucking Honduras makes that an easy thing to be."

"He called Myla this morning. He's on a plane moving to an undisclosed location. I need to know it's not here."

"Have you traced the call? It's doubtful, but that might give us an originating point."

"Not yet," I say, my eyes landing on her phone on the nightstand, "and Blake, man, if I give you the number, Kara cannot call her."

"Give her some credit, man. She knows she's operating like she's undercover. She gets the psychology of it all."

I grab the phone and look at the caller ID. "The number he called from was blocked, of course," I say, "and I have no fucking clue why I haven't asked her for his number."

"He won't have one," Blake says, "but I have magic fingers. I can do a lot with her number. What's her number?" I hesitate and he knows. "Give me the fucking number, Kyle, or I will come there, bring Kara, and get it myself."

Grimacing, I give him the number. "If he shows up here—"

"Kill him," he says. "We have the locations where the women are now. We'll get them out. You just keep him the hell away from Myla."

"We both know we can't be sure we'll save those women that way."

"We will save them."

"Just fucking find him, Blake," I say, hanging up, my gaze lifting to the doorway where Myla now stands holding two cups of coffee, her expression unreadable. "I talked to Royce first," I explain as if she's asked, "but bottom line. He's one of the best hackers in the world. We need him looking for Alvarez."

"I understand," she says, crossing to hand me my coffee. "I promise."

"He wants to know if you have a number you call Alvarez on," I say, accepting the cup.

"No number."

"Ever?"

"Ever," she confirms.

"What comes up on your phone when he calls you?"

"It's always blocked." She changes the subject. "Is Kara with Blake?"

"She is and she's trying to help." I sip my coffee. "Perfect. Thank you."

"Of course," she says, her expression solemn. "Now I feel like I need to talk to Kara."

"No," I say. "You don't."

"No?"

"No. Your instincts to say you shouldn't see her now were right."

"Why were they right?"

"You know that answer."

"Because I'll worry about her and I'll get reconnected to a world I can't quite have yet."

"Exactly," I say. "You can't reconnect with the real you, or you'll make mistakes. And Kara knows this. Blake just told me she does."

"He did?"

"Almost Scout's honor, sweetheart," I joke. "Seriously though. He did. Kara's fine, but I do want you to meet the people protecting you. You need to know who they are and feel good about them, and since we can't risk an in-person meeting, Royce and I just had a quick conversation before I talked to Blake about doing a Skype. Are you okay with that?"

"I am. When?"

I glance at my watch. "It's only six-fifteen. When do you want to get to the office?"

"Nine."

"Then let's just do this now." I motion to the desk where I have a monitor set up with Skype already.

We move in that direction, claiming side-by-side seats. "Who am I meeting with?" she asks, sipping her coffee, seemingly relaxed, but there is an edginess to her I can't quite define.

"Asher, Jacob, and Royce." I send a Skype ping and the reply is almost instant, with Asher appearing on the screen, his long blond hair tied at the nape, his short sleeved t-shirt showcasing his brightly colored tattoo sleeves.

"Myla," he greets, his tone friendly. "I'm Asher. How the hell are you?"

"I'm better now that I have help," she says.

"Everybody's better with help unless that help sucks and we don't suck."

"That is true," she says, the sound of her laughter that follows is welcome in the aftermath of Alvarez's call.

"Myla," Jacob says, moving into the screenshot, the contrast of his short buzzed hair and stoic personality to Asher hard to miss. "I'm Jacob. I just wanted to say that we've got your back."

"Hi Jacob. Thank you. You both know Kara?"

"We do," they both say.

"I've worked with her quite often," Jacob offers. "I'd trust her with my life or anyone else's."

"Count me in on that one," Asher agrees. "Your sister's kick ass. Have you heard what she did to Kyle?"

I grimace at the memory I can't escape. "No she has not," I say, while Myla gives me a curious look.

"It's nothing," I say. "It was before—"

"She dropped him like a rock," Asher supplies, "or more like a ten-foot tree." He holds up his hand and mimics me falling as he adds, "He fell like a timberland."

"I wouldn't know how I fell," I snap, "since I was drugged and passed out."

Myla faces me. "Why'd she drug you?"

"Because I was trying to keep her from going after Blake, who was going after Alvarez."

There are voices off-screen before Asher says, "Royce wants to talk to Myla." Then giving her a nod he adds, "Myla, nice to meet you." He firms his voice. "And all jokes aside. I have your back. You have my word."

"Yes," Jacob adds. "We have your back."

Both men disappear and Royce appears, his long, dark hair tied at the nape, his trademark hard stare and the hard set to his square jaw in place. But when he says, "Hello Myla," his voice is gentle, and friendly. "I'm Royce. I'm sure you have questions. What do you want to know?"

He's asking if she wants to know about Kara, testing her to see if she's distracted by personal matters. "Did you check out the locations I gave you?" she asks, proving her focus is crystal clear. She wants to save those women. She wants to get Alvarez.

There is just a flicker of surprise in Royce's eyes that he quickly replaces with hard focus. "We've been up all night working on it. In every location we have trusted contractors, we confirmed active locations. In most of the others, we've found missing person trends that support a location in the city."

"Then what's the plan to get them out?" she asks.

"At this point," I say, "we want to put together a mass raid that happens at all locations at the same time we extract you, which will be at the moment Alvarez appears."

"That's going to require manpower and support," Royce adds, "which means we need to call in the FBI."

"If you hand this over to them and they delay to act or make even a small mistake," she says, "those locations will be gone. And if anything happens to him, and they're not already under your control, they'll be gone. He's taken precautions for everything."

"Without the FBI involved," Royce says, "we'll be delayed. With them we'll have the resources to monitor, prepare, and raid those locations."

"In other words," I offer. "Even if the location is moved, we'll have eyes on it, and move with it."

"We're on this, Myla," Royce says. "And thanks to you, we're going to finally get this bastard, and all his minions. But if you don't mind, can I have a word with Kyle alone?"

My jaw clenches at the request sure to stir discomfort in Myla, though her reply is quick and cordial. "Of course. And thank you for your help."

"Thank me in person when you are no longer in prison."

She gives a nod and without looking at me, rounds the chair and heads to the door, exiting and shutting it.

"Whatever this is," I begin, only to be cut off with, "Holy hell, Kyle," Royce snaps. "Is she fucking wearing your shirt? She's Kara's fucking sister."

My irritation is instant, and while I would gamble he's guessing on the shirt, I don't even try to deny it. "I seem to remember Lauren ending up in your t-shirt when you were guarding her."

"She wasn't traumatized by a madman," he bites out. "And she wasn't Kara's sister. And yes. You are right. Lauren's my wife. She wasn't just a fuck and a conquest on an undercover job."

Now he's pissing me off. "Myla isn't just a fuck and conquest."

"You just met her."

"I've been looking for her for a year."

"You look for a lot of people. You don't take them to your bed."

"Exactly the fucking point. Back off, Royce. And now, unless you have something other than a lecture, I'm going to open the door before I end up losing the trust I want from her."

"If you hurt her—"

"If I don't die saving her life, feel free to finish that sentence." I end the connection, scrubbing my now heavily stubbled jaw, then do the same of the now longish layers of my hair that need a cut as bad as I need a shave. Inhaling, I walk to the bathroom, brush my teeth, and then stare into the mirror. I wait for the self-flagellation to start, for regrets over Myla to follow, but it doesn't happen. I don't regret touching her any more than I question why she's important to me, beyond the obvious family connection. She just is. And I damn sure don't regret the year of looking for her that created this connection I feel to her in the first place, because I found her, and I'm going to take her home.

Pushing off the sink, I cross the room, exit to the hallway, and seek out Myla, finding her standing in the kitchen, leaning on the counter, where she seems to stare at the wall. Seeming to sense my arrival, she turns to face me. "I heard what he said to you. I stayed by the door and I listened and I shouldn't have, but I did. The man thinks I'm a loose cannon. And how dare he decide who can be in my bed, after all I've dealt with. How dare he—"

I'm in front of her before she finishes the sentence, my hands on her shoulders, my lips on her lips, my tongue doing a deep slide before she sighs and says, "You taste like spearmint," telling me that I've successfully brought her mood down at least one notch.

"That was just to make sure you know where we stand, but he was just being protective. He cares. And I told you. He's gruff around the edges but a good man, Myla."

"I get that," she says. "I do. I just don't need anyone doubting me right now. I can handle this. I *am* handling it."

"Like a champion," I say, "Now. Let's take a shower together. Yes?"

"Yes," she says, and she's barely spoken the word before I've scooped her up and started walking toward the bedroom, my action meant to tell her that I'm here to carry her if she needs me. And she will. Maybe not now, but later, because what I don't say to her, what I can't tell her now, but I know all too well, is that once touched by a monster, that beast stays with you forever. All I can do is make sure he doesn't get the chance to add to her scars.

Chapter Seventeen

KYLE

It's eight-thirty, half an hour before we need to be at her office, when Myla steps into the doorway of the bedroom looking sexy as hell in some sort of peachy looking dress she's cinched with a belt at her waist, her long, dark brown hair silk around her shoulders. "You ready?" she asks.

"You look beautiful, sweetheart," I say, shutting my computer, and picking it up to take with me, before standing and closing the small space between us.

"Thank you," she says, sliding her hand over the light blue tie I've paired with my navy suit. "I like this. And since they say the man makes the suit, you absolutely do."

"A compliment from a future famous designer," I say, taking her briefcase from her, her shiny lipstick a perfect match for her dress, and the only thing keeping me from kissing her. "I'm honored."

"I don't want to be famous," she says. "I just want…" Shadows settle in her pretty green eyes. "I don't know what I want anymore."

"You want to design your clothes, your way," I say. "And you will, on your own label."

"He owns some of my favorite designs now."

"He's not going to own anything when this is over. Now." I tilt my head toward the hallway. "Let's go get another day of playing this ridiculous game over with, and then we'll come back here, take a run, get naked, and then watch Dexter while we eat pizza. Then we'll do it all again."

She gives me a tiny smile. "Dexter again?"

"He'll feed your fantasies about killing Alvarez, I promise." I shift to preparation for the day. "Do you have your gun?"

"Yes."

And back to her and us. "Let me see," I say softly.

"You want to see?"

"Yes. I want to see."

"All right," she says, giving me a shy, sexy smile as she reaches for her zipper, "My design, by the way," as she pulls it down. "I should market it as easy access to your handgun."

"Or to other things," I murmur, as she reveals her ample cleavage, a black lacy bra, and the gun, all of which has my cock thickening and my gaze lifting to hers. "I'm not sure what I'm going to think about the most today. This moment or the one where you were naked and holding a semi-automatic rifle in your hands."

She zips herself back up. "I can't believe I was holding that gun while I was naked."

"Just know I'll be a happy man every time I think about

it today," I tease, tilting my head toward the hallway, amazed at the flush of her cheeks that I catch before she turns and heads to the door. Somehow, some way, Alvarez took her body, but she's managed to deny him her soul.

"Let's assume there's a camera to go with the recording device Les installed last night," I say, joining her at the door, and flipping the lock. "I want you to drop your purse to force us to linger at the door. That will make our conversation we want them to hear seem natural."

"And what is that conversation supposed to be?"

"Be snappy with me," I say. "Act irritated that I'm around."

She shakes her head. "No. That's doesn't fit me. I never do that, even with Juan."

"All right then. We'll stick with me being cold and you being uncomfortable. Just follow my lead and let's ride the elevator down that has cameras and continue the same tone."

"Got it," she confirms, and I open the door.

Myla immediately exits the room, dropping her purse, which manages to open and spill the contents to the floor. "Oh my God," she murmurs, squatting down to start collecting her items. Instead of helping her, I shut the door, and step closer to her, towering over her, and watching her efforts.

"These kinds of delays and mistakes, are dangerous," I say. "It allows someone time to grab you."

"I didn't do it on purpose," she says, sounding flustered, and glancing up at me. "Do you have to hover?"

"It's my job to hover," I reply dryly.

"It's making me nervous," she says, popping to her feet and shoving her purse to her shoulder. "What is it exactly that you're protecting me from?"

"As I keep telling you. Everything and everyone that isn't me."

"Can I have my briefcase? I want to look at my sketches."

"And I want your hands free in case you need to use them to protect yourself."

"My hands? I can put the briefcase on my shoulder."

"Not and hold the sketchpad. We need to move along."

She glowers at me and turns on her heel, beginning the walk to the elevator, smartly holding her character, her steps a bit too fast, her body language stiff and uncomfortable. "Behind me," I instruct, when we step into the elevator. "Always behind me. I'm in front to take any fire that comes before you would."

"What fire?" she asks, as the doors close. "Who wants to shoot me?"

"It's not my job to name names," I say. "It's just my job to ensure no one hurts you."

She says nothing else, remaining where she stands, her acting skills a testament to how she's survived. The game is as second nature to her as it is for me to step forward first when the elevator doors open to the garage, and immediately know something isn't right. An instant later, my gaze lands hard on Juan, looking shorter than usual, because he's leaning on my fucking Mustang, just asking to get hurt. I reach for Myla, my hand closing around her arm, as I pull her to my side. "Why is he here?" she murmurs, as we start forward.

"Trying to get his balls ripped out," I say, not releasing her until we're at the car, and I'm standing a foot in front of Juan. "Get in the car, Myla," I instruct, clicking the locks open.

LISA RENEE JONES

"That won't be necessary," Juan counters. "She and I need to talk. I'll drive her to work."

She stops walking. I keep my eyes on him, and repeat, "Get in the car, Myla," and this time, she does exactly what I say, moving to the passenger door.

"She's going with me," Juan says. "You work for me. Myla! Come back."

"I work for Alvarez," I say, as the car door slams with Myla inside the Mustang. "You're just the messenger, and you should know: my car is my baby. Lean on it again, and I'll have to defend its honor."

"You're very protective of her," he says. "Maybe too much so."

"I paid a hundred thousand dollars for that car. You're damn straight I'm protective of her."

"I mean Myla and you know it."

"I was hired to protect her or die. I'm not getting my balls cut off over you, but right now you should know I'm thinking about where to hang yours." I walk to the driver's side of the car.

"I'm not done talking," he says.

I get in the car, lock the doors and hold up a finger to warn Myla the car might be bugged. She inhales and nods, facing forward. Juan remains on the back of my car, apparently thinking he's going to stop my departure. I rev the engine and still he stands there. I shift to reverse and roll just enough to knock the shit out of him, which earns me loud cursing and his butt getting the hell out of the way. I back us up and get us the fuck out of the garage, handing Myla the scanner from my pocket. She eagerly accepts it, turns it on and sweeps the car, during which time my mind is conjuring all kinds of reasons to turn around and run Juan over.

"Why would he want to see you alone?" I ask, the minute we're clear. "Is that a regular thing? Does he—"

"I know what you're thinking," she says. "And no. That was one time, but he likes to play with my head. He taunts me. He was not pleased when Michael decided to bring in a bodyguard."

"Interesting," I say, glancing over at her, and hating the way she's hugging herself again. "Are we sure Juan isn't making a move against Alvarez?"

"They're family," she says. "I can't imagine that to be the case, but it's Juan, so maybe."

"You will not go with him anywhere. In case I haven't made myself clear. That means, you shoot him if you have to. Understand?"

"Yes. I understand."

But what I don't understand are Juan's actions and motives, which brings me back to him telling me Kara's FBI, not ex-FBI, when Alvarez is obviously concerned about her contacting Myla. Maybe he was testing me. Maybe it was a slip of the tongue. Maybe he's just an asshole who's a fool. But assuming so could make me the fool and get us killed.

• • •

MYLA

The minute Kyle and I walk into the lobby, our timid little blonde receptionist takes one look at Kyle's hard-set expression, and jumps to her feet. "Can I get either of you some coffee? Or some...something?"

"I'll make some in my office, Heather," I say, "but thank you, and don't worry." I indicate Kyle. "He's my personal stalker, I mean bodyguard. He won't stay up here and stare at you." It's weak humor, but the best I have in the "feel good/comfort" category after the Juan incident that seems to have left Kyle worried, rather than just agitated. Maybe that's because he's just not used to Juan's behavior, but he's honed years of instincts I've only been using for a year. Maybe there is something about Juan I've been missing that he's picked up on.

Whatever the case, the two of us make a beeline for my office, where Kyle unlocks the door, flips on the light and does a quick scan before he allows me to enter. The instant I'm inside, I cross to my desk, feeling a punch in my chest at the sight of my mother's photos. I settle my purse in my desk, unsurprised when Kyle shuts the door, sets his MacBook on the conference table, and removes his scanner from his jacket. Also unsurprising, by the time I've pulled my sketchpad out, flipped through my presentation for today, and looked back up, that he's already found a recorder by the Keurig and destroyed it.

There's a knock on the door, and he immediately returns the scanner to his jacket pocket and walks to the door, opening it, his big body blocking me from seeing my visitor. "The bodyguard is back," a female voice I recognize as Barbara's says. "And he even answers doors."

"But I don't make coffee for anyone but myself," he says, stepping back to allow her to enter. "Don't ask." He delivers this with such a dry, flat tone that I'm not sure if he's joking or serious.

And from the look on Barbara's face when she enters

the room, and her awkward reply of "I…of course not," I am pretty sure she isn't either, especially when Kyle actually walks to the Keurig and inserts a pod, proving he knows how to take his comment, and his cold, hard-to-read bodyguard routine to perfect extremes.

"Good morning," I greet her, pulling her attention back to me, and noting how lovely she looks in a baby blue sheath, with her sleek gray hair piled on top of her head.

She seems to shake herself into action, walking to my desk. "What is his deal?" she whispers, as if he can't hear her.

"Robot," I say, as she perches on the edge of one of my visitor's chairs. "It's the only explanation I have for that man."

She laughs good-naturedly. "I do believe you're right. He's a robot. That explains so much."

"He," Kyle says, "is still in the room, and not going anywhere." He sits down at the conference table and opens his MacBook. "And I'm not programmed to refrain from commenting should this conversation continue."

We both laugh, and then Barbara looks at him, her cheeks flushed, her eyes warm with fondness that has me deciding she's quite taken by Kyle, which can only work in our favor. I hope. "I'm not staying anyway," Barbara replies, focusing on me. "I just wanted to give you a heads up that I'm going to have the model agencies send you spec sheets this morning and I'm hopeful you pick some models you want to see this afternoon."

"Actually," I say, deciding not to ask but rather tell her what's going to happen. "I don't want models. We don't need them and they're expensive and high maintenance anyway."

She looks dumbfounded. "But the campaigns."

"I have a solution I am quite pleased with," I reply, showing her my sketches, to which she gives a critical inspection before her expression lights up.

"I'm blown away," she says. "I love the concept of "We design. You make the style." Everyone is going to love it. I'll get with the art departments at the magazines right now, and find out what we need to do."

"I still have a few ideas I want to elaborate on," I say. "I need to finish these sketches."

"I'll have the appropriate people work through it with you," she says, standing, "and really, this is a load off. We can focus on other things now. I'll be in touch in a few." She turns to leave, but Kyle stops her progress.

"Before you leave," he says, drawing her attention and mine, since I have no idea what he's about to say. "There's going to be a security team coming in late this evening to install a new system and cameras," he continues, clearly intent on giving his team full access to the building and being prepared for whatever comes our way. "I'm asking them to complete the task after hours as to not disrupt your work, but if you could make sure all appropriate people know as to not be concerned."

"Of course," Barbara says, her tone saying that her mind is clearly elsewhere at this point. "We appreciate the extra protection." She's gone by the time she's spoken the words, leaving Kyle and I alone.

I grin and pick up my sketches, pointing to them, and feeling quite proud of myself for my morning success. No models. No more victims. Kyle winks, his eyes alight with understanding and support, and as I walk to the Keurig, I have this sense in that moment of really not being alone anymore. Unbidden though, when I reach for one of the chocolate coffee pods Michael had arranged for me, I hear his voice. *Does it please you?* The photo shoot comes to my mind, and I toss the pod in the trash, walk back to my desk, and reach for my sketchpad, pretending to work to hide my reaction from Kyle, who I can't tell about this. He won't want me to do it. I know he won't, but if I refuse, there will be consequences none of us want to pay.

•••

The day ends without a photographer or any contact to explain why, but that is not unlike Michael when he travels. His unpredictability is part of what makes him elusive to his enemies and the authorities. Kyle and Blake are determined to change that, though, planning a virtual hack party tonight, delayed by the need to keep my routine looking "normal" if anything about this life could be called such a thing. The instant we arrive in our room, Kyle and I change into workout clothes and head to the gym, even bypassing a scan of the room.

It's on the treadmill, with Kyle by my side, that the photo session starts bothering me again and I'm not sure why. These are the kinds of control games Michael plays with me to prove he owns me. About ten minutes in, I decide I'm worried because I know this is going to upset Kyle, despite the fact that there is nothing dangerous about pictures. I can't even call them demoralizing, considering the things Michael's made me do or done to me. Twenty minutes into the run, I don't think that's what's bothering me at all, but I don't know what is. Thirty minutes in, I still can't figure out what the heck is grinding at my nerve endings.

At the forty-minute mark, I have an epiphany that hits me like a heart attack and I punch the stop button on my machine, grab my towel, and force myself not to visibly show how freaked out I am right now. Kyle does the same and glances at me. "Are we done?"

"Yes. And I just remembered something I need to tell you back at the suite."

"How important is this something?"

"I think you'd rate it as a "Why the fuck didn't you tell me?" moment."

"Okay then," he says, wiping the back of his neck. "We'll talk in the room where I can react accordingly."

And we stick to that decision, enduring the ride upstairs and the walk down the hall to the room, in silence. Once we're in our private space, Kyle flips the locks, points to the bedroom, and follows me inside. "Tell me," he says, the instant he joins me.

"Don't we need to...?" I motion to the room for a scan.

"We cancelled housekeeping and set up an alarm on the door today to let our team know when someone enters," he says. "We're clear. Tell me."

"Michael—"

"Alvarez," he bites out. "Call the fuckhead Alvarez."

"Alvarez," I say, thinking Kyle really isn't going to be reasonable about those photos. "He told me that if he couldn't come to me this weekend, he'd have me go to him."

"And you said?"

"That I really didn't want to leave before the store opening and I really wanted him to come see my work."

"And?"

"He said he'd try but then he wanted to have photos taken of me today, but the photographer he was arranging didn't show up."

"What photos?"

"The photos aren't important," I say, going back to my point. "What's important is that the photographer didn't show up. Maybe he didn't set it up because he's coming here after all. And if he comes here now, there's no way the FBI is ready. Royce was just calling them today."

"He did call them and they're actively involved," he says. "We'll be ready for him."

"He could show up tonight for all we know."

"Everyone is on standby for that possibility and if he's flying in here tonight, Blake and I will find him." He sits down at the desk and keys his computer to life.

"I want to help, then," I say, joining him. "Tell me what to do."

"Order us some food," he says. "I'm starving."

"That's not helping."

"I'm pretty fucking starving, sweetheart,"

"Okay, aside from the food. What can I do?"

"Start making a list of every detail you can remember from this past year. Any name, place, person, or company Alvarez ever associated with. Even favorite foods and restaurants are noteworthy. These things help more than you know."

I key the other computer to life and pull up a Word document. He turns my chair around and faces me, his hands on the arms of my seat. "Food first, sweetheart."

"I just want to do something to make a difference."

"You have and we are. We're going to be ready. I promise."

"What if he insists I go to him this weekend?"

"Then we get those women out and we get out."

"If we don't get him, he'll come after me and Kara, which means everyone in our circle, your circle, Kyle."

"Not if he thinks you're dead."

"Yes well, about that plan," I say, logic hitting me where hope had blinded me before. "Why do we believe he'll think me dead any more than you did? If he wants me to go to him this weekend, I have to go."

"You're not going," he says, his tone absolute. "We'll find him." He cups my face and kisses me. "I've got you now, sweetheart. You aren't getting away."

• • •

Kyle and Blake don't find Alvarez, any more than the FBI does. For three mornings in a row, I wake up in Kyle's arms with the knowledge that every effort we've made the day before to find him and be ready for what he does next, has failed. In fact, Michael is not only missing, but completely silent, zero communication with me at all. The possibilities are night and day: He's either in hiding, something he does when he's under an imminent threat, or planning to surprise me by showing up here this weekend.

With this in mind, come Friday morning, we are all up at the crack of dawn, preparing for what could be the day Michael shows up to see me, or sends someone to take me to him. I retreat to my bedroom to shower, and Kyle lets me, mostly I think because he's talking back and forth with Royce and struggling to get in the shower. Alone for the first time in days, I remind myself that this is all bigger than me. I am not what's important. Michael Alvarez is dangerous and even if we save those girls he's kidnapped, there will be others if he escapes. The idea that I can stop him is a powerful drug, one I've lived on for a long time, and it fuels me now.

I dress with a potential confrontation in mind, choosing a black, fitted dress, the last one I have with me that reflects my obsession with front-zippered bodices. And while it allows for easy access to a weapon, I hesitate before I attach the gun to my bra, nervous about Michael finding out I'm wearing it. If he does, and I can't shoot him and still protect those women, it could be me who dies.

Not allowing myself to think of such things, I flat-iron my hair to a sleek brown shine, and take extra care with my make-up to hide how sleep deprived I am, choosing a shiny red lipstick to draw attention from my tired eyes. Finally, I make coffee and head to Kyle's room, finding him at the bathroom sink, having just put a light blue and black striped tie through the collar of his starched white shirt.

"Coffee," I say, walking to him and handing him his cup.

"Thank you," he says, accepting it from me, his blond hair laying in long, sexy layers, his green eyes giving me a keen inspection. "How are you?" he asks, sipping from his cup, and sighing. "Damn, I needed that."

"I thought you might," I say. "You haven't slept at all. How are you?"

He sets the cup on the counter and pulls me in front of him. "I'm fine. And you just avoided telling me how you are."

"No. I didn't. I'm just...here. That's how I am when I'm preparing for him. Just here. I want to get this day over with."

"I understand," he says, and he does mean it, but he

doesn't understand. No one can understand what Michael Alvarez does to me, except me. And I don't want them to ever have to understand. "Tonight, we might not even be here anymore. You might be—"

"Don't, please," I say, flattening my hand on his chest. "I can't think like that. I have to accept being here, to keep being here, you know that."

He gives me a grim, reluctant nod. "I do," he agrees. "Give me five minutes and we'll leave."

"Okay," I say, and when he kisses my forehead, his lips lingering on my skin, I feel his dread merge with mine.

I slip away from him, entering the bedroom, and sitting down at the computer, and my heart squeezes with the message that appears in the live chatroom. **It's from my sister:** How is Myla? It reads next to her name. I don't even hesitate to answer. **I type:** Nervous but good.

Kara: Define good.

Again, I don't even think. **I just type something our mother used to say:** Splendid, darling.

Kara: Myla?

I type: Yes. My chest tightens and I add: I love you. I miss you but if I talk to you—

Kara: I know. Stay focused. Stay strong. I want to pull you out of there, but I know I can't and it's killing me. But I am so very proud of you for what you've made possible. You've already saved lives. I love you.

I swipe at the dampness on my cheeks and stand up, only to find Kyle standing right behind me. "You saw?"

"I saw," he confirms.

"It just felt like time."

"Then it was time," he says, but I see in his eyes what

I already know. I just told him I couldn't connect with the possibility of an outside world, but I just did just that. And I know why I did it. I was afraid that when this day was over, I wouldn't be able to tell Kara I love her.

Kyle pulls me to him, and says exactly what he did three nights ago. "I told you. I found you. I'm not letting you go." I believe him, but what I don't say to him is that if it means protecting him and Kara, as well as all of those innocent women—if it means destroying Michael Alvarez so he can't hurt anyone else—I might have to let *him* go.

Chapter Eighteen

MYLA

Nothing happens. All day we wait, and wait, and wait some more for word from Michael, but nothing happens. Evening arrives, and Kyle and I linger in my office near closing, in no hurry to leave, simply because the building is surrounded and we're protected. Finally though, it's inevitable that we leave.

"He'll be waiting for me at the hotel," I say, packing up my briefcase. "That has to be what's happening."

"We'd know if he was there," Kyle says, stepping to the front of my desk, his back to the open door.

"Like the FBI knew where he was the past fourteen months?"

"We'd know," he reiterates.

"Forgive me if I'm not confident," I say. "But I'm not confident."

"Knock, knock."

At the sound of Heather's voice, Kyle steps aside, giving me a view of her holding up a white box with a red ribbon. "I was about to leave when this came for you," she says, grinning with the excitement of the unknown, while my stomach knots with the certainty that Michael is near. "It looks exciting," she says, rushing forward and setting it on my desk. "Can I see what it is?"

"I think it's one of those gifts you look at by yourself," I say, aware of Kyle's heavy stare resting on me and the package.

She laughs, shoving long blonde hair behind her ear. "One of those fun packages. I'm jealous." She eyes Kyle, who's standing to the left of her, looking stoic and unaffected, when I know better. "Ah well, then," she says. "Goodnight."

"Night, Heather," I say, watching as she leaves, Kyle right behind her to shut the door.

I grab the card on top of the box, trying to open it, but my stupid hand shakes. Kyle is there in an instant, opening it for me, and much to my distress, he reads it out loud: *This is for your sexy photo shoot, bella. Another surprise to follow. Michael.*

He gives me a hard stare, and grabs the box, and opens it to reveal a red lace bra and panty set, with garters. "What the fuck is this?"

"I told you—"

"You said there were some kind of photos, not that he wanted to turn you into a porn star."

"I design lingerie, too."

"Why didn't you tell me this?"

"Because it's pictures, not him touching me, and if that's what it takes to keep him happy and finally end his reign of horror, I'll do it."

His rejection is instant. "No, you won't, he could use those pictures on porn sites. Hell, he *will* use them."

My throat thickens. "He won't."

"You don't know that," he bites out.

"He has pictures of me," I spit out. "Horrible pictures, and you haven't found them while you looked for me. He wants to own me. I'm his possession."

He presses his hands on the desk. "You are not his possession and I'll find the pictures—"

"Please don't. I can't bear the idea of you seeing them."

"Myla," he says softly. "That does not matter to me."

"It matters to me. And I have to do this."

There's another knock on the door, and he firms his voice again. "You will not do this and you will listen to me."

"You can't—"

"Don't think I can't stop you, because I will. You take my lead on whatever happens next. The end." He doesn't wait for a reply, walking to the door and opening it.

"What do you need?" he all but growls.

"I need to talk to Myla."

At the sound of LeeAnn's voice, I welcome anything that might give me an excuse to work late and perhaps miss the photographer that may well show up at the hotel. It's impossible to know with Michael. "What is it, LeeAnn?" I ask, forcing Kyle to take a step back and let her enter.

"I was instructed to take you for a little surprise," she says, her tone less than pleased. "It's inside the new store."

"Instructed by who?" Kyle asks.

"Mr. Alvarez," she says, brushing a wavy lock of red hair out of her face. "He's been planning this all week. He said you should bring the gift he sent you as well."

"Oh," I say. "Of course." Then saying what Michael would expect, I add, "This is fun," only I sound more like it's torture.

LeeAnn doesn't seem to notice, giving a smirk. "Right. Fun. He said you'd say that." She eyes the box on the desk. "Grab your gift and let's get going."

"I'll carry it," Kyle says, scooping it up.

"That won't be necessary," LeeAnn says. "She's to come with me alone."

"That's not happening," he says, removing his phone from his pocket to look at a text, his expression unreadable.

"We're inside the facility," she argues. "Didn't you have security installed a few days ago?"

"The security for Myla is me," he says, typing a return message to whoever contacted him and then returning his cellphone to his pocket.

"She's just going with me," LeeAnn snaps irritably. "It's no different than her walking down the hall with Barbara."

"Aside from Barbara actually liking her?" he asks dryly. "She's not going with you alone."

LeeAnn doesn't deny his statement. "Fine," she says, turning her attention to me. "Follow me." She rotates on her heel, and I inhale a deep breath, my gaze colliding with Kyle's. He motions me forward, his expression hard, his mood dark and focused. I want to ask about his plan and about the text message, but I am aware that Michael could be here, and catching him could make the timing critical.

And so I walk forward, entering the hallway, my heart thundering in my ears. And considering the storefront is on the other end of the building, it's not a short trip, nor does LeeAnn slow or look for me even once. Even when we arrive at the entrance, and she faces us, she focuses on Kyle, not me. "You can wait out here."

"Not happening," he says.

She makes a frustrated sound. "This is private," she says. "Not for your eyes."

"Vague statements get you nowhere with me," he replies. "What's inside?"

"Her newly decorated storefront for her viewing."

"And what else?" he asks.

"At Mr. Alvarez's request, we're doing a private photo shoot of Myla in her clothing line."

"We being who?" he presses.

"We have a photographer and several models," she says, and I know that means that I'm expected to "perform" with them for the camera.

"Those people are in the storefront now?" I ask.

"Yes."

"I haven't met them, or checked them out," he says. "In other words, this "surprise" is put on hold." He shoves the box in his hand at her.

"Mr. Alvarez will not be pleased," she says, forced to take it, and finally looking at me. "You know he will not be pleased."

Kyle's hand comes down on my arm. "She doesn't have a choice. I'm in charge, per Mr. Alvarez. If he has a problem with my decision, tell him to call me." He turns me and starts walking.

"Kyle," I whisper.

"Not now. Not here."

"But—"

"Not now, Myla," he warns, his grip on my arm holding

steady all the way back to my office. "Get your things," he instructs as we enter, "and don't ask me anything else yet."

I do as he says, while he grabs his computer, then directs me out of the office, and the instant we're outside, he shackles my arm again and leads me to the passenger door of the Mustang, where he helps me inside.

The instant he joins me, I twist around to face him. "What is going on?" I demand.

"Give me a minute, sweetheart," he says, revving the engine and putting us into drive, multi-tasking to dial his phone. "Are we sure he wasn't there?" he asks whoever answers, almost immediately. He listens a minute. "No," he replies. "He wanted Myla to do something for him I didn't let her do." Another pause. "Yes. Right. That's the plan." Another pause. "Are we sure he isn't at the hotel? Just be fucking sure." He ends the call.

"Is he in the city?" I ask.

"We don't think so," he says, "but we can't be certain." He stops at a light. "We're going to have a conversation before this night is over about what happened back there."

I brush away his anger, focusing on the real threat. "He's going to be furious."

"Good," he says. "Then maybe he'll get his ass here where we need him."

"The FBI is involved now" I argue. "They aren't ready for the full outreach yet."

"They have an emergency plan," he says. "They can be ready if it means ending this."

"What if he just decides to kill you for defying him?"

"He won't."

I twist around to look at him. "You don't know that."

"Calculated risks are necessary. I just took one."

I shut my eyes and face forward, inside a Mustang that might not be spinning out of control, but I sure feel like we are.

• • •

KYLE

To say that I am pissed at Myla trying to sacrifice herself again is an understatement. We walk into the hotel room, and I head into the bedroom while she takes off for the living area. I dump her briefcase and my computer, and tell myself to calm the fuck down before I go after her, but fail in my effort. I pursue, catching her arm before she reaches the living area and push her against the wall, my legs framing hers.

"You will never do that again," I growl. "You are not disposable. You are not porn."

"And yet, you just put yourself on the assassination block? How is that different?" She grabs my jacket. "How is that different? You tell me to trust you. You tell me you aren't letting me go, but then you invite a bullet to the head."

My fingers slide under her hair, my hand wrapping the back of her neck to pull her mouth to mine. "I'm not letting you go," I say, my mouth slanting over hers, my tongue stroking against hers in a hot, possessive claiming I don't even try to tame. "He doesn't get to kiss you." My hand slides to her backside, melding her to me. "He doesn't get to touch you. And he damn sure doesn't get to see you in fucking lingerie. The only reason I get those things is because you let me, because you choose me."

"I do choose you, Kyle."

"Then no more him, ever. Say it."

"No more," she whispers.

"No more ever," I say.

"No more ever," she repeats, and we linger there, breath mingling, heat flaring between us until we are suddenly kissing, both of us wild with need. I barely remember how my zipper is lowered, how the thick pulse of my erection is between her legs and her panties are in my hand, torn away in a hard yank. But I damn sure remember lifting her and pressing inside her. Holding her against the wall and thrusting deep, hard, fast, the soft, sexy sounds she's making, the way she clings to me, driving every move and pump of my body. She drives me wild, and it's her who takes us over the edge, her body spasming around me, pulling me into release, taking me there the way she takes everything I am, and I can't seem to find a reason that's a problem. When it's over, we melt into each other, our breathing slowing, and I carry her into the bathroom of my bedroom, sitting her on the sink, and handing her a towel. Neither of us speak as we clean up, but once she's tossed the towel, I press her knees together and settle my hands on top of them. "Myla," I say softly. "I don't want this for you anymore."

"This is bigger than the two of us," she says. "We both know that. That's why you put yourself on the line. That's why I might have to as well."

"You've done your share. It's time for someone else to do theirs."

"And that's you? You die instead of me? That's unacceptable and if I have to take some damn pictures to protect you, me, and other people, it's nothing compared to what I've endured."

"Sweetheart—" My phone starts to ring and I reach for it. "Fuck. I have to—"

"I know. Get it."

I glance down at the caller ID to find a masked number, turning away from Myla to answer. "This is Kyle."

"Hola, Kyle," comes a heavily accented male voice. "Explain to me why Myla is not at the photo shoot I set up for her."

I walk into the bedroom, and sit down at my desk, **keying in a message to Royce:** Alvarez on my phone.

"My understanding was that you wanted her to stay alive and frankly, I plan to stay alive myself."

"How does a photo shoot get either of you killed?"

"My understanding is that if she dies, I die. And you have enemies. I had no idea who was in that store, what they intended, or what they might do to hurt her. Not to mention that you're fucking LeeAnn, who hates Myla and wants to replace her in every way. I assume since you're paying me a million dollars to protect Myla, you don't want that to happen."

He's silent for several beats. "We'll postpone the photo shoot. What's happening with Myla and her sister?"

"Myla wants nothing to do with her sister," I say.

"How can you be sure?"

"My professional opinion," I say, "and I have zero indication that I'm wrong."

"You're tracking her communications?"

"I have the records I can send you, but I am curious. Why did Juan tell me her sister is FBI when she's ex-FBI?"

"FBI, ex-FBI. Semantics. And if you couldn't figure out where she is and what she is, that would be a problem."

"So you know where she is?"

"New York, married to Blake Walker, a pain in the ass, ex-ATF agent, both of whom I plan to kill when the time is right."

So Myla is right. He's setting Kara, and it seems, Blake up. "Which is when?"

"When they come for her, and they will."

"Don't you think I needed to know this?"

"Unless she tells her sister that she's alive, they won't come for her until we go public with the fashion line. I've yet to decide if you'll be around when that time comes."

"Well since my contract ends before that date, I'll be gone."

"I might make it worth your while to stay."

"I might consider an offer," I counter.

"We'll talk when I get to Dallas."

"Which will be when?"

He laughs. "Do you really think I'd announce that? Just do your job. Keep my woman safe."

"About your woman," I say, that term grinding on my nerves. "I assume Juan's trusted with her?"

"Of course, Juan's trusted."

"Then he has special privileges with Myla?"

"What does that mean?"

"She's afraid of him. I think he's touched her and he tried to get her alone today, but I didn't let it happen. I don't want to interfere if you share her with him."

"No one touches her. She stays with you. Period. And if you touch her, I will cut your hands off. If you fuck her, I will shoot your dick off."

"Okay then, I think we're clear. If Juan tries, should I follow that protocol?"

"I'll deal with Juan. What do you know about the FBI nosing around my operations?"

"Aren't they always?"

"Present day and you knew what I meant."

"I'm paid to protect Myla. I know nothing about the FBI investigation of you."

"Two hundred thousand dollars says you do. Make this count. What do you know about the FBI nosing around my operations?"

"Someone close to you is talking."

"How close?"

"I always say, look to the man trying to fuck your woman, and you find your enemy."

He is silent, seconds ticking by like hours. "I'll be in touch."

The line goes dead and I dial Blake. "Alvarez knows you and Kara are married. He's planning to kill you. Go to Italy now."

"Fuck, fuck, fuck, fuck, fuck. I'll get Kara on a plane, even if I have to tie her up to do it. Are you sure he's not playing you? Does he know who you are?"

"I've been off the grid since joining Walker. He doesn't know me and Royce covered everyone's tracks when they came here. We're good. You're not."

"Be sure. Be really fucking sure."

"I just talked to the man. I'm sure."

"You talked to him?"

"I did and just go. Now." I end the call and rotate to find

Myla sitting on the bed. "You heard?"

"Of course I heard. They're leaving?"

"Yes. They're leaving. And Alvarez now trusts me and doubts Juan."

"He's smart. If he knows about Blake, he will know about the entire family."

"But he doesn't know we're here. I'm sure of it."

"He knows the FBI is looking into him, right? Is that what I heard?"

"Yes. He knows and he thinks Juan is behind it."

"He'll go underground for a few days and evaluate," she says, "and if he decides he has to stay there, he'll come for me. He'll take me with him."

"He'll come for you and I'll kill him. Then this is over."

Chapter Nineteen

MYLA

Michael Alvarez is lying on a table. He is naked. There is plastic wrap over his body. The room is wallpapered with the images of all the women he's turned into sex slaves and all the kids who overdosed on his drugs. There are more on the ceiling, so many they are overlapping each other. I am in the outfit I wore the night I met him. The shirt pink. The jeans black. The boots with tiny silver buckles. I stand over him, a knife in my hand.

"Bella," he murmurs. "Don't do this. You love me. I love you."

"I hate you," I say, looking around the room. "They hated you."
I raise the knife, waiting to feel guilt over what I am about to do, but I do not. I want him dead. The world is a better place without him. But then something happens. The image shifts and it is me naked on the table, him standing over me, holding the knife.

"You betrayed me," he says. "And know this, bella. I will kill everyone you love."

I gasp and sit up, blinking the television screen into view and an image of Dexter, holding a knife above his victim. "Easy, sweetheart," Kyle says from beside me, his voice bringing everything back to me. The living area floor. Chinese food. A Dexter marathon. Ten days of hearing nothing from Michael Alvarez. "You had a nightmare."

"No more Dexter," I say, pressing my face into my hands. "Turn it off. I just dreamed I was Dexter about to kill Alvarez, and then it reversed, and he was Dexter, about to kill me and everyone I love. How can he be this silent this long?"

He grabs the remote and turns off the TV. "You said he's done this before."

"He has, but I was always happy when he was gone. Now, I just want him to come here. I want to kill him."

"We're all fighting over that honor," he says, pulling me into his arms, my head resting on his chest, his heart thundering beneath my ear, his hand on my head. I shut my eyes and the nightmare slams into my mind: *You betrayed me,* he says. *And know this, bella. I will kill everyone you love.*

I sit up. "Kara and Blake are still in Italy, right?"

"You were with me when I talked to Blake tonight. You know they are."

"Right. Yes." I lay back down and stare into the dimly lit room.

"That's it," Kyle says, sitting up and taking me with him. "You are making yourself crazy."

"Dexter made me crazy. We've watched it every night for over a week."

"You were obsessed," he reminds me. "You wanted to watch it."

"Because you got me addicted to it."

He glances at his watch. "It's midnight. We need a plan to relax you. A hot bath. Cartoons."

"Cartoons?"

"No serial killers. Guaranteed."

"Good point."

"Or there is always my favorite distraction. Naked, wild, hot sex."

"I vote for naked, wild, hot sex."

He stands and pulls me to my feet. "A woman after my own heart." He scoops me up and starts walking toward his bedroom, despite the master suite being closer. We avoid that room, I think because it reminds us of Michael Alvarez. It does to me and I don't know why. Michael has never been here or in that bed. And hopefully he never will be.

• • •

DAY ELEVEN

Still in my pink silk robe, I'm standing at the bathroom sink flat ironing my hair when Kyle walks in, already dressed in a blue pinstriped suit and looking like sin and sex. He leans on the counter next to me. "I have something for you."

I set down my flat iron and face him, frowning as he holds up several jeweled bobby pins. "What are those?"

"A special tracking device the FBI has been working on for you," he explains. "The first two have the actual chips in them. The third is just a hair clip that you can give to the staff and tell them you want it to be a part of your accessory line. That will keep it from looking odd that you're wearing them all of the time." He indicates his watch. "I have a tracker here as well."

I take the bobby pins and fold my hand around them. "You're afraid we'll get split up."

"I'm not going to let us get split up," he promises, his hand settling on my hip. "But if we get ambushed and Alvarez is not present, we're going to have to let them take us to him." He gives me a keen look. "Are you prepared for that? Because if you—"

"I am. I can. Whatever it takes to get him."

His expression fills with what I think is admiration. "You are so very brave, Myla."

"No. I'm just pissed off. I'm angry. Whatever it takes to get him. Let's do it." I turn to the sink and slip those bobby pins into my hair, and I revel in the idea that I am now the single most dangerous person Michael Alvarez ever met.

• • •

I wake on day twenty-four of Michael's silence in Kyle's arms. Yesterday was day twenty-three. Tomorrow will be day twenty-five. I wonder if this is a test or a strategy to make us both crazy. "Do you know what I want?" Kyle asks, letting me know he's awake and knows I am as well.

Rolling around to face him, I curl my fingers on his freshly stubbled jaw. "Coffee?"

His lips curve. "Coffee is good, but I was thinking bigger."

"Pancakes again?"

"Yes and no. I want to wake up with you in my bed."

"I am in your bed."

"My real bed in New York. My apartment is only a few miles from where Kara and Blake live."

"I'm curious about your man cave. Take me there."

"I will, Myla. I am going to take you there."

I smile, and it is a smile I feel to my soul, but it fades quickly.

"What's wrong?"

"I'm afraid it won't happen. I'm afraid. I hate that I'm afraid. How can I be afraid of so much when I lived so many months without that emotion?"

"It's called waking up," Kyle says. "I've lived it after a few undercover operations. It's bittersweet pleasure. You're you again, but what you did when you weren't is still there, haunting you, sometimes clawing at your soul."

"There is something to be said for what you don't know, or let yourself realize, not being able to hurt you," I say. "It worked for me."

"But it can hurt you," he says. "It just takes you off-guard when it does, and when that happens, that's when you're broken."

I sink deeper into the pillow, not sure how I feel about that, because I am waking up, and when Michael returns, I'll be awake to live it.

• • •

On the twenty-seventh night of silence, three eves before the opening event at the store, I remember falling asleep in Kyle's arms, his heart thrumming beneath my ear. But it is not long before a fit of nightmares follow, mostly about my months with Michael Alvarez. I remember Kyle comforting me. I remember falling back to sleep. I remember the first moment of tragedy in my life.

I am in the corner of the closet, fifteen going on twenty until this moment, when I feel ten, tears streaming down my cheeks. Kara, not much older than me, is hugging me. "Shhh," she whispers. "Don't cry." The sound of my mother's scream fills the air, and I sob, but Kara covers my mouth. The memory flashes forward, to the funeral. *I am dressed in black, on my knees in front of my parents' caskets. Kara, is beside me, hugging me. "We will always have each other. Remember that, sis. We are not alone."*

I sit up straight, looking around the brightly lit room, to find Kyle missing. Throwing off the covers, I hurry through the apartment and find him in the kitchen in nothing but pajama bottoms, his chest bare, his hair a sexy, mussed up mess. His eyes light on me and then narrow with concern. "What's wrong? Aside from a night of nightmares."

"I need to talk to my sister."

"Are you sure?"

"I said what you don't know, or let yourself realize, can't hurt you, but you were right. It can and if it takes you off-guard, you are broken. If anything happens to me, and I was keeping a distance to play some role with this monster of a man, it would break her."

Understanding fills his eyes. "Now?"

"Now."

He reaches in his pocket and removes his phone, punching in a number. "I need Kara, Blake." There is a pause. "Kara," he says his gaze connecting with mine. "I have call for you."

I hear her sob from the distance and my eyes start watering. My hand shakes as I take the phone and press it to my ear. "Kara."

"Myla," she whispers. "I can't believe it's finally you."

I turn away from Kyle, walking toward the living area. "I'm sorry I haven't called. I can't explain what kind of mess my head is. I mean, it's not. I found a place to put it all, but I just...I didn't know how to be both people."

"I don't care. I am just so very ready to hug you again. And I want to ask so many questions, but I know this isn't the time."

"Not yet, but I'll tell you."

"Are you okay? How is it with Kyle?"

"He is...I am..."

"Oh no. Or, oh yes. You're in love with him."

It's not until that moment that I know the truth. "It's soon. It is but...."

"You are."

"Is that bad?"

"Are you kidding? He's the greatest guy. I love him too."

"Is that why you drugged him?"

She laughs. "Serves him right for trying to be a macho man and protect me." She goes on to tell me the story, and then all about Blake. When we hang up, I find Kyle in the shower and join him, hugging him.

"How'd it go?" he asks.

"She says you're pretty great."

"What did you say?"

"You're pretty great."

His lips curve. "I'll take that for now."

"For now?"

"There's more to come," he promises. "Wait and see."

I press my head to his chest, and let myself believe that

the "more" that is to come is good. It's not plastic, knives, and serial killers. It's my sister. It's Kyle. Maybe it's even me designing clothes. But when I get dressed, an odd sense of foreboding begins. And when I pick out my dress for the day, I choose the peach one again that zips all the way to the waist, and gives me easy access to my gun.

Fifteen minutes later, my hair pins in place, similar ones now in production, Kyle meets me at the door, his gray suit and silver tie perfection, but for just a moment his gun peeks from beneath his jacket, indicating he's left it unbuttoned. He feels it too. We take the elevator in silence, the edge of expectation in the air. Now I know why I needed to call my sister so badly. Today is the day Michael Alvarez returns. We both know it.

Chapter Twenty

KYLE

The instant we're in the Mustang, I hand Myla the scanner, rev the engine and get us on the road. "What am I feeling?" she asks when she's cleared the car. "Because all of a sudden I'm ready to crawl out of my own skin."

"The same thing I'm feeling," I say. "It's instinct. It's what made you survive this long." My cellphone rings and I glance at the caller ID. "Blake," I say, since she's so nervous, and I answer the call on speaker and set it on the console between us.

"You're on speaker with me and Myla," I answer.

"Myla," Blake says. "Nice to finally fucking be meeting you."

"Hi Blake," Myla says, laughing. "You do like the "F" word, don't you?"

"Don't tell me you're going to ride my ass like Kara on

that, because we're going to have a problem if you do. Okay, scratch that. I'm going to have a problem."

"The problem," I say, "is me and Myla are really on edge this morning and we don't know why."

"I've picked up some odd chatter that doesn't make me feel like the fucking king of the world myself today considering Royce has no idea what the hell is going on."

"Holy hell," I grind out. "Tell me the FBI hasn't gone rogue on us and set us up for a problem."

"Oh no," Myla says. "Please say no."

"Don't start fretting now, sweetheart," Blake says. "It may be nothing of consequence. I'm still working through my data here and Royce is a beast when he's pissed. He's on this. He'll bust some balls and get things in check. In the meantime, we put extra coverage on you today to be safe."

"Copy that," I say, pulling us into the parking lot of the factory. "We're here now. Keep us posted." I end the call, and maneuver us into a spot near the front door.

"If we're on edge, and Blake's hearing chatter," Myla says as I kill the engine, "that has to connect. It has to mean today is the day."

"You've always thought he'd show up for the opening of the store," I say, remembering comments she'd made over our late night dinners and TV sessions, and sticking the scanner in my jacket. "It's close. It's time to be on high alert anyway." I reach for my door handle. "Stay where you are and let me come around and get you." I exit the Mustang, scanning the parking lot, which is still mostly empty at this early hour, round the Mustang and open Myla's door.

"The longer he's gone, the more I worry that he's not going to just visit. He's going to send someone to grab me and take me to him."

"He's trusting me to protect you, and he instructed me to keep Juan away from you," I say, pausing before opening the front door. "He'd have me bring you to him."

"With ten other men holding guns on us," she says. "He won't trust you that easily."

"Relax, sweetheart," I say. "We have an army watching us."

But as confidently as I relay that message to her, I'm more than a little relieved when she steps inside the lobby, and even more so when we're inside the controlled environment of her office. "Get comfortable," I say, sitting down at the conference table and opening my MacBook. "We're going to call this room home for the day until we hear more from Royce."

"More than fine by me," she says, pulling out her sketchpad, and keying her company computer to life, only to have Barbara appear in the doorway.

"Oh good, you're here," she gushes, her cheeks as pink as the silk blouse she's wearing. "We need you in the storefront."

"Why the storefront?" I ask.

"Why?" she asks incredulously. "We're about to open to the public in a few days. We have to have everything perfect." She motions Myla forward.

"We'll be right there in a few minutes," I tell her, which earns me a glower, but encourages her departure, but not before she gives Myla a pleading look and a prod of, "Hurry please."

I shut my computer and motion Myla forward, meeting her at the door. "I just wanted to warn you that the storefront has cameras and recording devices. And stay away from the front door."

"Where will you be?" she asks as we exit into the warehouse to start our lengthy walk to the other side.

"I'll be right by your side. I just want you on high alert."

"Right," she says. "High alert."

I want to say something to comfort her, but I don't. Comfort doesn't protect her and protecting her is all that matters right now.

• • •

The instant we walk through the back door of the store, Barbara is in our path. "There you are," she says, lacing her arm with Myla's and guiding her forward, leaving me to pursue.

Keeping them close, I scan the store, the half-moon shaped register desk in the center of the space, piled with clothes, while various employees work to hang them on display racks, the front display windows stacked with boxes. Myla and Barbara, on the other hand, disappear beyond an arched entryway near the rear of the space. Following, I find them in the center of a lounge-style sitting room surrounded by a half dozen dressing rooms. Confirming there is no separate exit, I leave them to fret over what several mannequins are wearing and claim the leather chair on the wall just outside the dressing room.

It's nearly noon, and I'm still sitting there when Royce calls. "I have you on camera. I know you can't talk, so just listen. The FBI staged a raid on several low-end Alvarez targets. The raids went down over the past few nights and amounted to pretty much nothing."

"Why the fuck would they do that and not tell us?" I ask, because just listening already isn't working for me.

"I blasted them, but the plan was a good one. It makes Alvarez feel they're focused on low quality targets that do nothing to harm him, thus he can come out of hiding."

"Let's hope like hell that works."

"Blake's picked up further chatter he feels indicates it has. He believes Alvarez is on the move."

"Based on what?"

"I have no fucking clue," he says. "He was talking that hacker shit you two talk, but he says this is the first time he's ever pinned down anything he believes indicates Alvarez's possible movement. He must plan to surprise her for the grand opening."

"Too obvious," I say, choosing my words cautiously.

"What are you thinking?"

I watch the UPS man walk in the door and start chatting with Barbara. "Today. My gut says today is dangerous."

"I'll sharpen our guard and alert the FBI."

We end the call and I stand, rounding the corner to check on Myla as I have a half dozen other times since arriving to the store. She's alone in the lounge now, standing a few feet from one of the mannequins, her gaze taking in the pale pink dress it's wearing, pure pride in her expression. It's her creation, her dream that she's looking at in that moment, and I vow to make sure that Myla has her fashion line, no strings or monsters attached.

• • •

Myla and I return to her office mid-afternoon and spend the rest of the day there, but the anticipation of what might happen, and hasn't, is wearing on Myla. Come six o'clock, Myla grabs her purse from her desk and sets it on top. "I'm ready to leave." She glances over at me where I sit at the table. "This is when it will happen, right? When we leave."

I give her a slow nod. "That would be my expectation."

"Then let's leave."

As ready as she is, I give her a nod, and quickly key a message into the chatroom I have live with our surveillance team: **We're headed out the door**, receiving an immediate: **Copy that**, in return.

Shutting the lid to my computer, I stand, meeting Myla at the corner of her desk. "It's over after this. Remember that."

"I do," she says, her chin bravely lifting. "And I have never wanted something as badly as I do this moment, other than his death."

"I want to kiss you right now," I say softly.

"I'll taste better when he is no longer on my lips."

I don't tell her that he isn't because she is the one who has endured his torture, much of which I haven't asked her to talk about. One day, maybe she will, but that day will be easier if he is no longer a threat. "Remember your gun," I say, before giving her space, and she doesn't hesitate. She moves forward, but instead of exiting the office, she pauses by the door and stares at the photos on her wall of her mother. I step behind her, close but not touching her, silently letting her know I am right here with her.

"I hate that he used her like this," she whispers, expressing what I've always thought but not said, but she doesn't give me time to reply. Her spine straightens just a little more, and she steps forward, sureness in her pace that tells me those photos have destroyed her fear and enraged her anger. I step to her side in the lobby, the receptionist's desk already shut down for the night.

We exit the building into an exceptionally humid March Texas night, and I stay close to Myla again, our shoulders all but brushing, surveying the area for trouble, which is nowhere in sight. She slides into her seat, and I seal her inside, and in a matter of a few seconds, I'm inside with her, doors locked, while I shove my computer under the seat. Automatically now, she grabs the scanner and checks the car, her task complete by the time we're out of the parking lot.

"Maybe he's waiting at the hotel," she says, clearly remaining as certain as I am that tonight is the night, while my gut says an ambush is headed in our direction.

"We're not back there yet," I say. "And we'll know if he's in the room or the hotel."

She doesn't reply and I eye the rearview mirror, spying the car I know Asher is in, now in our line of sight. I'm also aware that Royce and Jacob are at the hotel, waiting on us, and watching for trouble. Five minutes passes slowly, and we arrive at the Ritz without incident. I pull into the garage, driving to our normal spot and parking. I reach under my seat for my computer, but instinct has me thinking better, leaving it under my seat and my hands free.

"I'll come around and get you," I say, unbuttoning my jacket and preparing to pull my weapon.

"I just want out and to get inside," she counters. "I'm getting out with you." She glances at me. "Okay?"

I give her a nod and we open our doors, meeting at the trunk. We never get the chance to take a step further. A black sedan backs out of a parking spot, pulls in front of us, parks, and two men get out, pointing guns at us, one of them Juan. At the same time, two men get out of another parked car and aim their guns at us.

"Alvarez requests your company," Juan says, a smirk on his lizard thin lips.

I take Myla's arm and pull her to me. "She's not going anywhere without me."

"You're in luck," he says. "You're both invited."

It's a small piece of the puzzle that goes in our direction, unless Juan intends to kill me. "We'll follow you," I say, clicking the locks to the Mustang to allow Myla to get inside.

"That's not happening," Juan says.

"We're not riding in a car with two people," I say. "One driver only."

He wants to refuse. I see it in the glint of his eyes and the set of his jaw, but the hesitation tells me Alvarez is really behind this not him and Alvarez wants me with her. He leans inside the car and speaks to the driver then shuts his door, with him on the outside. He then motions two men toward us. "You ride alone, but only after we search you for wires and tracking devices."

"No one is touching Myla," I say, pulling my weapon and shackling her arm. "And I'm not giving up my gun. Not when I spoke to Alvarez personally, and was to protect her. No matter what that requires."

Juan's eyes glint hard but he spits Spanish at the men and all but one backs off. "He gets her purse and both of your phones."

"We'll leave them in the car," I say, clicking my locks, but really, nothing on my phone is traceable. I just want him to feel he wins when he refuses.

And predictably he does. "This isn't up for negotiation," he says. "You give them to my man. You have them back later."

I hesitate long enough to make it seem like I care. "Give me your purse, Myla," I say, taking it from her, and handing it to the man, who snatches it from my hand. I reach for my phone, but the man yells at me in Spanish, telling me to put my hands to my side. I step away from Myla, doing as ordered, my gun still in my hand. "Right pocket," I say, but of course, he not only grabs my phone, but searches me for a second one, that I don't have.

The minute he's done and steps toward Myla, I grab her arm pull her to me, my gun aimed at him. "Try it. Please."

Juan orders the man to back off, and then glares at me. "Get in the fucking car."

"Let's go," I murmur to Myla, holding onto her and helping her into the back seat of the car, with me instantly beside her.

The driver eyes me in the mirror and I lean forward, indicating my gun I have yet to holster. "Where are we going?"

"I'm following another car. I have no idea."

It's a smart reply that may or may not be true, but gives me no room to argue. I lean back in the seat, reluctantly holstering my weapon, as the car starts to move. I don't look at Myla, nor does she me. We just endure the ride, and it doesn't take long for me to figure out why Juan didn't push to search us. Not only are we sandwiched between two cars, we're headed to a small airport outside the city, and once we're in the air, any such device will be inactive. No one will be able to find us. We have to hope like hell that Alvarez is on that plane, and we never leave the ground.

I know the minute Myla realizes the same, her fingers curling on her lap, then sliding down to the seat where she discreetly presses her hand to my leg, like touching me comforts her, like she needs to reassure herself I'm here. And holy hell, I want to grab her and hold her, and it hits me that there are things I need to say to her in case anything goes wrong. Somehow, some way, I have to find that moment, and make it happen.

We pull into the private airfield, and Myla leans closer to the driver. "Is Michael here? Is he in the plane?"

"I have no idea," the driver claims. "I just drive."

And he does, straight onto the airfield where a large private jet awaits us, the car in front of us halting, as we do the same, followed by the sedan behind us. Our driver gets out of the car and knowing we may not survive this, I gamble there's no bug, turning to Myla, and discreetly grabbing her hand. "I need to tell you something."

"I'm nervous," she says. "I don't know if I can still fake it with him anymore. I've been away from him and—"

"You can. You will. And this is not how I wanted to tell you this, but I love you. I am so fucking in love with you. I think I was even before I met you, as crazy as that sounds even to me."

"Why are you saying this now? Stop staying it like it's goodbye. It's not goodbye."

The door opens behind her, forcing me to let go of her hand, and she mouths, "I love you, too," before she rotates to exit the car. I stay with her, ready to grab her if necessary. Hell, I just go ahead and do it.

I step to her side and shackle her arm, while Juan appears in front of us. "Inside the plane," he orders.

"Is Michael here?" Myla asks eagerly.

"Go inside and find out," Juan says, a snide taunt to his voice, his eyes meeting mine, a challenge in their depths I plan to counter with a bullet between his eyes.

My hand goes to my gun. "She's not getting on that plane until I talk to Alvarez."

"Do you really think you can resist at this point?"

"Do you really want to risk her getting hurt in the struggle?"

His thin lips get thinner and he pulls his phone from his pocket, punching in a number and then listening a moment. "He wants to talk to you." Juan hands me the cellphone.

"Kyle here," I say.

"Had you let her get on that plane without contacting me," Alvarez says. "I would have killed you."

"Why am I taking orders from Juan?"

"I have plans for him," he says. "Don't worry about him."

"I seem to remember we discussed the opposite."

"That order stands."

"So I do need to worry about him?" I ask, looking directly at Juan, and making damn sure he knows we're talking about him.

"Keep her close and him at a distance."

"You realize what a conflicting message that is?"

"That message will become crystal clear in about four hours. Let me talk to Myla."

"Where are we going?"

"I repeat. Let me talk to Myla."

I hand the phone to Myla. She presses it to her ear, her

gaze going to Juan, who's staring at her, which prompts her to give him her back. "Where have you been?" she asks, eager. "I was worried." She is silent for several beats. "Yes. I'm glad. See you soon." She rotates forward again and hands me the phone. "He hung up."

Juan reaches for it, yanking it from my hand. "Angry much?" I ask, with an arched brow.

"Just get in the damn plane."

I shackle Myla's arm and we start walking, two men, one of which is Ricardo, flanking us. Myla walks up the stairs first, with me on her heels, and I can tell she is unsteady, anticipating Alvarez might have tricked us and be inside, while I'm preparing to reach for my gun and kill him. Myla enters the plane, with me there immediately after. She turns to look at me, giving me a shake of her head, telling me Alvarez is not here.

I glance over her shoulder, eyeing several rows of leather seats. "All the way to the back," I instruct.

"Myla, you're up here with me," Juan says, appearing in the walkway.

"That's not happening," I say, motioning for her to get moving.

Juan's hand comes down on my arm, and I pull my gun, pointing it at him. "Touch me again and you're dead."

Ricardo is suddenly beside him, pointing his weapon at me as well. Myla steps to my side. "Michael hired him. He wants him alive. Pilot! Call Michael."

"Don't call anyone," Juan calls out. "Holster your damn weapon, Ricardo." Juan lifts his chin at me. "Go take your fucking seat." Ricardo lowers his weapon, moving to sit down.

"Go sit, Myla," I order softly, lowering my Glock.

"She's protective of you," Juan observes. "Michael isn't going to like that."

"Is that a threat?"

"I don't need to threaten you. Not when Myla is this close to you." He walks to his seat and claims it.

I back away, moving down the aisle with my gun at my side, re-holstering only when I'm sitting next to Myla in the seat at the back of the plane. "Sig island, right off Long Island," she says. "That's where we're going."

I hold up a hand, silencing her, certain we are being recorded and maybe even filmed. She inhales and sinks into the leather of her chair. I do the same, hoping like hell our team heard her tell them our destination. That is the question we'll both be asking for the next four hours in the air.

Chapter Twenty-One

KYLE

Hours of sitting next to Myla, wanting to touch her, wanting to talk to her, pretty much kills me. I manage to randomly touch her, though, trying to send her the message that we're together. We're okay. The plane finally starts to descend, and she takes off her seat belt. "Bathroom," she says, standing and heading toward the back of the plane.

I follow, knowing this is one of the only locations where I can talk to her, and even if it's bugged, we're at the end of this trip, and it's worth the risk. She enters the tiny room, and I catch the door before she closes it.

"Easy, sweetheart," I say, and noting how pale she is, I add, "We're okay. This is all going to happen hard and fast but when it's over, it's over."

"You can't know that. We can't know our people heard our destination."

"They did," I insist, "which means they're in place, and ready to attack the minute we land."

"Everyone is in Texas."

"Luke, and many of our men, are in New York, not to mention plenty of Feds."

"It's an island," she says. "How do they get to us?"

"Water and air," I say, though it's a problem I too have been concerned about during our travels, but I'm not about to tell her that. "Find your zone," I say, "and let's get ready to end this." I shut the door, standing guard and giving her time.

It's not long before she appears again and gives me a nod, the look in her eyes, stronger now. "I'm ready," she says, and I believe her. She is. We are.

I let her see the admiration in my eyes, and the love, stepping out of her way to allow her to return to her seat, with me closely behind her, both of us reclaiming our seats. It's not even ten minutes later when we make our landing approach, near midnight if our destination is indeed an island in New York, when we approach a singular runway and tower, that seems to make that a pretty acute assumption. The fact that we hit the pavement, and top pretty damn hard and fast, also indicating an island and water, or that's my guess.

I unhook my belt, and Myla does the same, clearly as eager as I am to get out of this metal box, that makes us sitting ducks. "Stay behind me," I order softly, standing and waiting for her to join me, before I start down the aisle, my hand settling under my jacket to rest on my gun.

Juan stands, moving around in the front of the plane, as does Ricardo, and a couple of other men who've come along for the ride. Two of them line up to exit, but they're pushed back when a stocky, short Mexican with a permanent scowl on his face and a machine gun at his hip, enters, pointing for them to sit. Whoever he is, they obey, and when I stop walking, the man motions me forward, as if he knows who I am, or simply wants me under his thumb.

There is a shift in the air then, a prickling at the back of my neck, moments before it happens. The ghost of a man I've seen pictures of but have never met enters the plane. He stands in the center of the aisle, his black suit expensive, his salt-and-pepper hair wavy and longish, and when his eyes meet mine, evil radiates from their depths that is like nothing I've ever felt, which is saying a lot considering the filth I've arrested and killed. His gaze shifts to the gun at my hand, a silent command that I take my hand off my weapon, and it kills me to obey, but that machine gun-wielding man beside him will shoot me, and then Myla will be on her own.

I continue forward, my body sheltering Myla's, dread in me for the moment I will have to let her go to him, and I will. I may even have to let her walk off this plane with him, and I hope like hell my team is waiting when they do. I stop several feet in front of him, Juan, Ricardo and the other men in the seats dividing me from Alvarez.

"Finally we meet, Kyle," he says. "I owe you money and appreciation for caring for my woman. We will discuss our arrangements later, but as you can understand, I'm eager for you to allow Myla to pass. She's safe now, though we will certainly discuss your services for her return trip to Dallas."

Every muscle in my body fights this moment, but somehow, I rotate to let Myla pass.

"Michael," she gushes, playing her role, and hurrying past me into his arms. His hand flattens on her back, and I can almost feel her skin crawling with his touch, but he does not hold her for long. He grips her arms and looks down at her. "We need to discuss something before we retire for the night."

"What is it?" she asks, sounding nervous, while I step just a little closer, my hand itching for my gun.

"Is it true that Juan touched you?"

"What?"

"Is it true that Juan touched you?"

"He...I...."

"Then it's true," he assumes.

"He said he'd tell you I invited it, but I swear—"

"I believe you."

Juan moves into the lane just in front of me at the same moment that Alvarez sets Myla aside. She flattens on the wall behind her, and the machine gun guy is watching me, keeping me from offering her any comfort. "She's lying," Juan claims. "She tried to fuck me to get her freedom."

"And you wouldn't tell me?"

"I didn't want to upset you."

"That never happened," Myla says. "Never, ever, would I do that."

Juan goes for the gun at his hip, and afraid for Myla, I step to him and cover it with my hand. It's at that moment that Alvarez grabs Juan's shoulder, and then the unexpected happens. He shoots him in the cock. Juan screams, a horrific, pained sound, then falls against me, the small lane I'm in making it almost impossible to see around him, while I can think of only one thing. Getting to Myla.

I rotate his body, bringing Alvarez into profile, Myla out of my eyeshot. Juan's screams go silent, and I shove him to the ground, while Alvarez holsters his weapon and grabs Myla's arm.

"A car is waiting on you outside, Kyle. We'll talk tomorrow." He moves toward the exit, and I take a step toward Myla, but the machine gun guy exits in front of me.

I follow him, my hand back on my gun, but as soon as the machine gun guy clears the stairs, two armed guards step into my path. My gaze reaches beyond them, to where Alvarez is leading Myla across the runway toward a black sedan, but I can't get to her without ending up dead. "Alvarez!" I call out, trying to buy us time.

That's when the first explosion happens, shaking the ground around us, and part of the runway goes up in flames. The guy with the machine gun and the guards rotate, looking for the source. The two men in front of me do the same. Another explosion goes off, and men swarm the runway, some in FBI jackets, others in military gear. Smoke is everywhere, and I run in the direction Myla should be, hearing a helicopter coming in low that I pray is one of ours. I clear the haze, and holy fucking hell. Alvarez is climbing onto the chopper, and pulling Myla onto it with him. I run for it, burning every muscle I own, but it's too late. They lift off.

• • •

MYLA

I fight Michael when he pulls me to the chopper, but he is too strong. "What is wrong with you?" he demands. "Did you betray me? Is that it? Did you bring this raid on me?

"I did nothing of the sort, but they will shoot us down. We have to land."

"We are in the air," he says. "Calm down and we will be fine." He shoves me into a seat and turns to talk to the pilot, and I know then that I have seconds to act.

I unzip my dress, and I waste no time, pulling out my gun. He turns back around and I shout over the engines. "Tell him to land."

"We aren't landing. Put the gun down."

"Land the chopper!"

He takes a step toward me, more like a lunge, and I shoot him, not once, but three times. He falls, not forward, but out of the door. I rush forward to the pilot and hold a gun on him. "Turn around and land."

"You can't kill me," he says. "You need me."

"I can shoot your leg," I say. "You don't need that to land. I killed Alvarez, so if you think I won't—"

"I'm landing, you little bitch." He turns us and we've gone such a short way that we are quickly coming in low on the runway, and we are not even on the ground when the FBI swarms us. I rush to the door and Kyle grabs me, pulling me into his arms.

"Thank God," he says, against my hair. "Thank God. You have no idea how scared I was for you."

"I killed him. I killed Alvarez."

He takes my gun. "I know you did. We saw him fall but I had a moment when I thought it was you that will give me nightmares for the rest of my life." He kisses me, another helicopter coming in low. "That's our ride out of here. Come on."

• • •

KYLE

Myla starts to shake when we get in the air, in shock, but with good reason. She's been through hell and back. But the ride is short and we land at a private airstrip off Long Island, where there's a surprise waiting on her that even I didn't know about until minutes ago. I get her the heck off the chopper, and Luke rushes forward, offering her a warm blanket, which I wrap around her shoulders.

"Myla, I'm Luke," he says. "You kicked ass today and you're safe now."

"You look like Royce," she says, her teeth chattering.

"But better looking, right?"

She laughs, but it's a choked sound. "Yes," she says, "but I'm going to tell him the same thing."

Luke laughs now too, and looks at me. "You're fueled up and ready to go."

"Thanks, man."

"We'll see you both back stateside." He steps around us and we start for the plane.

"Where are we going exactly?" Myla asks as we approach the plane.

"Out of the country until we're sure everything with Alvarez is cleaned up." I motion for her to head up the narrow stairs and follow her up.

She rounds the corner into the plane and it's Kara's screech of joy that tells me the surprise is now revealed. I enter just in time to find the two sisters clinging to each other, tears flowing, the two of them settling into seats just inside the door. I move past them and Blake greets me, his hands on the luggage bins, mine on the seats on either side of us. "Fuck, man," he says, sounding emotional. "I can't believe he's dead. I feel...I don't know what the fuck I feel."

I flash back to Blake holding Whitney, rocking her in a pool of her own blood, and I know this moment is surreal for him, "It's over," I say, "and as pissed off as I am that you came back to the States and didn't tell me, I'm glad you're here now. Italy will be good for Myla. She needs a safe escape to heal. And she needs time with Kara."

"You and Myla—"

"I love her, so if you're going to lecture me..."

"No, man. Just don't hurt her. Then I'll have to pull your fucking balls out through your throat."

"Kyle."

At the sound of Myla's voice, I turn and she hugs me. Kara's standing behind her, and when her eyes meet mine, there are tears of thanks in them. I give her a nod and bury my face in Myla's hair, holding onto her and planning to never let go.

• • •

MYLA

We arrive in Italy to discover that seventy women were saved through our efforts from various parts of the United States and Mexico. It's balm to my soul, but not the entire cure. It seems there is a process I must endure, and my detox begins. It's as if Michael was a poison my body and mind are rejecting. There are nightmares and bad memories, but Kyle is there for me at every turn, as is my sister, and even Blake, who becomes like a big brother. And then there is Ella, who Blake and Kara were hired to find, but she's another story. I have moments when I worry that I have no job or money, but between Kyle, my sister, and Blake, I end up with a sketchpad in my hand and they force me to design again. Royce takes the lead with the FBI to get all my designs back, but it's like all such things. Time will tell. It's healing and so is just getting to explore the Italian fashion world.

Three months pass and Kyle asks me to live with him in New York. How could I say no? I have two best friends now. Him and my sister.

We arrive on a hot June afternoon, our taxi pulling up to the high rise tower near Central Park. A doorman takes our luggage, and is even delivering it to the tenth floor, where I'm pretty excited to realize I now live with him. His arm drapes my shoulders and he guides me toward the sliding glass doors. "I can't wait to see the apartment you chose for yourself," I say.

Kyle's hip is pressed to mine, his faded jeans hugging his powerful thighs the same way his "Italy" t-shirt hugs his defined upper body.

"Just remember we can redecorate," he says as we enter the lobby, the cool air washing over me, seeing the fancy art deco paintings on the wall, and thinking suddenly that my sparkly black flat sandals aren't enough to dress up my own jeans and t-shirt.

"I need to make a stop here on the lower level," he says, angling us down a hallway, and into what appears to be a retail area. "We have shopping right here in the building?" I ask, eager to dive into the New York fashion world and find out where I can take my designs.

Kyle stops at a closed door in between two stores, and I figure it must be some sort of storage area. He opens it and motions for me to go inside. "Is there a light?" I ask, stepping into the darkness.

"Surprise!"

The light flips on and every one of the Walker clan, an extended clan I've met at some point in person, or by Skype, are in a vacant retail store. There's at least twenty people. Not only are they here, but so are all the mannequins from the Alvarez store sitting around the room, with my designs on them. I turn to Kyle. "What is happening?"

"I bought the store for you," he says. "And Barbara wants to come and work for you if you want her. I didn't promise her anything. We can plan a launch and—"

I push to my toes and kiss him, while the room erupts in cheers. "You are amazing, Kyle. So good to me."

"Does that mean you'll marry me?"

"What?"

He goes down on one knee and presents me with a box he opens. It contains the most stunning oval-shaped diamond I've ever seen. "Marry me, Myla."

"Yes," I say. "Yes."

He slips the ring on my finger and stands, his hands cupping my cheeks, his lips finding mine as the room once again erupts in cheers. "I love you, Myla."

"I love you too," I whisper.

"I'm going to interrupt," Royce calls out.

"Because why wouldn't you fucking interrupt," Blake adds. "That's what family is for."

Kyle and I laugh and he slides his arm over my shoulder,

turning me toward the room. Royce is standing directly across from us with his wife Lauren, a pretty petite brunette, next to him. "Some of you know that Lauren and I tried to start a family last year," he says, "and it didn't go as well as we'd hoped. We waited a while to try again. And we didn't want to say anything until we were sure it was going to work out this time."

"We're four months pregnant!" Lauren shouts.

More cheers erupt and before I know it, I'm being hugged left and right, but of course, Kara is the first, with Blake following. Asher and Jacob, are here too, and even more Walker Security men are present.

"I love fashion," Julie, Luke's wife, tells me, when we finally get some time to chat. "I'd love to help you launch the store. If you don't mind?"

"I'd love help," I say.

"Can you design baby clothes?" Lauren asks, joining us.

"I would love to design for the first little Walker baby," I say.

"And we can help with the wedding," Julie offers.

Kyle steps to my side and takes my hand. "I'm stealing my future wife," he says, leading me to a private office, shutting the door and pulling me close. "How do you feel?"

"Happy," I say. "When I never thought I'd be happy again."

THE END...

AND COMING LATE 2016 IN THE WALKER SECURITY SERIES

BOOK 2:
Pulled Under
(ASHER'S STORY)

In order to be alerted to the ebook pre-order please text:
LRJones to 313131
This will also serve as future communications for my
upcoming releases and INSIDE OUT TV news!

THE TALL, DARK AND DEADLY SERIES

Book 1: Hot Secrets (Royce's story)
Book 2: Dangerous Secrets (Luke's story)
Book 3: Beneath the Secrets (Blake's story)

THE WALKER SECURITY SERIES

Book 1: Deep Under (Kyle's story) – available now
Book 2: Pulled Under (Asher's story) – coming late 2016
Book 3: Falling Under (Jacob's story) – TBD

Want more BLAKE WALKER? Read the INSIDE OUT series in which he is a very prominent character and his brothers make an appearance too!

The INSIDE OUT series is now in development for television with producer Suzanne Todd (Alice in Wonderland, Must Love Dogs, Austin Powers, The Boiler Room, and more)

STAY TUNED TO LISA'S WEBSITE FOR UPDATES ON THE TV SHOW!

www.lisareneejones.com

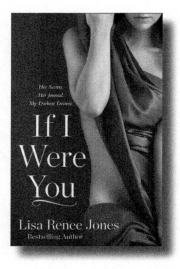

Her Secrets.
Her Journal.
My Darkest Desires.

If I Were You

Lisa Renee Jones
Bestselling Author

Start the INSIDE OUT series with IF I WERE YOU.

Available now!

*He is dark passion and sweet
obsession...Her journal.
My darkest desires. I was looking
for her and I found him.*

A journal comes to Sara McMillan by chance, when she unexpectedly inherits the key to an abandoned storage locker belonging to a woman named Rebecca. Sara can't resist peeking at the entries inside...and finds a scintillating account of Rebecca's affair with an unnamed lover, a relationship drenched in ecstasy and wrapped in dark secrets.

Obsessed with discovering Rebecca's destiny after the entries come to an abrupt end, Sara does more than observe the players in the woman's life; she immerses herself in the high-stakes art gallery world Rebecca inhabited—and is magnetically drawn to two men. Both will want to possess her but only one -- the dark, mysteriously sexy, Chris Merit, will win her heart. But where is Rebecca? And is Sara trusting the wrong man?

Visit www.lisareneejones.com for more information

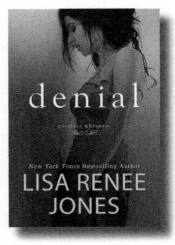

Ella Ferguson awakes alone in Italy, unsure of who she is, and a gorgeous man has claimed her as his own. He's tall, dark, and sexy, with money and power, the kind of man who makes a girl want to be possessed. And he does possess her, whispering wicked wonderful promises to her, stealing her trust and her heart. Soon though, the past finds her, yanking her from a cocoon of passion and safety. Everything is not how it seems. The truth will shatter her world, but it can set her free, if it doesn't destroy her first.

ALSO BY LISA RENEE JONES

The Inside Out Series
If I Were You
Being Me
Revealing Us
*His Secrets**
Rebecca's Lost Journals
*The Master Undone**
*My Hunger**
No In Between
*My Control**
I Belong to You
*All of Me**

The Secret Life of Amy Bensen
Escaping Reality
Infinite Possibilities
Forsaken
*Unbroken**

Careless Whispers
Denial
Demand (May 2016)
Surrender (December 2016)

Dirty Money
Hard Rules (August 2016)
More information coming soon…

*eBook only

Missed Royce's book – HOT SECRETS?

GET A SNEAK PEEK!

"You're not alone now," he said softly, brushing his fingers down her cheek, sending a tingle of electricity through her body. "I'm here and no one is going to scare me away."

"Have you met my father?"

He laughed. "Not even your father."

"We'll see about that one."

"Yeah," he said. "We will. I'm not going anywhere unless you make me." He turned to his side to face her. "I know I said this before, but I'm going to say it again. I'm not here because of the threats. If they didn't exist, I'd still be here, if you'd have me. I'm here for you, Lauren. I'm here because there is something about you I can't escape, and I don't even want to try."

The rain pelted against the windows, the fire crackled in the fireplace. Electricity sparked in the air, intimacy thickening with it.

"I'm glad you're here, and not because of the threats."

She hesitated. "Okay, maybe I'm a little glad you're here because of the threats. I'm rattled, Royce. I don't know why; it's not like me, but I am. And I wouldn't tell anyone else that, but I am. And I feel like I can tell you that without it becoming everyone else's knowledge."

"You know what I think?" he asked, lowering his head slowly, his breath warm, teasing her with the promise of intimacy. "I think you need something else to think about." His lips touched hers, a soft caress that traveled her nerve endings. Her nipples tightened, and heat pooled low in her belly.

Nerves fluttered in her stomach, with the awareness of where this was going, but his tongue, his hands, his touch, drew her deeper into the fog of desire. She lost herself in the moment, savoring the feel on him, a soft sound of pleasure escaping her lips as his tongue swept against hers. He deepened the contact and she wrapped her arms around his neck. His hand traveled her back, scorching her with heat, melding her closer. She could feel the desire expand between them, consume them, and leave her with only him.

Royce pulled Lauren into his lap to straddle him, the V of her body pressing against the thick ridge of his erection. He wanted this woman, wanted her like he had not wanted in a very long time. Wanted in a way like he'd never wanted. Her hair was soft on his face, and that damn vanilla and honey scent was driving him wild. So much of what she had told him had twisted him in knots. Her ex cheating on her explained the insecurity he'd seen in her, the fear of intimacy.

He drank her in, kissing her, making love to her with his tongue, and vowing to be the man who showed her just how sexy she truly was.

"You're beautiful," he murmured against her mouth. "And your ex was a fool."

"Royce, I—"

He swallowed her words, working his hands under her shirt to her soft skin, not allowing her to reject his words, showing her how much he meant them. She reached behind him and tugged loose his hair, twining her fingers into it. Her touch was like silk and fire at the same time, soothing him even as she ignited his hunger. He touched her, filled his hands with her high, full breasts and shoved down her bra to tease her plump nipples.

She shifted on top of him, arching against his cock, and he moaned with the ache and pleasure that crashed into him. He tugged at her shirt. "Take it off."

She leaned back and stared down at him, and he saw vulnerability wash over her face. He wrapped his fingers around her neck and pulled her mouth to his. "You. Are. Beautiful. And I want to feel you next to me." He reached over his head and tugged his shirt off, trying to make her feel more comfortable by undressing first.

Her gaze swept his chest, her teeth sinking into her bottom lip. "You're beautiful," she said, her hands splaying over his pecs, his arms.

He kissed her, hard and fast, caressing her sides, her breasts, before easing her shirt up again. "Take it off. Let me feel you next to me."

She pulled it over her head and tossed it and he cupped her breasts, teasing her nipples even as he unhooked the front clasp of her bra.

Her lashes fluttered, her hands covering his. He rolled her to the ground and eased her legs apart, settling his hips between her legs and going down on top of her.

Their eyes locked and held, the connection, the desire he felt with Lauren, expanding inside him, feeding a possessive need to pleasure her, to protect her, to hold her. He kissed her, trailed lips down her neck, taking his time...

Visit www.lisareneejones.com
for more information on HOT SECRETS
– available now!

Excerpt from Luke Walker's book
– DANGEROUS SECRETS –
available now!

Luke Walker watched the only woman who'd ever rocked his world sashaying her sexy little behind toward the plane, remembering another goodbye, and wondering if she was remembering it too. It had been two years ago and he'd been headed back to active duty after a month off and in her arms. She'd taken him to the airport, even walked with him inside. They'd stopped at security and stared at one another, long seconds of silence heavy between them, and he'd been unsure what to say. Their time together had been a short-term thing. They'd both been clear about that, no strings, no tomorrows, but he didn't want it to end. He squeezed his eyes shut, reliving the past.

Julie leaned into him, her hands on his chest, scorching his skin through his shirt. She pressed to her toes and brushed her lips over his and it was all he could do not to kiss her like it was his last kiss in this lifetime. "Don't die, soldier," she whispered. "The world needs more men like you, not less."

He'd wrapped his arms around her and held her close.

"And you? What do you need?"

She blinked up at him and he saw the uncertainty in her face for an instant. "One last kiss," she said, her mouth finding his again for a feather light kiss that was over too soon. She pushed out of his arms and turned away, half-running toward the exit. Regret and disappointment filled him.

Luke scrubbed the tension at back of his neck. As time had ticked on, one thing about that day had replayed over and over in his mind. There had been no goodbye.

An announcement sounded over the intercom, snapping Luke back to the present. His flight was cancelled. The doors to Julie's plane hadn't closed. He had a gut feeling she wasn't going anywhere either.

He walked to the counter and found the attendant. "Is this flight going to take off?"

She sighed. "They're trying to get clearance but it's not looking good."

"If they don't, since you put them on the plane, will you put them up in a hotel for the night?"

"We won't pay for the room since weather is an act of God," she said, "but we'll get them to a reserved room if they want it."

"Which hotel?"

"The Royal Blue," she said. "If you're thinking about staying there, I'm not sure that will be possible. The airline reserved a large block of rooms. You should check around quickly before everyone is sold out."

"Understood," Luke said. "Thank you." He turned away and started walking. The airline wasn't the only one with a Royal Blue contract. Airport administration and security had one as well, and he had a security clearance badge that gave him priority reservations. He was headed to the Royal Blue and he wasn't giving Julie a chance to run away to a different hotel.

He'd see her when she arrived.

Visit www.lisareneejones.com for more information on DANGEROUS SECRETS – available now!

And now our favorite bad boy,
BLAKE WALKER, from his book
BENEATH THE SECRETS
– available now!

Blake shut the door behind him, sauntering into the room to find her tossing her purse and briefcase on the typical luxury room high back chair by the window. He shrugged out of his leather jacket and tossed it on the king sized bed separating them. "You have my money?"

"I'll need to review the file."

He crossed the room, stopping at the desk and pulled the chair out, putting them within a few steps of each other. Blake opened the drawer and removed the file, setting it on top of the desk. He tapped the top of it. "Now you show me yours. Full exposure at the same time."

Her lashes lowered, and he could almost hear her thinking about her next move, before her brown eyes met his and for just an instant he saw trepidation in her eyes. She blinked and it was gone, but he'd seen it, recognized it for the hesitation and fear that it was, and silently cursed. Holy hell. He was her first gig like this. She wasn't even sure this was where she belonged but something made her desperate enough to do this. Fuck me. He was going to try and save her.

"All right," she said, and she reached for her briefcase but instead of removing the file, she carried it with her towards him. She stopped at the chair and set it down, but didn't reach for the file. Instead, she stepped around the chair, close to him.

Blake didn't wait for her to act. He pulled her to him, and maneuvered her against the wall. "Why are you here?"

"I thought we were pretty clear on that point?"

"I'm not." He pressed one hand to the wall beside her, his body framing hers but not touching it. He wanted this woman, but if he could scare her the hell out of this room without touching her, it would be in her best interest. "Spell it out."

"I have something you want. You have something I want."

His body responded to that tease, his cock thickening against his jeans. "And yet you're in my room, alone with me. You have to know that's asking for more than a simple exchange."

"It's as simple as it gets. You brought my boss a file. If I like what's inside it, I'm to make sure you're rewarded. So I suggest you show me your file, Mr. Wright. Otherwise, you won't be getting anything."

She delivered the seductive promise with such Grande that he almost—almost—believed he'd been wrong about her, but not quite. "You don't have to do this, you know?"

"You're right," she said. "I don't. I can walk out of here with my envelope and leave you with yours. I just choose not to."

"What is it he's promised you to make you willing to sell

your soul and your body for him?"

Her hand slid to his chest. "I have a choice." She leaned into him and pressed her lips to his. She tasted like the same tangerine of her lipstick, sweet and tangy, tempting.

He didn't respond at first, thinking through what came next, what he should do. She was inside Alvarez's operation. He had no reason to trust her, or help her, and he wanted her more than he remembered wanting anyone in a very long time. So, why was he hesitating to take what she offered?

With a low growl, he slid his hand to her back and called her bluff. If he was right about her, he'd scare the shit out of her and have one hell of a cold shower afterwards. His mouth slanted over hers, tongue delving past her teeth, hand settling on her back, molding her soft curves to his hard body.

She melted against him, a soft moan sliding from her throat, her arms wrapping around his neck. Holy hell, he thought again. He could make love to this woman. Make her feel soft, sexy, and pleasured, and enjoy every damn second of it, seduce her into helping him. They had chemistry and attraction that would make this easy to blow off as a hot night that wasn't as dangerous as it was for her future. But that wouldn't save her, and she needed to be saved. He didn't know why he knew this, but he did. The only way to help her was to scare the living shit out of her. To take her places she wouldn't want to go and force her to see that this wasn't where she belonged. That meant this was going someplace down and dirty, and hard and gritty.

His hand caressed over her side and upward, until he palmed her full, high breast, his fingers finding the already stiff peak of her nipple under the soft silk of her dress and, surprisingly, barely there bra. She arched into his touch rather than pulling away and he knew this was where he set the stakes higher. Where he pushed her.

He set her back from him, his eyes meeting hers, searching her face, searching her lovely, passion filled face, and damn it, he wanted her to stay all soft and wanting, just like she was now. But in all good conscience, and he hated he still had one, he couldn't let that happen.

Blake backed away and sat on the edge of the bed, and damn she looked sexy with her hair down. "Take off your clothes."

She blinked at him, and her creamy ivory skin paled even further, but she recovered quickly, drawing in a breath and reaching for the zipper running up the front of her dress. His blood thundered in his ears like he was some kind of randy teenager who hadn't seen plenty of hot woman, and hot flesh, before. What the hell was it about this woman that set off a firestorm inside him? But he knew. His gut twisted with just how well he knew. She was gorgeous, out of her element, and she needed to be saved. Like someone else he'd failed to save. And damn it to hell, he thought he had enough distance from this to be calculated and cold, to finish this once and for all.

The dress shimmered down his new temptation's hips and fell to the ground, leaving her wearing a cream-colored bra and panties set with little diamond sparkles, thigh-highs and heels. He drew in a heavy breath, reeling in the desire he knew he had to control. There was so much more on the line than sex, mostly for her.

She reached for her bra and he moved quickly, surprising her, and shackling her wrist. She was flat on the mattress, and beneath him in an instant, one of his legs between hers, because both would have been too much to bear. As it was, that scent of hers, all sweet and flowery, was like fire licking at his limbs. And his cock, which was against her hip, throbbed with the promise of how close he was to the also sweet V of her legs.

"You don't have to do this," he told her.

"I thought we already covered this?"

"Not well enough. You aren't too far gone to turn back."

"This coming from a man who has me almost naked in a hotel bed with him?"

"Almost, sweetheart. I didn't think you'd have the courage to really strip for me. Whatever it is you think working for this guy will fix, it won't. What do you need? Money? I'll give you money if you promise to walk away from this and never look back."

"So I'll work for you instead of him?"

"No strings. You never have to see me again."

"Are you seriously trying to save me?" she asked.

"Yes. I am."

She studied him a long moment before her fingers curled on his cheek, the simple, delicate touch, sending a rippling sensation through his body. "You know what they say about those who try too hard to save other people?" She didn't wait for a reply. "They say they need saving themselves."

His hand slid to hers. "I'm way beyond saving, sweetheart."

"So am I," she whispered.

"I don't believe that."

"Then you're looking too hard for something that's not there."

"I don't think so."

"If I can be saved then so can you."

His lips twisted cynically. "We aren't even in the same universe. Believe me. I'm lost. You can still be found."

"You sound so sure." She reached up and stroked his hair from where it already began to fall from the back at his neck, his fingers tugging it forward. Every time she touched him, his entire body burned. She had no idea how much willpower it required for him not to slide between her thighs and settle in for a long, hot night. "I wonder," she contemplated, studying him with big, gorgeous eyes, he could get lost in forever, "if maybe we should both try to save each other and then in the morning, pretend we didn't?"

Or maybe, Blake thought, in the morning he'd fly her off to some tropical paradise, away from this wicked winter hell of Alvarez's world, and convince her she never has to come back.

The Negotiation...

Blake's mouth came down on hers, and this time he didn't hold back. He wanted to save her. She wanted to save him. She didn't have a chance where he was concerned, but the wicked heat of her kiss, the delicate play of her tongue against his, sure as hell would go a long way in helping him forget why that wasn't possible, at least, for tonight.

His hand slid down her neck, over the soft silk of her shoulder and he tugged her bra strap down with him. Her skin was cool and he was hot. He wanted her hot in a nearly consuming way. It was illogical but he really didn't care. His mouth traveled the delicate line of her shoulder blade and downward. Her fingers played in his hair, her touch affecting him far too easily, but then there wasn't a lot of softness he let in his life. Normally, he'd snatch her hand, and hold it over her head. He'd do the touching, not her, so why wasn't he doing that now? Why wasn't he stopping her? Why the hell was he lingering at the sweet spot at the base of her throat when he could be ripping away her panties and burying himself inside her?

After all, he'd been on the edge before he'd ever met her, ready to finally get what he wanted, what he'd craved for two years. Knowing he was still too far away. His need for an escape, for something hard, fast, and furious, should be driving him. Instead an inescapable, dangerously distracting, need to save this woman, to please her, consumed him.

His fingers traced the clip in the center of her bra and unsnapped it, closer to having her completely bared to him. He wanted her bared to him. He wanted her naked, panting, and screaming his name. Blake caressed away the silk of her bra and framed her high, full breasts with his hands. She arched into him, and moaned when his mouth closed down on the rosy peek of one nipple. He took his time, teasing her, licking her, enjoying her, rather than ravishing her, slowly kissing his way downward, until he peeled her panties down her hips.

Something dark and needy expanded inside him at the sight of the dark, well-groomed triangle of hair between her thighs. He slid off of the bed, and took the panties all the way down her legs, at the same time he went to his knees, pulling her towards him.

She rose up on her elbows, her big brown eyes wide with emotion, without arousal, and yes—there it was again—just a hint of trepidation. No matter how hard she tried to hide the truth, a night with a stranger wasn't the norm for her.

Not even close.

His gaze raked over her lush breasts, his cock thick and pulsing, and he tugged his shirt over his head and got rid of it. He tossed one of her high-heels and then the other. "No shoes, keeps you from running away."

"Then maybe you better take yours off," she commented.

"I never run."

"Neither do I," she said. "But even the score. Shoes off."

His lips quirked at her challenge and he gladly complied. "Satisfied now?" he asked settling her feet back on his thighs.

"Not yet," she said. "But I have high hopes I will be."

He laughed at that bold statement. She was a contradiction of fearless and fearful that intrigued him. "You will be," he promised, and one by one, he rolled the lace-topped silk slices down her legs, skimming a path down her long, shapely legs. The woman had a killer body that would have had any man begging to be right here, opening her legs to him. And open she did as he settled one delicate instep on each of his shoulders.

Visit www.lisareneejones.com for more information on BENEATH THE SECRETS – available now!

About the Author

New York Times and USA Today bestselling author Lisa Renee Jones is the author of the highly acclaimed INSIDE OUT series, which is now in development for a television show to be produced by Suzanne Todd of Team Todd (Alice in Wonderland). Suzanne Todd on the INSIDE OUT series: Lisa has created a beautiful, complicated, and sensual world that is filled with intrigue and suspense. Sara's character is strong, flawed, complex, and sexy—a modern girl we all can identify with. I'm thrilled to develop a television show that will tell Sara's whole story—her life, her work, her friends, and her sexuality.

In addition to the success of Lisa's INSIDE OUT series, she has published many successful titles. The TALL, DARK AND DEADLY series and THE SECRET LIFE OF AMY BENSEN series, both spent several months on a combination of the New York Times and USA Today bestselling lists. Lisa is presently working on a dark, edgy new series, DIRTY MONEY, for St. Martin's Press.

Prior to publishing Lisa owned multi-state staffing agency that was recognized many times by The Austin Business Journal and also praised by the Dallas Women's Magazine. In 1998 Lisa was listed as the #7 growing women owned business in Entrepreneur Magazine.

Lisa loves to hear from her readers. You can reach her at **www.lisareneejones.com** and she is active on **Twitter** and **Facebook** daily.

CPSIA information can be obtained
at www.ICGtesting.com
Printed in the USA
BVOW07s1434010516
446322BV00005B/91/P